marc spitz

a novel

Too Much, Too Late

 THREE RIVERS PRESS • NEW YORK

Published in the United States by Three Rivers Press,
an imprint of the Crown Publishing Group,
a division of Random House, Inc., New York.
www.crownpublishing.com

Three Rivers Press and the Tugboat design are registered
trademarks of Random House, Inc.

Library of Congress Cataloging-in-Publication Data
Spitz, Marc.
    Too much, too late : a novel / Marc Spitz.—1st ed.
       p.   cm.
    1. Success—Fiction. 2. Rock groups—Fiction. 3. Rock
musicians—Fiction. 4. Male friendship—Fiction. I. Title.
    PS3619.P582T66   2006
    813'.6—dc22

                                        2005026384

ISBN-13: 978-1-4000-8293-3
ISBN-10: 1-4000-8293-5

Printed in the United States of America

DESIGN BY ELINA D. NUDELMAN

10   9   8   7   6   5   4   3   2   1

First Edition

Too Much,
Too Late

Also by Marc Spitz

How Soon Is Never?

We Got the Neutron Bomb: The Untold Story of L.A. Punk
(coauthor with Brendan Mullen)

For E.D.G.

acknowledgments

Thank you, friends and family. Special thanks to Carrie Thornton and James Fitzgerald. Thanks to Brandi Bowles, Jim Walsh, Hal Horowitz, Jay Sones, Bill Adams, and Anne Garrett for all their hard work. Thanks to Gideon for the DVD. Parts of this book were written in the attic at James and Camille Habacker's house in Swan Lake, New York, and in the Davis Alumni House at Bennington College, Bennington, Vermont (the latter on the recommendation of Jared Paul Stern). Thank you for making me feel at home.

PART ONE

prologue

Some of you already know my name, or can remember it after a bit of jostling.

"Oh, yeah . . . *him*."

Then you'll probably hum the melody to "Let's Go Steady Debbie." Most do. Although it's only been in release for two years, that song has become a classic. These days, everything moves so quickly that a really good song tends to cross over into that canon inside of a month. Fourteen-year-old kids are writing "pop standards," and greatest-hits packages tend to get released after an artist's second album. But that doesn't take away from "Debbie," or shouldn't. And happily, it hasn't. Not yet anyway. Two summers on, it's still a prom song. And a yearbook quote. It shows up on lists. Top Fives. Top Tens. Top Fifties. One Hundred and One Most . . . (or Least . . .). In magazines. On television countdown shows. Web sites. "Debbie" makes them all.

Top 200 Most Hummable Oldies Ever Written That Somehow Never Annoy

106. "Spooky"
107. "Let's Go Steady Debbie"
108. "Windy"
109. "Stormy"

I can't remember where I saw that one, but it made me laugh. I'm proud that "Debbie" walks that fine line. Even though I didn't write the song. I played percussion on it. With my band. The Jane Ashers.

Do you remember the Jane Ashers? "Oh, yeah . . . *them*."

After the humming, maybe you'll worry for half a second about getting old yourself, losing your time. Then you'll laugh with just a trace of nerves and ask, "Whatever happened to them?"

I don't consider myself a has-been, I consider myself a *was*. It's a miracle, really, that I ever made it onto your lists or your radio at all. But from a purely existential standpoint, nobody wants to be asked, "What ever happened to you?" It hurts. The inquiry causes genuine physical pain: an uncomfortable tingle around your solar plexus. When I first started fielding the question, I used to wait till whoever had posed it walked away, then I'd secretly dig the nail of my pointer finger into the flesh of my opposite forearm just to confirm that I was not, in fact, a ghost. I suppose I'm writing this memoir partly because I don't want to keep doing that. It leaves marks.

Although I made a lot of money in the last couple of years, I didn't move to New York or Los Angeles. I still live in Dean, Ohio, my hometown and the birthplace of the Jane Ashers ("Where?"). Here, in Dean, I never have to remind people who I was. What I've done. Here, it's harder to be forgotten.

I was born in 1967 to one of Dean's two Jewish families. I'm the only child of Albert and Minna Klein. In a town of 14,000 Roman Catholics, Baptists, Lutherans, Methodists, Presbyterians, and Greek Orthodox, being one of seven Hebrews who believed that Jesus died for somebody's sins but not theirs doesn't really make a kid feel like one of the Chosen. It does, happily, make him a vaguely proud outcast . . . and perfectly primes him for a life in rock'n'roll.

The only other Jewish boy in Dean was Rudy Tunick, whom you now know as the Jane Ashers' guitarist. Rudy and I had been friends since we were in diapers. My parents were the pioneers, settling in Dean a year before the Tunicks. When they arrived, Rudy's parents and my mom and dad immediately became close. They were obliged to bond. Nobody was burning crosses on our lawn, but we didn't exactly put the lit menorah in the window every December, either. Happily, we all genuinely liked each other. We shared meals and even carpooled into Cincinnati to spend the high holy days in an actual temple.

As we entered our teens, a time when kids may start to pull away from their old friends and familial trappings, Rudy and I grew even closer than we'd been as children. It was no longer circumcisions and an acquired taste for sour cream that made us soul brothers. It was a massive, sleepless, uncontainable passion for *Rubber Soul* and *Revolver* and *Quadrophenia* and *The Wall* and the Kinks' live album *One for the Road*. Rudy had grown his black hair long and greasy. His left eye was slightly lazy, and it seemed to wander as his attention span evaporated. When he was playing or listening to rock'n'roll, it wandered back. Around the time I got my first kit for Chanukah, he'd acquired a candy-apple-red Flying V2. Used. It was only eight years old but looked twice that. Rudy didn't bother to restore it. He liked the fact that it was beat up, or rather he liked the fact that it wasn't new and antiseptic kind of irked his parents. Rudy didn't even carry it in a case but dragged it down the pavement by the neck like a strangled goose.

I think Rudy Tunick was a punk before we'd even heard of punk. He was certainly young, loud, and snotty.

Rudy never had a job. He never even washed a car or shoveled snow for a few singles. He was passionately lazy. His sister, Nell, was the exact opposite. She had a before-school job at Joan's, the bakery, and she volunteered at the hospital, playing cards with the elderly. Rudy's mother and father had a serious work ethic. Mr.

Tunick ran a plumbing supply outlet, and Rudy's mother, Barbara, worked at the *Dean Beacon* in the ad sales department. They both knew the riches a ten-hour day brings to one's character and bank book, but for some reason they indulged and spoiled their son. Probably because, unlike Nell, who was sweet but a bit blunt, Rudy was whip-smart. His rim-shot-worthy sense of humor was pitch black and delivered with perfect timing. The Tunick family thrived on his wit. When sober, Rudy brightened up every dinner conversation, adding a pungent spirit to what would otherwise be a somewhat dreary domestic scene. But once he found that guitar, and his records, and beer, and pot, Rudy stopped caring whether his verbal cutlery was sharp or dull. He'd made those daffy old Jews laugh enough, he figured. It wasn't exciting. Not like the Rolling Stones were exciting. He'd started relying on oldies, which were met with polite titters as the small TV flickered on the kitchen counter and the sour cream was ladled out on the latkes.

"Ronald Regan . . . he . . . he used to . . . he was in a movie with a chimp. Chimps. Har. Harf."

It wasn't worth it anymore. Rudy preferred to smoke pot and slow down that fierce mechanism in his head. I should also mention that in addition to being too smart to work, he'd become too smart to bathe. Anyone in Dean could scrub up with white soap. Not us. We were . . . evolving.

I'm attempting to explain that I did not change my name from Sandy Klein to Sandy James because I was ashamed or anything. I know some people strain to point out that Bob Dylan's real last name is Zimmerman and Winona Ryder's birth certificate reads Winona Horowitz like they've uncovered some deeply buried secret about them (these people usually take pains to point out that Bruce Springsteen is *not* a Jew). I won't speak for Dylan, because Dylan clearly hates people who speak for him, but I'm fairly certain that transitioning from Horowitz to Ryder doesn't mean Winona's a self-hating Jewess. It means that she, like me (and Moses Horwitz, who found fame as Moe Howard, the most irascible Stooge), is in show business. Horowitz is a fine Jewish name but a bad show-biz name (apologies to Vladimir Horowitz). Nobody in "the biz" is named Klein besides Robert Klein, and he's not funny. There's Patsy Cline, whom I love, but that doesn't count either. Nobody in rock should answer to Klein. I have a lot of rules about rock'n'roll, as you'll come to understand if you keep reading.

One of them is that you must respect Winona. She's suffered for rock, I think. The music has moved her to do foolish things, and that is, in its way, somewhat noble—to feel so much that your rational thoughts melt away and you find yourself shoplifting or dating the guy from Helmet. She is our muse as a result, and nobody can fuck with her. Other rules? Okay, lead singers should never start out with beards. It's okay if they grow beards, like Fat Jim Morrison or Paul McCartney during the *Let It Be* period did. There are dozens more, and they're all rigid, but I'm getting distracted. . . .

I was Sandy Nista during a fervid Clash phase circa 1982. Armbands. Mohawks. Calling the sheriff a fascist and screaming, "This is a public service announcement . . . with guitars," every time someone crossed me. Then Joe Strummer kicked Mick Jones out of the band and lost me in the process as well. One night after way too many bong hits, I insisted that I was Sandy Duncan and demanded a box of Wheat Thins, some glass cleaner for my eye, and more pot. Sandy Jones stuck for a while. I decided I'd take David Bowie's given name (he changed it to Bowie so as not to be confused with Davy Jones of the Monkees, who were then much more popular). It was kind of a cool inside joke, but I got tired of explaining it to everyone, and it really made no sense unless Bowie knew about it and provided some commentary. I wouldn't meet Bowie for another 22 years or so.

Finally, about three weeks before Harry and I formed the Jane Ashers, I became, and will forever remain, Sandy James. No reason. James is a good outlaw rock'n'roll name. There's Jesse James, of course. James Brown. Tommy James. Rick James. You could say that Klein was my slave name. James is the name I took after playing real rock'n'roll set me free. You *could* say that. I don't, but you could. And I'd like it if once in a while you would. Say anything about me. Just don't forget.

I know what this is. I want you all to know that I know what this is. And that I'm not ashamed to be doing this, even though it's a poor substitute for playing drums in the band. My arms are still huge. Disproportionately so. They always will be. My arms beg for anchor tattoos, but then someone would have to hack off my limbs when I die and bury them in a gentile cemetery somewhere . . . and you couldn't hack off my fucking arms with a chain saw. I will be an old man with

Bill Wyman wrote one about the Rolling Stones. Brian Jones just died and became a legend.

Noel Redding wrote one about Jimi Hendrix. Jimi choked on his own spew and became a legend.

There are about fifty such things, all worthy in varying ways, if at all. All sad in the same way. And all completely necessary in one way or another to their shell-shocked author getting through the long, lonely night in whatever town works for him or her these days.

I never thought I'd be writing one of them myself, but this is the cheesy rock'n'roll memoir I'm writing about my lead singer, Harrison August Vance Jr. Songwriter, visionary, mouth organist, and ultimately destroyer of the Jane Ashers, the biggest middle-aged rock'n'roll 15-year overnight sensation in history. Harry is not dead, but he's already legend.

I know this may sound defensive, but I swear I'm not doing this just for the money. I've got plenty. More money than I ever thought I'd have in my savings account, anyway. I'm set for life . . . provided I only live another eight years. I even give away some of my fortune to worthy charities—hound rescue, gripe relief— or at least my accountant claims that I do. There are selfless reasons why this book exists. I believe that in light of what transpired, our fans really do deserve to know the truth about why there's not going to be any more Jane Ashers music. Harry's not going to tell them why. Not with Neil Strauss. Not with any other ghostwriter. Not ever. He won't even tell me. I think that he's in denial that it ever happened in the first place.

I'm doing this for him. Harry is the most pigheaded person I've ever met. And although he must suspect it,

I'm sure he won't accept that ending it all abruptly and without any reason the way he did has only made his legend greater. The more he hides, the more he'll have to hide. Just ask J. D. Salinger. Or Syd Barrett. Or Sly Stone. Or Axl Rose. Maybe this book will satisfy everyone and erase all that mystery. Maybe then Harry can finally disappear completely. Go quietly. But he won't wanna do that either. He never did.

They say it's better to burn out than fade away, "they" being Neil Young. Nobody ever asked, "What happens if you come close to both but ultimately do neither?"

There is an answer. You get an agent. You write a cheesy book. Then you go back on tour. Only this time you rock the cafés at the chain bookstores, and I'm sure it's relatively peaceful backstage. It could be worse. The book, I mean. I think it's pretty good. My life now, as a was, could not be worse. Please, enjoy.

suckers, and book some extremely capable and eager musical entertainment.

I'm being cynical now, but back then Eggfest '92 was our largest show yet, and we weren't taking it lightly. No longer would we crash the thing, screaming, "Eggs! Eggs!" in homage to Edie the Egg Lady from the old John Waters movie *Pink Flamingos* (which we loved), and spooking the pony. With the thirty to forty stragglers who'd wander up each year and justify the following year's Eggfest, we'd be performing for 500 people easy. I was nervous. I was already getting used to folks being nice to me because I played drums in a real band, and I was hungry for more. And for eggs.

The Jane Ashers had formed in my garage two years previously, in the summer of 1990. I was five years into my post-graduation from Benjamim Harrison High but I'd yet to send one college application out there for consideration. None of us had after-school jobs yet either. And I wasn't joining the army. I had the notion in my head that college was bullshit, and there was nobody around to challenge that. Not in my house anyway. My friends, they didn't have the grades or the money. And the notions in their heads were limited to "hungry," "girls," or "pot." I didn't know what I was going to do with the rest of my life. I decided to give myself a year to figure it out. By the time I turned twenty, I told myself, I'd know my future. And if not, I could always try college. In the meantime, I had plenty of hobbies. I was building my own computer from spare parts. Eating frozen pizzas and drinking my dead dad's Jim Beam bourbon out in the garage. I had my drums out there too. My Frankenstein's monster of a kit. A third-hand

Ludwig bass. Dented Pearl tom and snare. Cracked Zildjian cymbals I stole from the band closet at school and dropped during my getaway. My drums were hand-painted a sort of orange, the shade of a burnt cake—I'd never seen another kit quite the same color. I remember taking pains to come up with something odd when I was mixing the pigments and getting high. I didn't care if it was ugly, and it was. I just wanted it to be one of a kind. My things were occasionally unreliable. But they were also unique. Like me. Who needed higher education? I wasn't bored yet. Life was good enough.

I lived alone with my mother, whom I adored, even though she was trouble. Ma had dropped off the grid just over a year after my father passed away in the fall of 1985. She made an attempt at proper widow behavior for a little while, probably for my sake. Minna was good-looking. I got her light hair and blue eyes. I guess everything else came from my dad: obstinacy, alcoholism, and this nose. Anyway, once it was proper, about two months after the funeral, the men came. Nobody local, out of respect for my father, who was well loved in Dean whether he worshiped the Son or not. I wondered where these men with their oily hair and powder blue two-piece suits were materializing from, because nobody in Dean would dare violate Artie's legacy in such a rude and horny fashion. Were they traveling salesmen passing through Dean on their way to Cincinnati or Toledo or Chicago even? More likely they were just blank, common men, half in the bag and vaguely wanting to nail my grieving mother after buying her a few rounds of inexpensive vodka at Tate's Grill out by the interstate turnoff. I even followed

too much, too late

her in a friend's car and spied on her as it all went down. Minna drank gimlets and smoked unfiltered cigarettes like someone hastening her own demise. I remember her catching me with a stolen Pall Mall out in the garage and beating me with a Goody hairbrush until it snapped in two. And there she was, getting loose and lighting one cig with the end of the last, swaying and falling into the arms of these highway wolves with their Japanese cars full of regular gas out back. I didn't judge. She was bereft. Only 38, and left alone for all time.

"I don't even like them, Sandy. I don't like them touching me." I'd found her in the bathroom with a bottle of Smirnoff vodka, a notebook, a pencil, and an open bottle of sleeping pills. This after a particularly empty interlude. I screamed like a girl.

"What are you doing, Ma? You'd just leave me like that?"

"I'm having a drink."

She stared up at me. The corners of her lips twitched involuntarily. There was a sparkling ring of snot around her right nostril. She wiped it away.

People told my father that he looked a lot like Glenn Ford, the actor from *The Blackboard Jungle*. He was solidly built. Strong. Craggy. Maybe I'm thinking of William Holden. I don't know. My point here is that he was a bull. He fixed the car. We didn't pay a mechanic. He had a big gray toolbox. Now it's mine. Dad followed some girl named Jennifer Blake from his native Cleveland to Dean after college, then ditched her and married Ma, who was in high school at the time. All I know about Jennifer Blake is that she was very tall, with straw-colored, almost white hair . . . and after Dad had spent a few days in Dean, she was very gone. The way I heard it, although they didn't repeat it much, was that Artie spotted Minna at the counter in Bix's drugstore, walked to the pay phone by the gas station, put a coin in, and broke it off with Jennifer immediately. Then he went in, sat down, ordered a bottle of cola and introduced himself. He won over Minna's parents with his no-nonsense demeanor and some rudimentary Hebrew he remembered from school. At the time the Roth family were the only Jewish settlers in Dean, although they put up a tree every December and tried almost too hard to assimilate, changing the name on their mailbox to Ross. Unlike Winona, they were not in show business and they may have been slightly ashamed of their tribal roots. Who knows?

Minna's family had a business selling materials for countertops, and Artie went to work there. After starting in the yard, he moved into the office and ended up taking over the business inside of three years. He could sell scratchproof Formica made from the new miracle plastics developed for the last two war efforts like nobody else. By his late 30s, he'd built the company into a chain. I remember marveling at his ability to maneuver long sheets of material even in his silk suit and gold Baume et Mercier watch. He ate his meat rare. No dessert. Just coffee, black, and an unfiltered Pall Mall cigarette. Artie Klein was the toughest Jew who ever lived. Certainly not the kind of guy you'd expect to get killed by a bumblebee. He'd lived 49 years, 5 months, and 12½ days without knowing that he was allergic to bee stings. How would you know if you've never actually been stung by a bee? It was just fate he hadn't, I guess. They thought it was a heart attack at first when he keeled over in the garden, his neck all swollen and red, eyes bulging, tongue purple and bitten nearly in two. When the doctor told us what really happened, that a little fuzzy bee took down my indestructible father, I vomited. Nothing made sense. I understood Minna's need to find something meaningful after having her marriage and basically her whole existence reduced to some kind of black irony. But she wasn't going to find it the way she was looking.

I should confess here that I was the one who got my own mother strung out on pot. Ma wasn't a party girl in the '60s, when everybody else was supposedly feeding their heads. She became one in her late 30s. Until my dad died, Ma was "Mrs. Klein," as straight as any middle American housewife and mother. She kept her hair in a ponytail. Bought the groceries. Fed the goldfish. Washed the dishes. Dried the dishes. Tipped the gardener. Lit the menorah. Never flirted with the postman.

"Come with me, Ma." She followed me into the garage. With the first few steps, I gently grabbed the vodka bottle. With the last few, I angrily confiscated the pills. I sat her on the old man's workbench, grabbed a cassette out of the pile I'd brought out there and never bothered to return to the shelf in my room, and cued up a track. It was "Have a Talk with God," by Stevie Wonder, off the *Songs in the Key of Life* double album.

I pulled a half-smoked joint of skunker weed from my jacket pocket. Rudy had let me keep it, and I'd planned on lighting up a bit later and watching *Re-Animator* or something. Instead, I lit up then, took a pull, and handed it to my mother. She took it without asking what it was. She put it to her lips, and I guess it was there that the healing began. Call it medical marijuana. After the joint and three or four tracks, Minna was begining to come around. I nodded as I saw her getting it. Getting happy. "And he's *blind*," I reminded her. Very soon, rock'n'roll started to make sense to Minna when nothing else did anymore.

It wasn't like she became a stoner overnight. I even think she hit Tate's a couple more times before deciding that the only time she'd felt like herself since her husband died was when she'd gotten stoned with me. I was tinkering with my computer out in the garage about two weeks or so after the bathroom incident. I'd had a blinking cursor on the monitor for more than twelve seconds without the box surging and dying, and I was trying to figure out what I'd done right when I noticed her standing there.

"Ma?"

"I want some more."

"More what, Ma?"

"Grass, Sandy. Do you have any?"

"No, Ma. I'm dry."

"How come you're dry?" she scolded.

"Well . . . it's expensive. And sometimes I just run out."

She reached into the pocket of her gray plaid skirt and pulled out two brand-new $50 bills.

"Will this get me some fresh grass?"

I pocketed the bills.

"Certainly."

"How do you get it?"

"I have a dealer. I can call him. I'll call him."

She began thumbing through my cassettes. "What's good here?" She held up a copy of *The Who Sell Out.* "Is this good?"

"Yes."

"Can I borrow this? And these?"

She dispayed a tape of *Forever Changes* by Love. Then she picked up *Darkness on the Edge of Town* by Springsteen like it was an orange or a pear at the produce stand. I nodded again. She randomly pulled Bowie's *The Rise and Fall of Ziggy Stardust and the Spiders from Mars, Life's Rich Pageant* by REM, and *Horses* by Patti Smith from the collection.

"Those are all amazing," I told her.

She smiled. It was the same warming, maternal expression I remembered from my early childhood. I wanted to run to her and hug her. But she was jonesing. A little stiff. I was kind of scared of her, I have to admit. But I called my guy and he came over and sorted my mom out for bud.

She didn't leave the house much after that. Not for lunch or shopping or doctor's appointments or anything. She just dropped out. Everything was delivered. Our dealer—let's call him Barry—got a lot of business out of Ma. His biweekly deliveries soon became daily. One day he disappeared, and I had to find Minna another supplier. Later we discovered that Barry'd gone off to Pennsylvania to study dentistry. I always wondered if some of his tuition didn't come directly from my fiending mom's purse.

The downside of saving my mother's life with rock and drugs was that the entire house started to look like the garage. Nobody wants a dirty hippie for a mom, but soon I had one. I didn't bring my friends around, even Rudy. The house was pretty roughed up. Ma'd be all zooted and break a glass and not bother to sweep it up or warn anyone that the kitchen floor was hazardous. I still have some microscopic shards in my toe. Every once in a while I'll jar one loose from a callus, push it into a nerve, and wince.

Before we befriended Harry, Keith Richards of the Stones made us take the possibility of being a real band a bit more seriously. Or rather Keith's spit did.

When the Rolling Stones came through town on their *Steel Wheels* tour, we all went down to see them at Riverfront Stadium in Cincinnati. Rudy, who like many rebellious teenage guitar players was wholly obsessed with Keith, had already started weaving little trinkets into his high-piled rat's nest hairdo: pieces of yarn, tiny bottles lifted from his little sister's dollhouse tea sets, fetishes of all kinds. It was Keith's new look, and so it became Rudy's too. Rudy was chubby or at the very least well fed, but by the time he was 21, he'd lost about a third of his body fat, mostly by spending months consuming nothing but cherry Jell-O and weed. He kept it off by replacing the weed with Ritalin. The Jell-O remained the same. The resulting malnutrition did a number on his teeth, but Rudy liked that. He said it made him look like Keith in '68 around the time of the film *The Rolling Stones: Rock and Roll Circus* and that great "Jumpin' Jack Flash" video where they're all in makeup and ladies' big sunglasses. When the bicuspids started falling out, Rudy agreed to supplement his diet with some applesauce and a couple of chewable vitamins, smashed to powder and ceremoniously ingested like they were pulled from a sack of opium with a pirate's dagger, rather than a childproof bottle with a Flintstone or a Rubble on it.

You'd think a smack habit would be easier, but nobody knew how to get any good drugs in Dean. This didn't stop Rudy from pretending to get the shakes and wheeze "You Got the Silver" from the *Let It Bleed* album. Call it air DTs. After a while, he did actually start to resemble Keith—from a distance or a great height.

So the Stones and their support act, the black rock group Living Colour, rolled in, and we all showed up a few hours early to try to get backstage. I accompanied Rudy as far into the concrete bowels of the arena as the cops and the Stones' private security force would permit (about twelve paces), then stood with my hands deep in my too-thin leather jacket. Rudy didn't seem to feel the cold, but I was shivering inside that man-made wind tunnel as he pleaded with the old-school brick-wall men who'd been keeping Mick Jagger, Keith, Charlie Watts, and Ronnie Wood away from the likes of us since the mid-'60s.

"Come on, Rudy, man. Let's go inside and get a hot dog. It's fucking cold like ass out here."

"I need a luuuuuv to keep me happay, bay-bay!" he'd sing, then rush the guard one more time. It was "Happy," Keith's song off *Exile on Main Street.* The goon, one of those muscle men with embarrassingly chubby cheeks that stand out among all the chiseled tissue, seemed uninterested but not unkind. He even offered his hand to pick Rudy up each time he knocked him on his behind. Rudy'd push away the hand and carry himself up, bruised and hoarse but no less determined to meet Keith.

"You're missing Living Colour, kid," the guard warned as we heard a muted wave of applause roll up from inside the stadium. It sounded like it was echoing from ten miles away.

"Fuck fucking Living Colour, man."

"What are you? A racist?" The guard laughed. "You don't think niggers can rock'n'roll?"

"Nah, man. The niggers can't rock'n'roll."

The guard knocked Rudy down. This time there was no helping hand.

"Niggers! Niggers! Niiiiggers raaaahk! Whoooooooo! Hoo!"

The guard kicked him in the gut. I thought I heard ribs snap.

I knew Rudy didn't believe a word of what he'd said—he was just baiting the guy because he wasn't getting his way. Still, I said, "Rudy, man! Take it back!" But he wouldn't.

"I gotta see Keeeeeeeeeeef! I need to talk to Keeeef!"

After 45 minutes or so, some barrel-gutted, old-school Stones crewman with tattooed, lobster-red skin and 17 chins emerged from the hallowed locker room, hauling a couple of boxes of garbage.

"Keef! Keef, man! Keef!"

The security guard and the old crewman exchanged a knowing look and started guffawing together.

"No bitches?" the crewman wondered. The guard shook his head disappointedly. Somewhere, maybe, one of his co-workers was getting his rocks off. All he got was me and Rudy.

"Keeeeef! Hey! Hey! Keeeeeef!" Rudy grabbed the old man by his dirty blue socks.

"Yeah, I just seen him. He says, 'Keep on rockin',''' the old guy croaked.

"No way, man!" Rudy grinned. "Come on. Listen . . . listen . . . listen . . . listen . . . listen . . . uh . . . I gotta see Keef tonight, man."

"You better go around to the gate, then, 'cause that's the only way you're gonna see Keith Richards, kid."

"Aw, man! Man!"

The crewman stopped and pulled something from the box of garbage. He gave the guard a conspiratorial look, then returned his glance to Rudy, who was drooling.

"Lookit," the red man spat, "I got some of the guys' garbage in here. Was gonna toss it all."

"The Stones' trash?"

"Yeah."

"The Stones' . . . uh . . . rubbish?"

"Whatever."

"Keef?"

"Yeah. Keith. Charlie. Mick. You want it, it's yours." Rudy pounced on the box and rifled through it, throwing empty cans of tomato juice and hardened cheese rinds all over the floor, then apologetically, gratefully stooping to pick each item up. Desperate and semi-cognizant of the old guy's barely contained laughter, Rudy finally pulled out a wadded napkin and unraveled it. He held up a hunk of spent cinnamon-flavored chewing gum.

"Whose gum is this? This Keef's?"

"Yeah. As a matter of fact, I seen Keith chewing on that not two minutes ago. Must have taken it out to light up a cigarette." He exchanged another wink with the guard.

"Rudy, man," I warned, "don't put that nasty shit in your mouth."

It was too late. Rudy was chewing Keith Richards's discarded gum with the widest, toothiest smile I've ever seen.

"It's Keef's, man. I can feel Keef . . . seepin' into me."

"Yeah, all right. Can we go now? I'm dyin'."

"Keef's inside me, man."

"That's awesome. Let's go."

"He's passing something on to me."

"What?"

"I can't tell you, man. It's a secret."

I don't know what Rudy did with that piece of gum while he slept—stuck it on the wall, maybe—but the message Keith was relaying (maybe it was "Get a life, ya twit") must have been slow to unfold, 'cause the guy kept that nasty hunk, which had probably been in the teeth or on the shoe of a roadie, in his mouth forever. Keith's gum. Keith's DNA. Keith's secret. Keith.

It was always about the Stones. They were the bedrock. Them and the Beatles, Kinks, and Who. But that summer it was all about cock rock. Hair metal was enjoying its lame-duck year of cultural relevance. Not that we knew or cared about culture at the time. We just found *Sonic Temple* by the Cult and *Dr. Feelgood* by Mötley Crüe better records to play along to than, say, Fugazi's *Margin Walker* EP or *Doolittle* by the Pixies. We loved those records too, but trust me, when you're fantasizing in a garage, it's more fun being a cheeseball. It was how we'd learned to play, anyway. I only started counting and remembering certain beats or patterns that year. And that was on a dare. We'd mouth the vocals 'cause neither of us had much of a singing voice. I reiterate that none of this activity was afforded any more or less importance than a night of drunken vandalism, and much less importance than screwing girls, which we did when we could, and we rarely ever could. If you'd have asked me then if I wanted to be in a band, I would have shrugged and mumbled, "Sure. Yeah." But I can't tell you that that's the reason why I didn't go to college.

The first time I ever shook Harry Vance's hand, I noticed that his nails were bitten down so deeply that hard, piglet-colored scar tissue had started to form over the nubs. That shake happened on the big lawn in Hunter's Park.

Once or twice a week, whenever my muscles started to lock from hunching over the computer I was building, I'd gather up Rudy and some of my other guys, and like good Buckeyes we'd toss a football around Hunter's Park, the little acre of public pitch next to the market and the screen door factory. We'd play while the old men fed day-old bread to the chickadees and the younger men with blood and scratches on their cheeks ate their lunch on the curb before punching back in, putting on their thick gray gloves, and picking up the heavy wire cutters for another few hours. Some of the kids we'd graduated with had taken jobs there.

We'd play rough and sloppy and loud, fully challenging the notion that billiards and bowling were the only sports you could play while drinking and smoking heavily. That day, me and Rudy and Willie Rath, whose dad used to be the deputy sheriff, were about four Bud tallboys apiece in, and one man short for our semiregular game of two-on-two touch.

I'd seen Harry out there before, sulking under this big old tree, the kind where you can see the rounded roots bulging out of the ground, all twisted like thick nautical rope. He wasn't the kind of guy you paid any attention to, since he sort of faded into the landscape, but on that day, when my team was short, I'd somehow decided that he was a big boy and I was going to draft him.

"You know this is my oak tree you're sitting under," I informed him. "I've got one in Israel too. Someone planted it for my bar mitzvah. I got trees all over the world."

Nothing.

"You like this tree, huh? Like sitting underneath it? Yeah. It's a good one."

"Come on, Sandy!" Rudy shouted. "Is he in or out?"

Harry looked up.

too much, too late

"He's in!" I hollered back. Harry appeared concerned now. In what? In his mind, he was certainly out.

"Well, hurry up. I'm losing my buzz!" Rudy groaned, and searched his pockets for a stray roach or a pill.

"It's an elm." Harry's voice was shockingly raspy. The voice of a blues singer, really.

It almost threw me off my cool. "A prospector elm."

"Oh yeah?" I replied.

"Not an oak."

"Whatever," I whispered. "It's not really mine."

He looked back down again.

Around Dean, Harry was a minor bogeyman. There was talk he'd been away, some hospital in the city. Others said he was a drug casualty or a retard who'd eaten lead paint chips as a kid and now was "subnormal," violent, and prison-bound. I didn't believe any of that. I've been in enough extremely amateur bouts to know if a guy is going to be a problem or not, and Harry always struck me as a gentle soul, if a little sad. Not that I blame the old ladies, shop owners, and cops who were wary of him. He was a real wiggy sight, old enough to vote and die for this country but kitted up like a mom-dressed fourth grader: velveteen polo shirt buttoned to the top, those inexpensive perma-creased chino pants that look like they're made out of cardboard, thick black socks, too-tight suede sneakers, and one of those Timex wristwatches with the leatherette band they sell in Bix's drugstore, stacked in those revolving showcases. He had an unruly shock of brown-red hair, six inches high with clumpy licks darting everywhere like wild mushroom caps.

"Listen. We're playing some ball."

He didn't respond, his attention fully returned to his composition book.

"What are you writing there?" I asked. "That your diary or what?"

"No."

"Well, what is it?"

"It's nothing."

"Come on, lemme see." I tried to grab the book away, not too forcefully. He tugged it back and struggled to lock it up in the metal box.

"It's personal," he growled. "Sorry."

"That's cool. I've got personal thoughts too. Feelings."

He started opening up a piece of red hard candy, fiddling with the cellophane wrapper.

"You know those things'll rot your teeth out of your head. Terrible for you. All sugar. Chemicals."

I lit up a cigarette and offered him one from the pack. He stared at it.

"I don't smoke."

"Why not?"

"It kills you."

"Not right away."

He stared at me like *I* was the crazy one.

"You know who you look like?" I asked.

"No."

"You look a little like Dr. Who. You know Dr. Who?"

He looked up. His eyes were a little friendlier now, cautious but interested.

"You know what that is?" I asked again. "Dr. Who?"

"Yes."

"I really like Dr. Who."

"Seriously?" He looked surprised, like he'd thought I was the kind of guy who only watched wrestling.

"Sure. I love anything from England. *Monty Python. The Goodies. The Young Ones. Benny Hill.*" British rock came first. Then TV.

Harry loved both as well. We had even more in common. Single mothers, to be specific. My dad was dead. It seemed like his might as well have been. Harry's father, who was also named Harry Vance, left his mother when Harry junior was only two, and although he sent checks every couple of months for a while, Harry never saw him again. He had no direct recollections of the old man, and although she related a few details about his character when pressed, she never provided a real explanation about why they were alone. Probably because she didn't have one. Formulating any excuse would mean he was really gone, and Harry's mother wasn't ready to accept it in 1970, when he first split, or in 1989, when Harry was already a fully grown adult. Physically, anyway.

What Harry knew about his old man, and subsequently what I knew, was this: Vance senior worked in a patents, notarization, and incorporations assistance office. He was an amateur musician and knew how to play the piano and the trumpet—nothing you could make a career out of, but obviously more than a hobby. Maybe it was Harry's dad's appreciation for the beauty of music that didn't allow him to stay in an unhappy marriage. He knew there was more out there. The songs he played and the stuff he wrote down on his own whispered as much. They gave him the balls to leave. When he did, he left behind an old Hohner Marine Band harmonica for Harry. Not much at all but maybe, someday, it could provide good company and a hint at other more exciting possibilities.

Harry senior relocated to the Bay Area with a younger woman from his office pool and left his son and wife of three years in Dean. Maybe it was love. Maybe he had no choice. I guess after that, Mrs. Vance ran for the straight end zone as quickly and forcefully as Minna sprinted in the opposite direction, freak flag aloft. Hence Harry's perpetual fourth grader's wardrobe, which I knew she kept buying for him in increasingly larger sizes as he filled up and out.

Harry would soon get the balls to leave Mrs. Vance himself. And like the old man intended, it was the music that called him down the road. The first original song of Harry's I ever heard was "Who Told You You Knew Shit About Love?" The song, if you don't already know by now (it's the B-side to "Debbie"), is a simple, three-chord stomper with no middle eight. Worse, it's completely ripped off, if you ask me, from the far superior "Love Comes in Spurts," by Richard Hell and the Voidoids, but it was always fun to play. By the end of it, most times, I'd find myself standing upright, I'd pounded my kit so hard. That, to me, is the mark of a good punk rock song, and any more of a testimonial for "Who Told You" is unnecessary.

Verse:

You got your head in your tail and your below's your above.

Chorus:

Who told you you knew shit about love?

Harry could have sung "Sex Dwarf" or "Fish Heads." It was the singer, not the song, when he opened his mouth that day in our garage. Rudy and Willy had gone off to buy beer, and we were sitting around playing records and getting acquainted. I kept cajoling him to sing and play, and I guess he was worried that I'd hit him or something if he refused. Harry didn't know me.

And I didn't know he was a genius.

This isn't a rule. It's more of a spiritual belief, but you can add it to my list of rock'n'roll rules if you want. It's just my opinion, but if there is a God, I believe that he releases a great rock'n'roll voice only three times per decade. That's three in the '50s, three in the '60s, three in the '70s, three in the '80s. When I heard Harry sing, I knew I was hearing one of the ones that would mark the 1990s. It was simultaneously inviting and exclusive, haunted and joyous, wounded and defiant, soulful and trashy. I was only off by 15 years. Maybe someone else had taken Harry's slot for that decade, and God wanted us to wait. Maybe it was Weiland.

2

Archie Funz completed our original lineup. Archie was Mark David Chapman's pen pal. Now you might think, *Well, that's all I really need to know about the Jane Ashers' first bassist, Archie Funz,* but you need to know some more to really get what we were dealing with. Archie Funz became Mark David Chapman's pen pal so that he could lure him into a false sense of security, meet him in person whenever he was released from Attica, shake his hand, then shoot him dead like Chapman had shot John Lennon (we all approved of this, of course). Archie became a born-again Christian—in his letters, anyway—in order to facilitate a bond with Chapman (who had found God while serving his sentence). Rudy thought this was an ingenious scheme. Mark David Chapman and Archie became fast friends, bonded over their mutual sociopathy, I guess.

Archibald Funz was his real name. No need to change that for rock'n'roll. He was a Ritalin child who still did the stuff at 24. Nobody ever bothered to take him off it. He still had braces, too. Ironically, for all these trappings of arrested adolescence, Archie stank like an old man. He wore a black-turned-gray Joy Division T-shirt. Never took it off. I once asked him if he was obsessed with Joy Division or something, as some people are—mostly Jewish goth chicks. He shrugged and said, "Who?" I guess he just liked the shirt. Maybe he got laid in it once, although it was difficult to imagine anything like that. Archie's body was skeletal, his hair long and stringy and the color of dung. His skin was almost translucent, he was so pale. Like the Visible Man. If you stripped him naked and threw him into harsh sunlight, I bet you could have seen his weedy little organs pumping anemic blood, but trust me, you didn't want to strip him naked. He was the kind of spastic reject who runs in circles every time the doorbell rings. We sure knew how to pick them.

All this aside, I should mention that we were thrilled to have Archie Funz in our band. He was a natural bass player, and we didn't hesitate for a minute to hire him. Forget that he was the only one who answered our classified ad in the *Dean Beacon*:

Do you like English rock?
Can you play bass? Local band with big plans
seeking guitarist for gigs, recording.

We didn't really have big plans . . . yet, and the notion of recording was still pretty abstract, but we all figured that if we sounded ambitious, we'd attract the best.
We attracted Archie instead. Like I said, though, he was
talented, and it made us all overlook the fact that he was
wrong in almost every other way. When Archie played,
he was mysterious and dark, and his weirdness and the
smells sort of disappeared—for as long as he was
plugged in, anyway.

Another Funz selling point: he had a vehicle we could
hypothetically tour in. It was a gray 1969 VW bus, and
once we removed the rust from the white top and rims,
changed the tires, and cleared the cans of jellied cran-
berry sauce, toilet paper rolls, iguanas, chicken bones,
rocking chair blades, and empty tubs of Red Vines (now
filled with rainwater) out of the back, we could easily
load in our gear and get from one show to the next and
home again. I was willing to invest in Archie, a little
paint, and a lot of disinfectant, and so were Rudy and
Harry. Archie was in. We were a full lineup. A mobile
quartet. Troubadours, even.

"What are we gonna call ourselves?" Rudy wondered as he tossed his second beer can into the road.
He seemed to enjoy littering. He took comfort in leaving a trail of crushed Bud cans behind him like
some bread crumb path. It was his fake ID we used, so
I didn't hassle him about it. Harry nursed his beer,

then daintily placed the can in the bag to recycle later. I gulped mine but bagged it just the same. I sometimes fed myself for days on returned bottles and cans. Plus there's the whole ecology thing, which is cool.

"How about the Recyclers?" Harry offered sarcastically. "Because you're so totally into recycling."

"Why the fuck does everyone care about recycling? We're not really gonna save the earth," Rudy snipped, then patted Harry's shoulder to let him know it was affectionate.

A week or two earlier, Harry Vance never would have had the confidence to rib someone as sharp-tongued as Rudy. But he had moved out of his house the day after our first rehearsal, and I'd already noticed a change in him.

I'd offered him our old yellow velveteen couch, and he accepted. I know it seems fast, but that's the way it happened. I guess we both saw a way to help each other out of our respective ruts. I provided him with friendship and encouragement. He gave me inspiration. All of Harry's songs were about alienation and feeling lonely and sad and misunderstood, but they were sort of hopeful in between all those blues. Unlike many cathartic punk bashers, though, they all had very strong hooks that stuck in you long after you heard them. I found myself humming all these songs. I'd never hummed anything I'd played with Rudy before. None of our long jam lines or halfhearted attempts to write anything of our own was very compelling. They all sounded exactly like what they were: the product of two untrained but reasonably talented kids going around and around without focus before giving up and grabbing whatever was around—*Houses of the Holy,* Rush's *Moving Pictures*—and just aping to it. I'd never remembered any work of art created by anyone I knew. Not in school. Not ever. But Harry's songs were different. They were primitive, but his sense of melody was already strong.

"Minna putters around at night," I warned him. "She keeps weird hours sometimes, but she won't bother ya. Maybe she'll ask if you're hungry or who sang 'Tighten Up.' "

"What if I don't know?"

"Just make something up, man. That's what I do," Rudy said, and laughed.

"It was Archie Bell and the Drells," Harry informed us.

"Good. You'll do fine."

"Your mom is a record geek, Sandy?"

"Yeah. Every day something new comes in the mail. Mostly from New York or L.A. Sometimes London. Sometimes Jamaica. She's got like forty-five crazy mail order catalogs. And I'm not allowed to touch her shit— her records or her pot."

Harry slept on our couch in a fetal position, night after night, under an old, musty afghan that smelled vaguely of spilled soup. Ma watched over him. Harry's mom worked in the Olfactory, this makeup and perfume shop downtown. Mostly she did managerial stuff—opened the store in the morning, counted out the register, deposited the day's till in the safe. I'd passed by the store many times but thought nothing of it except that it looked painfully clean. I never saw any customers in there either. Maybe she just stood around smelling nice all day. Harry went and grabbed some clothes and all his journals with his lyrics in them while she was at the store. I waited outside the house, shifting from foot to foot and smoking. It took longer than I expected: three, maybe four cigs and a lot of worst-case-scenario-ing. Finally he emerged from the front door looking even more resolute than before. He locked it behind him, then hit me with a reassuring nod.

"Sorry. I wrote her a long note."

"What'd it say?"

"I told her I loved her but that I was never coming home again."

"How about the Homeless?" I offered.

"I'm not homeless," Harry protested, looking worried.

"How about I'm Not Homeless?" I modified.

"What would they call us? Like, what would be our nickname?" Rudy wondered. "The I'm Nots? I guess that's kind of cool."

"Holmes," Archie blurted out. "They'd call us Holmes."

The suggestions went on long into that night and through the better part of the next day. We were the Best-Dressed Soldiers before deciding that it was a better album title than a band name (it's a shitty album title). Then came . . .

Crud
Hate Laser

Oliver Reed

Hate Phaser

Plutz

Hate Taser

The Crud

Rather Fleshy Mushrooms

The Cheap Flowers

Don't Litter

Phenomenonsense

The Feeling Cavaliers

Frère Jacques and the Frère Jacqueses

We were already psyched to finally be in a real band, but all of us agreed that we needed the perfect name to make it official or we would surely be vulnerable to losing this newfound magic.

"What do we all love? Like, what's one thing we all agree on?"

"Beer?" Rudy replied. "Weed? Uh . . . girls? Football? Fried clams are good. Um . . . did I say weed?"

"Shit from England?" I tossed out. "Dr. Who? Benny Hill?"

"If we name ourselves after something from *Dr. Who,* that's kind of like naming ourselves after something from *Star Wars.* It'll marginalize us. But something Anglo would be good. The Bin Liners."

I vetoed that one.

"The Lifts. Uh . . . Beans on Toast. The Bog Standards?"

"Queen," Archie offered.

"Are you serious?" Harry wondered, a broad grin

creeping across his face. He had a weird smile. Each time he did it, it seemed like it was among his very first. Like he'd been waiting years to grin. It just looked . . . new.

In the name of research and science, we hit the video store, which was really just a section in the market, like cleaning supplies or produce, but they had a pretty decent selection. Always had the new releases and some good concert films, like *The Song Remains the Same*, that always seemed to go missing. I already knew the only two really English films available, but I pretended I didn't. Maybe I wanted to make this seem more like a search, a gang activity. Finding *To Sir, with Love*, starring Sidney Poitier, Lulu, and a bunch of Cockney schoolkids, would seem like a good omen if I kept my mouth shut. The other flick was *Alfie*, starring Michael Caine and Shelley Winters. Both of those movies were in the oldies section. We rented them both but only watched *Alfie*. There was no need to check out *To Sir*, except maybe to do a mock slow dance to the theme song. About a quarter of the way through *Alfie*, which really hasn't aged well, what with Michael Caine calling all his female conquests "it" and all, the actress Jane Asher appears. That was all we needed to see. Jane Asher crushed all four of us out pretty badly. Her bright red hair and eyebrows seemed ablaze. Add some bangs and a peaches-and-cream complexion and you've got flaming youth. Asher wasn't perfect. She had what looked like a slight overbite. She was also kind of dizzy-eyed, like the world overwhelmed her. But her green eyes cast a spell on Michael Caine, and we liked that she knocked out someone so prowling and cynical.

I'd like to say that that was the reason why we ended up naming our band the Jane Ashers. The real reason is that she used to date Paul McCartney. She was the muse who inspired him to write "Here, There and Everywhere." As we sat around our big old TV set—the one my dad had brought home for Chanukah in 1976, with clumsy rotary dials for both VHF and UHF (I'm pretty sure it gave off a semideadly level of radiation if you sat too close)—we agreed that if she was good enough for Paul, she was good enough for us.

"Jane Asher," I said aloud, passing around the bag of chips we'd stolen for movie food.

"She's ideal," Harry said with a nod. Rudy offered him a bong hit.

He politely declined it and stared straight into the TV screen.

I tried out a few variations. "Asher? The Janes. The Jane Ashers."

"The Jane Ashers." Harry smiled. "That's the best."

"How old do you think she is now?" Rudy belched. "Forty?"

"Fifty? I don't know." I shrugged.

"I wonder if she's still fuckable."

"*Jane* is a very rock'n'roll name," I pointed out. "Jane's Addiction. 'Sweet Jane.' "

"It's a good name," Harry agreed. "English and sexually ambiguous and just . . . good."

"Sexually ambiguous?" Rudy queried.

"Y-yeah, in a rock'n'roll way," Harry stammered.

"Are you gay?" Archie asked.

Harry gulped. "No."

"'Cause I've never seen you with girls."

too much, too late

"Girls don't like me."

Harry sat down next to me. He noticed my pack of Camels on the coffee table and gestured toward it. I nodded. He pulled out a cigarette, lit it, inhaled.

"You're smoking now?" I was surprised.

"I guess."

"How do you know girls don't like you?"

"They're never nice to me. I don't know. I'm not handsome, I suppose."

I lit a cig, then grabbed a beer from the fridge, shook it, and sprayed it in the air.

"Fuck that! You're the lead singer of the Jane Ashers now! You sing rock'n'roll," I reminded him. "And rock'n'roll makes you sexy! It just does."

"Are you guys with girls a lot?" he asked a little shyly.

"Fuck, yeah. We romp and drink and smoke and screw all the time!" I boasted.

"Some of the time," Rudy corrected. "Sometimes."

I decided that Harry needed a serious confidence transfusion. I don't want to be crass here, but the guy needed some pussy. It was time. Harry wasn't unattractive. He kind of looked like the bastard child of Buddy Holly and Ann-Margret. A little weird but . . . intriguing. To a high school girl anyway. But he'd never had a real girlfriend, and whenever the topic of sex came up with me and Rudy, as it frequently did, Harry'd always blush and demur. It confused Rudy and me. He was becoming our leader, but take him out of the garage and he was also a bit of a liability. Whenever there were females around, he'd recede into corners. We decided, after a few months of watching him twitch awkwardly while we'd step up and flirt with cheerleaders and home economics queens and chemistry teachers and lady bus drivers and PTA mothers, that it was time to do what Harry senior might have orchestrated if he hadn't tripped over his own prick on his way west.

Danielle "Dollface" Reese was the cocktail waitress at Pinheads, the local seven-lane bowling alley. When we were flush and it was too cold to play football, we'd hit Pinheads for a few drinks and a few games. Danielle was about 20 years older than us. Early 40s maybe. Imagine Marilyn Monroe if she'd lived another decade and started guesting on *Match Game PM* circa '73 or '74 and you have a pretty good idea of Danielle. She was a bawdy middle-aged bombshell of a lush with once-dangerous curves that seemed to broaden every year while retaining enough of their original shapeliness to suggest some kind of eternal hotness. Cheap white tequila was her drink—the sugary, viscous kind that smells like tequila but could be gin or vodka or any kind of poisonous swill. It had given her those W. C. Fields broken blood vessels around her turned-up nose. Years of liquor, sweat, smoke, and glass-cleaning chemicals had created a permanent rash of little red bumps across her ample chest. But that didn't stop her from wearing low-cut thrift-store party dresses to work every night. Under bar light among Pinheads' lounge decor of red velveteen, plastic oak, and fake gold, nobody noticed the bumps, only the cleavage, and that was the idea. These amazing frocks seemed to be made from the same material used to cover chaise longues and make patio umbrellas, but cut in the style of Monroe's famous *Seven Year Itch* dress. She wore them well, however. Danielle was always sweet and flirtatious with us when reasonably sober. After a few too many shots of tequila, however, she'd start ranting about how the Jews control the weather. We didn't mind. Rudy and I didn't really consider ourselves super-Jewish. Besides, we couldn't control ourselves, much less the sun and the rain. All of us had fucked Danielle. No, let me be real here. All of us had lost our virginity to Danielle. And I don't mean the Jane Ashers. I mean all the boys in Dean, once they hit a certain age. I'd been 16. Harry'd already blown way past the age of consenting to be cherry-busted by the bowling alley barkeep, but we decided that it was time for him to be initiated.

"Why now?" he sputtered as we casually informed him that he'd be going home with Danielle that night. "Why me?"

"We don't have any songs about fucking," Rudy explained.

"We only have songs about wanting to fuck," I elaborated. "We need you to write some songs about fucking."

"But I don't like that stuff."

"Well, then you don't like rock'n'roll, 'cause that's what it's all about."

"I like rock'n'roll a lot!"

"Oh, yeah? Prove it."

"He can stay," Danielle said as she pulled out her register drawer. Lenny, the security guard, all hair oil and tattooed muscles, had already motioned for us to get the fuck out. Closing time. But we'd tipped off Danielle

that Harry thought she was "cute." Which was, per tra-
dition, code for "he's ready." Danielle wasn't a slut. She
was single and lonely, like most everybody else, and
liked the attention, I guess. Liked to feel attractive.
Maybe she felt maternal. Far as I knew, she had no kids
of her own. We were like her bastard children.

Dollface went down into the basement to count out
her drawer.

"You going home with her?" Lenny asked Harry,
picking his nails with a long lemon-paring knife.

"I don't know," Harry answered weakly. He was a little loaded. We all were. But he seemed to snap into stiff
sobriety pretty quickly when we dropped the news.

Lenny laughed. "Wear two Trojans."

Harry and I agreed to take on part-time gigs in order to
fund equipment maintenance and rock'n'roll attire. I'd
started tutoring underclassmen at the high school.
Typing was the only real skill I had besides drumming
and shop, but there weren't many drummers, and most
of the kids who took shop knew what they were doing.
I was a lightning bolt on the QWERTYs and found it
almost pleasurable. Well, I found my own lessons pleasurable. I considered the thickheaded pupils with de-
ficient hand-eye coordination and attention deficit
disorder to be intolerable, and while they practiced I
would often excuse myself for a few minutes and steal
things out of their unlocked cars and lockers.

Harry, though, could not find employment at
Harrison. If he walked by cheerleading squad practice,

they'd probably call the sheriff. He was still much too shy then to assist anyone in a retail setting, so I suggested he investigate telemarketing.

"You can make a lot of money, and you won't have to look anyone in the eye," I assured him.

"What if they're ugly to me? People don't like being called cold. My mom . . . she gets ugly."

"Fuck 'em. Just be confident. You don't know what they look like. You don't care. And if they're pricks, just imagine they have humps or lobster hands and they're mean to everyone. You don't have to take any of it personally. Plus you can drink and smoke on the job. It's ideal."

"I don't know, Sandy. People really mess me up."

"You sound like a little kid. You're not a little kid anymore. You're a Jane Asher. We don't get messed up by people. We mess them up. Besides, Rudy needs a new guitar."

"Why can't Rudy get a job?"

"Rudy's . . . Rudy."

Fortunately, we didn't have to day-job it for too long. Things were happening out there, beyond the state line.

We didn't get our first four or five gigs because of Nirvana's surprise ascension to the top of the charts in the fall of 1991, but I should probably belatedly thank them for getting us our sixth through fortieth shows. And I don't mean to suggest that we ever met them or opened shows for them and shared beers and inside jokes or bong hits or anything. We were still only sharing those with each other. I'm just saying that a reasonably alternative rock'n'roll band did not have to be from Seattle to directly benefit from the massive cultural shift they were directing. You know that scene in the John Waters movie *Hairspray,* where Divine, playing a lumpy hausfrau, looks wistfully heavenward and says with utter conviction, "The times, they are a-changin'. Something's blowin' in the wind. . . ." That's kind of what it was like. Even the moms could tell. And I don't mean just my ma. Although Minna was the first one to play me *Nevermind.* She thought "Smells Like Teen Spirit" ripped off Hüsker Dü, not the Pixies, as Kurt Cobain later admitted. I memorized *Nevermind.* Listened to it in my dad's car. The speakers were pretty loud for an old man's vehicle. I was listening to it for pleasure, sure. It's obviously brilliant. But I was also trying to figure out what, if anything, Kurt Cobain had that Harry didn't, excluding a record deal. I already knew Nirvana's drummer played harder than I could ever hope to, but at the time I couldn't admit this and assured myself that I could take him. It was thrilling to decide that Cobain really didn't have much on Harry Vance. Both had voices that made the heat shoot down your brain and into the back of your neck. Both had a way with witty but honest lyrics, both punk-rock-direct and poetic. Both had bed head. Both sang about nutty chicks. Kurt was about a year older and a lot more famous, but that was about it. The closer *Nevermind* came to knocking Michael Jackson's *Dangerous* out of the number one spot on the charts just after New Year's 1992, the more it seemed the kids wanted to hear our kind of music. Well, most of them, anyway.

Rehearsal started a bit late the next day. We were all a little swollen from the cheap wine, a little slow. It was good to sweat out some toxins, but we weren't shaking much in the way of music. A wiggy jam on "White Rabbit" by Jefferson Airplane degenerated further with Rudy screaming improvised lines: "Remember what the dormouse said. Gimme head! Gimme head!"

"That's retarded," I sighed, flinging a stick at his head. "Like, someone's gonna blow a dormouse?"

"The dormouse of perception, man," he retorted nonsensically.

"Shut the fuck up."

"You're gonna regret being, uh . . . mean to me, Sandy."

"I don't think I will."

"Oh, yeah? Well, I think you will. I think you will a lot."

"Shut up, you 'tard."

He removed Keith from his mouth and stuck it on the end of his guitar, then lit up a cigarette and blinked at me. "Nuh-uh. 'Cause . . . I got us a gig."

"No way!"

Harry got up from the milk crate, picked up the drumstick and handed it to me, turned back to Rudy, and tried, as I was doing, to discern whether or not he was jiving us.

"It's true. Remember Lori Strange?"

"*Stange.*"

"Whatever, man. She's having a birthday party on Friday and she said we can play. Fifty bucks for an hour. That's not bad."

"That's fucked. Tell her we'll do it for a hundred," I barked.

"She said we can drink all the beer we want too. And maybe, like, cookies and shit."

"Fuck her cookies."

"It's a paying gig," Harry interjected. "It's not about the bucks, Sand. It's about the precedent."

"Okay, Harry. I understand that. I'm not stupid, you know."

"I know."

"Just a little hungover and irritable."

"Tell her we'll be there," Harry said, flexing his muscle as the unspoken leader. I don't know what would have happened if I'd challenged him on it . . . or anything. Maybe he'd've backed down. It didn't matter. I agreed with him because he had more to lose. He wasn't desperate—but he was very determined. Made him smarter.

"There's one condition."

"She's giving us conditions? For 50 bucks?"

"What's the condition, Rudy?" Harry asked.

"Well, they've got a list of covers they want us to learn."

"No, fuck that," I exploded. "We play Jane Ashers songs or no deal. We're not a fucking wedding band."

"What covers?"

Rudy reached into his dirty, skinny jeans and pulled out a slip of paper. He handed it to me.

"I can't read your handwriting. You write like a fucking hostage."

Rudy took the paper back and ticked off the list.

"Do Me" by Bell Biv DeVoe
"Pump Up the Jam" by Technotronic

too much, too late

"Opposites Attract" by Paula Abdul
"Unskinny Bop" by Poison
"The Power" by Snap

"Vision of Love" by Mariah Carey
"All Around the World" by Lisa Stansfield
"Nothing Compares 2 U" by Sinéad O'Connor

"We're learning 'Unskinny Bop,' " Harry announced. "We need to play out."

"We are not!" I shouted.

"And the Sinéad one. Come on."

"Suck my dick on that."

"Will you teach me 'Unskinny Bop'?" Rudy asked helplessly.

"I will teach you 'Unskinny Bop,' " Harry reassured him, and pulled Rudy's guitar strap. "Gimme." Harry took the Telecaster. "Can you hum the melody for me?"

Rudy hummed it as best he could from memory.

I smashed my sticks against the kit in defeat. I was gonna play Poison whether I wanted to or not. A precedent had to be set.

"Hit it, C. C.!" I spat mockingly, pointing my stick directly at Harry like my arm was a crossbow. Fortunately "Unskinny Bop" is an easy song to play, once you get over the indignity and nausea and shame. It's actually pretty fun. The Sinéad song, which is really a Prince song, as you probably know, is even easier. For me anyway. Slow, steady beat. Subtle or something. We all knew the lyrics 'cause it'd been a massive hit the year before. It's much harder on the vocalist, but Harry really wailed it. I would have had a tear in my eye if I'd had any emotions back then.

"Hello, Lori Stange's backyard! Are you ready to rock?" I shouted to absolutely nobody. We'd set up and started raving up too, but drew no crowd. We were competing with the newly tapped keg in the Stange kitchen and losing badly. We went through "Unskinny Bop" and managed to pull some 15-year-old with zits and a blue ski vest with the stuffing falling out. We were relieved. Harry played directly to him, Vegas-style, until we realized the poor underage kiddo had stumbled outside to puke. "It's better than being booed," Harry cracked through gritted teeth. We were all feeling the steepness of the hill and wondering if it was climbable at all.

"Let's do 'Shit About Love,' " Harry suggested, and I counted it off. It was a short song, so we played it twice. By the second version, we'd fattened our audience to five. Four dudes, one girl. They were sitting on the lawn chatting to each other about teachers they hated, students they hated, TV shows they loved. But they were bodies. We knew they were hearing us.

"Any requests out there?" Harry asked desperately.

"You got any weed?" one smartass kid with stringy blond hair and a goofy-looking blue and yellow striped turtleneck mouthed off. I stood up. Harry turned around to face me and shook his head. Spared the kid some damage for sure.

"Yes, we do have weed, actually."

"Cool."

"You bring ten of your friends out here and we'll share it."

"I'm not smoking those fuckers out," Rudy protested. It was his pot, after all. "Just you." He pointed to turtleneck boy.

"All right. Deal."

The kid ran into the kitchen and returned with two more friends. They were girls, so when he asked if they'd suffice, Rudy nodded. We struck up "I Wanna Eat Soup," the goofy old Ramones homage we had—a time killer and set filler. But fun to play.

> Keep your Peter Pan.
> Keep your eggs and Spam.
> Don't want no Froot-a Loop.
> I just wanna eat my soup.
> Soup is good food
> And I'm in a good mood
> So pass that spoon my way, momma.
> Pass that spoon today.

"We have some songs that aren't about soup, yeah," Harry promised. I could tell he was as frustrated as he was excited to be playing to live human beings. This was our big chance and it seemed, to him anyway, that we had nothing true to say.

We played our first public gig at Pinheads, of course. Danielle did some wheeling and dealing on our behalf and even slept with Archie Funz at the end of the night, which I still find amazing, as familiar as I am with the concept of chicks seeing ugly guys like us through rock goggles. From Pinheads we hit Cincinnati. We played Annie's, the Comet by the college, the Blue Wisp. Then Toledo: the Distillery, JJ's Aqua Lounge, Frankie's on Main Street. We played Neptune's Pizza Kitchen, which had awful pizza but a real sound board. We recorded our set there, slapped a photo of Jane Asher on the paper card a few days later, and that was our demo. We labeled it *Meatloaf, Loaded Guns, and Thick-Ankled Midwestern Girls* but decided that was too crude, like a bad Dwarves or Butthole Surfers title. We debated *Play to Shiver,* but that seemed way goth. Finally we just called it *Songs from the Deep End,* which referenced another Jane Asher film, a cult flick from 1970 where she plays a twisted London teenager's object of desire. It all takes place in a bathhouse and ends badly. We just liked the film. We didn't see its tragic ending as anything ominous.

At each tour stop we partied like mad. Harry took easily to partying hard. Maybe he needed to numb himself, or fake a little anger to get into the spirit of his old songs. Or maybe he was just lost and sad. All I know is he didn't eat food anymore. Just drank and smoked, and if there were drugs around, he drugged. Harry lost about 15 pounds in the first few weeks of his Jane Ashers tenure. No matter what it took to get him to sing, once he was in the mix, everything was right. The sheer rush of his voice falling in and out with my beats and Rudy's chords kept us all from keeling over, no matter what we ingested. In the early days of the band, that'd be beer and vodka. We also drank whiskey. We drank gin. We drank schnapps. We drank cooking sherry. We drank vanilla extract. We drank malt liquor. We drank Manischewitz. We drank Night Train. We drank Boone's Farm Strawberry Hill. We sucked the speed out of asthma inhalers. We ate NoDoz. We ate penicillin. We ate pot brownies. Macaroni and pot. Pot ziti. Corned pot. We ate frozen Snickers bars and smoked pot. We drank bong water and smoked pot. We

too much, too late

bought acid off African Pete, the hippie bagger at the supermarket who wasn't African, and ate that. We just wanted to stay high and play music. We weren't picky. We'd put anything in our body if we thought it would complement the main rush, the rock'n'roll. We'd eat guitar strings and drumskins if we thought it'd feel good. Better. Different. Interesting. We didn't care that it made it harder to play. Not yet. We were so high on what we had, we welcomed the challenge. Could we get through this song on a bottle of drippy roach snot and gum-wrapper-glue tea? What would "Roots" sound like if we played it on the moons of Jupiter? What would Elmer Fudd sound like if he sang "Straight Up" by Paula Abdul (Rudy) as a duet with Steve Marriott of Small Faces (Harry)? We were exploring. And at our age, you could snap out of a hangover quickly. More often than not, we did this by getting high and drunk all over again. It was elliptical and stupid, but in a weird and at the time very crucial way, it kept what we were doing private. It was the secret society of the "eat that." It was bonding . . . it created the Jane Ashers elite. Nobody else was as stupid and self-destructive and fearless as we were, so we must be special. I should also mention that we all slept with a different female Ohioan at each house party or bar gig, Harry Vance included. The difference between me and him was that I loved it.

Sometimes after a show, when everyone else had passed out or hooked up, Harry and I would find ourselves alone together, out in a parking lot, or up on some kid's roof. We'd look up at the constellations and pass a bottle or a smoke back and forth. He'd confess to me that he was very disappointed by it all.

"This can't be it," he'd laugh, sounding pained.

"This is pretty much it."

"I mean, it's good and all. It feels good, but it's just so empty, isn't it?"

"Hardly. It's awesome, Harry. What else do you want?"

"I don't know. Inspiration. Love, maybe."

"Who told you you knew shit about love?" I asked. It was probably the first time somebody had quoted one of his lyrics to him.

Harry laughed, but then he complained, "I might as well be singing 'Unskinny Bop' at every show. What's the difference between that and 'Soup'? They're both meaningless. Paul McCartney wrote 'Here, There and Everywhere' for Jane Asher 'cause he was in love with her. That song means something."

"Yeah, well, you can't hold yourself to that standard. That's Paul. You'll go crazy and do nothing with your life if you do that. You have good songs too. Forget about Paul. And John. They'll only stop you from becoming what you are."

"I feel like this is stopping me from becoming what I am. Those songs we're playing?"

"The ones everybody loves? What about them?"

"Some of them are so old, Sandy. They feel like they were written by someone else. Like . . . a little kid. I'm sick of them. They're not true anymore."

It was true. Nobody wanted to admit it because the songs sounded so good and that voice really did make them live, but if you had some kind of Geiger counter that detected jive molecules, there was a lot of horseshit going on that we didn't dare acknowledge . . . more death than life in our songs, covers excluded. More old news than the brave new. More sputter than spark. These were songs mired in the physical longings of puberty. And when that hormonal jones was finally sated, Harry wasn't really inspired by any of it. He needed something real to write about. Everyone can fuck. But getting satisfaction . . . that was much more complicated. Uncharted.

"What happens with those girls, Sandy . . ." He stood up and walked to the edge of the roof, staring out at the small town. "It doesn't make me wanna sing about anything."

3

Harry knew it was real, and he knew it fast. Ten seconds after meeting Debbie, he began to worry that one day (even if he lived to be 99) he was going to die, and she was going to die too (even if she lived to be 101). They would eventually, inevitably be separated, and this would not do. Harry started scheming about ways to avoid this but came up with nothing. I must allow that if anyone could get a young guy, just a few women into his sexual history, to obsess over extending his golden years, it was Debbie Andrews. At 18, she was all right in every way. The kind of girl you have to look over twice: the first time in admiration, the next in disbelief.

I couldn't find anything wrong with her myself. Well, maybe one thing: she never smiled. She was one miserable-looking pretty girl. She wore no makeup—didn't need to. She had the kind of clear and peachy skin that seemed permanently flushed and warm, like there was a candle burning in her skull, stuck to her spine with melted wax and fed with oxygen she inhaled through her Romanesque nose. She appeared preposterously healthy, excluding the grayish purple bags under each of her dark, almost black eyes. She had good proportions too. Figurewise, I mean. It's rare to find a petite girl with big tits that sit right. At least that's been my experience with girls and tits. Tiny hands, dainty feet, and a rack. It is strange, isn't it? I'm just pointing that out. Don't shoot the drummer.

Debbie's hair was a natural light brown that looked blond in the sun and deep chestnut under bar light. She wore black sweaters, even in warm weather. Tweed skirts. Wool tights, black or mustard-colored. Doc Martens boots, knee high. Smoked like cigarettes didn't give you cancer. She spoke in a knowing, humorous voice that was already a rasp, thanks to all the American Spirit Lights. She smelled like chocolate because she wore some fancy perfume with cocoa in it. But she didn't buy it at the Olfactory.

Debbie wasn't from Dean. She was born and raised in Cincinnati and still lived there, working at some fancy modern art gallery and planning to resume her study at Oberlin College, the state's biggest liberal arts school. She'd applied a few years before, been accepted, spent her freshman year there, then deferred just before the first semester of her sophomore year. Something was preventing her from moving on, graduating, ending up somewhere glamorous and nurturing like New York, or maybe Florence, Italy. She returned home, and that March she made a pilgrimage to Dean, as she'd done every March or April since she was a kid. Debbie Andrews had family here. Grandmother, I think. Maybe her great-aunt. She'd travel into town by bus. I remember seeing her by the station, wearing all black despite the bright sunlight, reading some thick hardbound book or the *New York Times*. I saw her at the newsstand a couple of times too. I'm sure I hit on her. Maybe I pointed and sang a verse from "Bela Lugosi's Dead" too. But we've never spoken about any of that, not even as a joke in hindsight, so who knows.

I don't know why Harry never spied her himself, or she him. Maybe she even passed him once or twice but didn't notice him until now. Before he led the Jane Ashers, Harry was easy to pass by. Regardless, every March or April this nutty goth chick would materialize in Dean, always hang around the same old house, three stories with a big brick chimney, clean white clapboards with navy blue trim, and a broad, well-kept lawn full of flowerbeds and bushes. Her grandmother or great-aunt or whatever had moved away or died long ago, but Debbie had some kind of understanding with the new tenants. They'd never call the cops when the strange girl appeared unannounced with a pair of shears and began trimming boughs off the big lilac bough in the front yard just as they started to bloom.

Lilacs, I've since been told, only bloom once a year, for a pretty short time. Then, like Debbie, the flowers would vanish.

The Andrews family had their unhappy living rooms and kitchens. And they had their funerals. Debbie's mother, Ruth, had been driving home from an Italian restaurant one night in the summer of 1985. She'd taken the wheel because she and Debbie's father, Paul Andrews, a big corporate lawyer with a lot of clients in the city, had had a lot of good red wine. It was decided that Debbie's dad was too drunk to drive. The problem was that Debbie's mother was too drunk as well. She ran off the road and flipped the DeVille in a concrete drainage ditch about three miles from their driveway. If they'd hit soft earth, she might have lived. It was just a freak thing that the roof landed on the hard concrete and buckled. Ruth broke her neck and died. Paul survived but sustained multiple injuries, some serious. Debbie, who wasn't in the car, was just 13. She was here in Dean with the grandmother or great-aunt, giggling, looking at photo albums, watching TV. Evidently Paul and Ruth were having marital trouble. It was whispered after the accident that that was why they'd been drinking. He was having an affair in the city. She'd found out.

Debbie Andrews wore black every day from then on, and I never saw her in a bright color until she hit middle age. I guess she'd tried to grieve and move on, but that wasn't to be just yet, so she stayed in the funereal garb just in case something else went down. And it did, about six or seven months after the car wreck: her dad had a stroke. He was all twisted up, but he was starting to recover. Debbie provided as much love and support as possible from someone who couldn't look at him for more than 30 seconds without becoming fitful and ill. She retreated to the lilac house in Dean as much as possible, even after it was sold. She was safe there.

Harry had been to the gas station and was just walking by on his way to band rehearsal, six-pack of beer in a brown bag by his side. When he saw her, he dropped it. The sound of breaking glass startled her.

"It's okay," was the first thing she ever said to him, although she probably wasn't looking his way just yet. "I'm allowed to do this."

Harry never delivered the beer he'd been running back. He went back to Cincinnati with Debbie on a sticky, hot bus and slept with her in her childhood bed with her invalid father muttering two floors below in the blue glow of some late-night horror film. I don't know if the sex came as fast as the love. Probably. Not my business. I know everything else came fast. When Harry returned to Dean the next day I didn't recognize him at first. And he looked at Minna and me like we were strangers too.

"What the fuck happened to you?" I asked. "You were supposed to get the beer!"

"Sandy." Harry smiled. "I wrote a love song."

He sang it for me and Archie. It was "Let's Go Steady Debbie," and it was . . . well, you know.

A few hours later Rudy arrived, chewing on Keith. He unpacked his guitar, plugged it in, and began playing the riff to "Who Told You . . ."

"Stop that," I demanded. It felt like an oldie.

"Huh?"

"We got a new one. Sit down. We'll work out it for you. And pay attention."

Harry sang. I provided a backbeat.

We turned to Rudy and waited for some derision. Rudy didn't like the sappy stuff. "Angie" was the only ballad he could tolerate. But even surly Rudy Tunick was smitten with this melody and started working out a chiming intro and that mock metal solo almost immediately.

"You know, this song could be a real hit or something."

Rudy grinned. "Like on MTV or . . . VH1."

"This could be our ticket out of Dean," Archie agreed.

"You don't live in Dean," I reminded him.

"Oh, yeah. Well, it could be *your* ticket out of Dean, and I can come. Right?"

I nodded. He flashed me some metal teeth.

"You think she'll like it?" Harry wondered aloud. He couldn't care less that he'd written something like a fucking American classic, on a par with "Walk Away Renee," "God Only Knows," "September Gurls," a song that anyone could cover and not ruin—even a teenage pop queen, someone who didn't know shit about love.

I know a little more about love today. All the hassles of being in love, all the elements that threaten the relationship—they're all born out of that first wave of excitement. The same one that feels like salvation. The panic and fear of death and poverty, the desperation to put your shit in order yesterday, the anarchy—they're born the same day your love song is born. The worst feelings in the world can crawl out, quietly, no fanfare, while you're cradling and guarding and nursing your best feeling in the world. And too much of a good thing can do your head in, make everything around you that's not perfect seem like a big black threat to your his-and-hers bliss. I can see how these threats are real if you make them real. At this point, we were doing fine as a band, moving along at our own pace, getting really tight and intuitive. But suddenly that wasn't enough anymore. And neither was starting rehearsal an hour late or knocking off an hour or two early to get fucked up in the park. And neither was Minna's comfortable couch, or sleeping together in the room above Debbie's gimpy old man's wheelchair. My lead singer now required a master plan, and we all had to adapt.

"She hates it at home, Sandy," Harry fretted as we sat in the diner. "She screams in her sleep."

"Maybe she's a mental . . . person?"

"Stop it." Harry pushed me. He'd never done that before. I shrugged it off. Punching my lead singer in the mouth, what would that do?

"I don't see why you have to move into your own place."

"Last night we stayed in a Motel 6 and she didn't scream at all. You know what she said? She woke up, stared at me, said, 'Turtles. I like turtles,' then laid her head down and went back to sleep."

"Great."

"That's an improvement!"

"I need more coffee."

I lit up a cigarette and blew a noxious-looking plume

across Dil's stained counter, right into his slap-happy face. I smiled. It felt good because I was starting to hate the guy. Maybe I was a little jealous. He'd been spending every minute of his free time over in the city. Sometimes he didn't even have enough money to get back to Dean for rehearsal, so he'd just wander around Metropolis all day, playing harmonica and waiting for her to get off work. It didn't even occur to him to play for change, pass a hat. I was getting really pissed. The only thing that saved his life when he'd show up days late for practice, wearing clothes that obviously belonged to a chick who shopped out of catalogs (and only bought the black articles, including boatneck sweaters and shiny blouses) were these new songs he'd have with him. "And It Made My Woman Happy," which you'll recognize from our album, you know . . . that could have been one of the folkier numbers on *Rubber Soul,* if you ask me. He wrote that one around that time. And whenever Harry walked a song like that through the door, I always forgave him for blowing us off. He'd sit down with Rudy and work it out, and suddenly our violently dispositioned rhythm guitarist, who wanted not ten minutes earlier to stuff and mount his lead singer, could only think about doing justice to this hot and beautiful new tune. Still, waiting for Harry was fraying us. Rudy and I finally decided we were going to give him an ultimatum: either he commit to us or we break up. Turns out he had an ultimatum for us too.

"We need to start treating the Ashers like a job or it's just not worth it."

"What?"

"Seriously, Sandy. This has to be a professional band. We need to play out. We need a manager. We need to start earning money off our music."

"When did you decide this?"

"Last night. In the Motel 6."

Apparently between screwing each other in cheap but private motor inns, lying naked under one of those tan foam blankets with the satin edges, Harry and Debbie had made some big plans for my band.

"I want to marry you. I want to have babies with you."

"I want to marry you too. But we can't raise our babies in a Motel 6," she told him.

She got up, padded naked across the gritty carpet in just her socks (black socks, I'm assuming), and turned up the air conditioner to drown out the bedlam outside. She jumped back in bed and pulled the covers up past her breasts, cocooning herself in the sheets. Harry started scribbling on the back of a newspaper. This wasn't the kind of place that gave you complimentary stationery.

"Hold me," she said. He did.

"We can live in Dean. It's so much cheaper. You can get a job there. Maybe my mother—"

"I like my job."

"I know. I'm sorry. I love you . . . but I can't leave the band."

"Why not?"

"I don't know. Sandy . . . he sort of . . . he and his mother . . . they sort of . . . they . . ." He sighed. "I really love you." She unspooled her sheet cocoon and sat up. She grabbed a cigarette off the woodgrain night table and lit it. Her voice was even raspier with fatigue, maybe a little urgent anger.

"Harry, if you told me that you can't leave because you truly believe that you guys can make it, that'd be one thing. If you told me that, I'd quit my job at the gallery and move into a shitty apartment in Dean with you. I'd put my plans on hold for a year and support yours."

"Really?"

"I would. Gladly. But instead you're telling me that I have to quit my job and upend my entire life because you feel a sense of obligation to your best friend's mother? I love you and I believe in you. But if you're going to play in a rock'n'roll band, you have to play in a rock'n'roll band for real. That has to be what you do. It's as genuine a job, as honorable a profession as anyone's. But all those professionals have real hours. They have rules. They're serious about them. I think you're really talented. Remarkably talented. Your voice melts my heart. But you need to figure this shit out, Harry. Because we can't keep doing this. I can't keep checking under these beds for dead bodies."

There was a faint lilac hue to the sunset the night Harry and Debbie first shacked up in Dean. They took it as an omen. Debbie paid first and last months' rent on a one-bedroom apartment by the railroad tracks, noisier but much less expensive. Not quite affordable, but Harry was determined to change that. He was a man with a girlfriend, an apartment, and a band, inside of one year. His loneliness and frustration and hurt, that was an '80s thing, he told himself. This was the '90s. This was how it was gonna be. This beautiful woman who loved him and cared about him had altered her course for him. And she would be the only one he would consider and protect and sing about in return.

Harry squeezed Debbie's hand as the taxi paused briefly at a stop sign in front of the lilac house. Tight sweat and blood on blood, the best feeling in the world, like Bruce Springsteen sang in "Highway Patrolman." Their cheap rental was only six blocks south of the big house with the purple flowers.

"We'll build a family in this place," Harry said, then pointed to the house as they cruised past. "One day we'll live there."

She squeezed his arm and stared out the window. "There used to be a trampoline in the basement. I wonder if it's still there."

"If it isn't, we'll buy one. I'm gonna make it, Debbie. We'll have everything you want."

"I don't want a trampoline, Harry."

"What do you want?"

"I'm not telling."

"Why?"

" 'Cause you're going to try to get it for me, and you need to focus on your art."

Harry'd never heard his songs referred to as "art" before. Certainly the Jane Ashers never talked such shit. His chest puffed up a bit involuntarily there in the backseat. He shone with pride. Then, after realizing things were good—very good, almost perfect—he flared with worry.

"Wait . . . Debbie . . ."

"Yes?"

"You can tell me. I want you to feel like you can say anything. Is there something you want?"

"I want to feel like things are getting better. Always. I want to feel like things are meaningful. Never just . . . empty."

"Okay."

"And I want pizza."

He laughed.

"With mushrooms and green peppers."

"I can't give you green peppers," Harry cracked, shaking his head. "It's disgusting."

She hit him.

"It is not."

"Solo maybe. Or in a salad. On a pizza, it just ruins everything. It makes it all taste hotter."

They ate pizza on the kitchen floor that night, green peppers on half. Harry was determined to give Debbie whatever she wanted even if it stank up a perfectly good pie.

Harry and Debbie continued to nest through the next few days, shopping in thrift stores, decorating, and exulting in first-apartment giddiness. You know, things like, "This is not just a dented orange teapot—this is our dented orange teapot." "This is *our* Reynolds Wrap. We place it in our cupboard and we will use it to wrap *our* leftovers. We own Reynolds Wrap. We are adults." Choosing what color toilet paper to put in the john: pink, blue, yellow, or classic white. Selecting soap (Debbie preferred Dr. Bronner's. I always thought people who got their shower soap out of a bottle and not a bar were a little suspicious). Deciding where to put the television set (theirs was on the floor, in the corner, and functioned mainly as a blue night-light). Does the Day-Glo Cure poster go in the kitchenette or the bedroom? Are the Christmas lights with the plastic bats a fire hazard if placed in the bedroom over the bowls of dried lilacs and the candelabra and the standing brass ashtray with the bloodred glass and all the smoldering cigarettes? (Probably.) Are the framed Edward Gorey prints a bit too Goth? (Certainly.)

The heat pipes were hissing and temperamental. The place could get quite cold at night, so they took to spending the whole day wearing old terry bathrobes they'd thrifted. This only contributed to the cozy, bohemian warmth. They spent most of the time in bed. The rest of their day revolved around either the card table in the kitchenette or the little study where Harry sat writing in his notebooks and staring out the tiny window or across at Debbie, who was making lists on a yellow legal pad.

> Call phone company
> Read want ads
> Oberlin application (Debbie)
> Groceries (stop ordering in—too X-pensive)
> Write songs—good songs (Harry)

"Harry, are you ever going to move your stuff in? We could put a nice bookshelf in that room. Maybe a desk. Piano bench too. I saw one out back in the trash. It's almost a piano."

Harry looked up from his lyrics.

"Yeah," he mumbled. "Piano bench."

"You're avoiding it."

"No. I'm just working on this—"

"You need to go over there. I'll go with you."

"No . . . no, that's okay. I'll go."

"You don't want me to meet your mom?"

"No. I do. I just . . . don't wanna meet my mom. Or see my mom."

"Ever again?"

"No. I—I don't know . . ." Harry stammered pathetically.

Mrs. Vance opened the door expecting to sign for a package. It was early, coffee and paper time. She had one earring in her ear and another in her left hand, black java in a yellow mug in her right. Stocking feet. Debbie was caught mid-yawn.

"Oh, hi, Mrs. Vance. I'm Debbie."

She extended her hand. Harry's mom shook it.

"I'm your son's girlfriend."

"Harry."

"Do you have another son?"

"No."

"We're living over on Metamora now. In case you were worried. We're renting a place together, 'cause we're in love. Do you have any more of that coffee?"

Debbie called a taxi and moved Harry's books, records, journals, and instruments into the car all by herself. It must have taken her a few hours. They weren't even boxed up. And Harry's mother didn't offer any assistance. She didn't even hold the door. Debbie transported Harry's belongings over to the apartment and had them set up for him by the time he returned from rehearsing with us.

"What did you do?"

"Now this is your home, Harry. I'm not going to have any half commitments here. Not when I quit my job and left the city."

"Okay."

He hugged her. Wiped some sweat away from his brow. Took off his glasses. Squinted.

"But how did you . . ."

"You need to talk to your mom, Harry."

"How . . . is she?" He fell into the chair and leaned an elbow on the card table.

"She's a mess."

"I know."

"But she's your mother."

"Yeah."

"My mother's dead." Debbie lit up a smoke, took a drag, and handed it to him.

"Are you happy?" she asked. He could smell the smoke on her breath, but it didn't seem to bother him. Everything that came out of her mouth seemed sweet.

"Yes."

"See, I thought so. I didn't tell your mother 'cause I wasn't sure. But she asked me, Harry. I think she wants you to be happy."

She took off her sweater. He watched her in amazement. "It's hot. These pipes are unpredictable."

She folded it and sat back across from him in her white tank top with the flowers embroidered around the neck.

At bedtime Harry lay on the bed and listened to the

too much, too late

faucet running in the bathroom. He didn't know what she was doing in there, but he assumed it was something routine, something domestic, something she never did while any other boy was in the next room, and it made him feel good. He wondered what their wedding would be like. If he could get an invitation to his dad somehow. If they'd hire a DJ or get the band to play some songs.

"I think we should have a housewarming dinner," Debbie said as she sat on the bed and started rubbing lotion into her legs. Harry was transfixed. He'd imagined what women did in private for a long time, and not always in a creepy way either—he was genuinely curious. Now he felt privileged. In the right spot. Treated to some fascinating female stuff.

"Are you listening to me? I can cook. We can have the band over. Maybe your mother."

"Not Mom."

"Just the Jane Ashers, then. I'll make spaghetti and we can get to know each other."

"Okay."

"How about Tuesday? We can get drunk on wine."

It never occured to him to correct her, to say, "Well, I am a Jane Asher too, technically." When he was with her, he was just Harry the man. Not Harry the lead singer.

"You don't remember me at all?" I was a little drunk already. Rudy and I had killed a six before we came by. Nerves maybe. We were worried it'd be stuffy. It wasn't. So I kept drinking the cheap merlot they'd bought at the supermarket. I was happy to see my friend so together.

"Debbie" was starting to really help our career. I remember thinking it was weird recognizing these strange faces at every new show. At first I'd wonder, "Isn't that the Chinese-looking girl from that bar?" and then I'd shudder as I realized she was there specifically to see us and not to drink or eat hot wings. We had real fans. And they made requests. Well, they only requested "Debbie."

We needed a band logo, for my bass drum. Debbie took a photo of Jane Asher over to the copy shop by the college, blew it up, and cut it into a near perfect circle. She glued it to the skin.

"That looks very cool," I encouraged her, then watched admiringly as she stenciled our name in a semicircle across the top of Jane's bangs. In less than fifteen minutes she had the logo right there. It's weird to see it now on T-shirts and stickers and stuff, 'cause really it was just something she did between American Spirits. Something that maybe kept her in touch with the artistic side she was essentially shelving in favor of supporting her man and his band. I was so grateful I made a point not to stare into her cleavage as she worked the markers and her breasts jiggled slightly under all that black wool.

We all thought it would be best if Archie Funz stood in the distance for our promotional photos. This sounds fancier than it actually was. We intended to send some out with copies of *Songs from the Deep End* but never got around to it, even with our new work ethic. But the *Dean Beacon* wanted to write up a feature tagged to the big Eggfest gig. Debbie volunteered to organize the shoot and take the photos herself. She even doubled as a stylist. She was watching Harry get dressed for rehearsal one afternoon and inquired whether or not he ever played in anything besides the old, tight black leather jacket he'd taken to wearing since leaving home and dropping some pounds.

"Why?" he worried. "You don't like it?"

"I just think a band needs a strong image. Look at Kiss."

"You think we should wear, like, demon makeup?"

"No. Maybe a little eyeliner, though."

"Eyeliner?"

"Not Siouxsie style. Don't worry. I don't want to goth you out. You'll end up in prison for a crime you didn't commit or something."

He stared at his boots. "I don't know, yeah. Maybe some eyeliner would be cool, I guess. I just don't know if anyone can see it behind the, uh . . ." He pointed to his thick glasses with a little shame.

"I think the glasses are part of the image, aren't they?"

"I guess. Mostly I need them to see."

"Right, but there's a precedent." Debbie was big on precedents. "Buddy Holly. Elvis. C, not P. Who else, Harry?"

"Well, Roy Orbison. He was supposedly an albino. Wore them to cover his red eyes. And Ian Hunter, from Mott the Hoople, he wore glasses because he was cross-eyed."

She kissed him and put her plaid cashmere scarf over his neck, studied it disapprovingly, and removed it.

"I'm just saying if you're going to wear them, wear them proudly. They're part of who you are."

He pulled the long scarf from her hand like a magician and tried to return it to his neck. She grabbed the end.

"No. I don't like it."

"But it's chilly."

"So . . . are you punks?"

"Not really."

"Are you new wavers?"

"Power poppers, I think. Sometimes just rock. Like we do a version of 'Shooting Star' by Bad Company." He giggled to himself. "It's pretty good."

She lit a cigarette.

"Power poppers."

"Yeah. We also like English things."

"What do Anglophile power poppers wear, Harry?"

"Suits, I guess."

"Matching suits?"

"I guess."

"Maybe that's the way to go."

"Nah."

"All right, not matching. But suits could work."

She padded across the room barefoot and pulled open the closet. She had a lot more clothes than he did, all black. Black sweaters. Black ski jacket. Black leather coat. Black blouses. Black winter hat. Black vintage fur stole with a black varmint head at the end. Tiny little rolled-up balls of nylon tights strewn across the clutter like jimmies on a scoop of ice cream. It took some time to find his clothes underneath all her shit. One rust-colored corduroy suit amid the hooded sweatshirts and striped polos that were now baggy. Everything else was just T-shirts and jeans. Under the leather jacket, he looked cool enough, but from a stage, before a crowd . . . she had a point.

"Maybe we should go shopping, Harry."

When the Janes posed for our first photos, we did look more like a power pop combo than before. But not slick like the Knack. The Replacements were more of a template. Scruffy but with a lot of style. Their jackets soaked with beer and stinking of cigs but still pretty natty. Sharkskin with the leather. Hairspray with the denim. And yeah, some black eyeliner, which is perfectly acceptable for a heterosexual rock'n'roll musican to shoplift from Bix's drugstore.

We gave Debbie a bunch of album covers we liked. *Rubber Soul. Aftermath. Blank Generation.* The first Romantics album. *Maggot Brain* by Funkadelic just to throw her a curve. She went to the big campus library over in the city and photocopied a bunch of portraits. Man Ray. Diane Arbus's shots of mentally retarded children. David Bailey's shots of swingin' London icons like Marianne Faithfull and Jagger. She did the homework, and the shots looked good. She even brought a Polaroid and took some test shots, like a professional. We felt sort of famous already as we posed, but when we picked up the prints from the Foto Shack a few hours later, those giddy waves seemed justified. We'd felt like a band. Then we sounded like a band. Now we looked like a band. Harry, although not as naturally handsome as me, took the front space in the shot we chose. You couldn't tell his hair was curly. It looked spiky the way it was caught on film, with a little help from the Aqua Net. His sneer and the crooked knot in his skinny tie were just punk enough to suggest a pissed-off but sensitive nerd-turned-troubadour. I stood to his left with my back leaning on him, wearing my bar mitzvah tie and a gold jacket with the lapels pulled up. Rudy was in full ectomorphic Keith mode, lazy lids, cig in the pout, skinny wannabe junkie arm over Harry's shoulder in blood-brotherly fashion. Archie crouched behind us. All you could see was the top of his shaved head and a cluster of zits that we couldn't afford to airbrush out. But fuck it. It made us real. Maybe that was part of our image too. Power pop/punk and pimply like you.

After the shoot, we all went to the diner, then over to my place to play. It was the first time Debbie had ever seen us perform. Even I was a little nervous. We knew she was a sharpie. She sat on a crate, chain-smoking. Maybe she was nervous too. She had, after all, invested a lot in this thing. Not to mention about $150 that very afternoon on film, various thrift-store suit jackets and skinny ties, and whatever else we couldn't steal. Also beer, Chee-tos, more beer, a couple of ham sandwiches, more beer, cigs, and four glittery shower curtains bound together with electrical tape for our backdrop. DIY, y'know.

We ran through what would become our set:

"I Mean You're Mean" (This would probably qualify today as an Ashers rarity. We never recorded it. But I believe the lyrics went a little something like this:

You're out on my limb like a kitten.
You're swinging your axe and I'm splittin'.
I got soul.

I got beauty, I know it.
But right now I'm worried I'll blow it.

It was not unlike the Violent Femmes' first album tracks
but way inferior. Not the best set opener in the pop universe.

"Who Told You You Knew Shit About Love"
"Tonsil Hockey" (A new song Harry'd written about,
well, kissing that we only played sandwiched be-
tween our two sraight-out punk songs so we wouldn't
seem super-wussed.)
"Roots" (Not about the miniseries. It's about dyeing
your hair.)
"Another Girl, Another Planet" (The Only Ones cover.)
"I Wanna Eat Soup"
"And It Made My Woman Happy"
"The Vampire Ghost of Frankenstein's Witch" (An
Archie Funz original, of course.)
"Louie Louie" (Only necessary when drunk. We did it
that night just for the fuck of it. Sometimes we'd do "I
Wanna Be Your Dog" by the Stooges or "Looking for
Lewis and Clark" by the Long Ryders 'cause we dug 'em
and it gave Harry a chance to blow evil harmonica and
us nonsingers to shout backup. Or "All Kindsa Girls" by
the Real Kids. Same reason. Sometimes "Cathy's Clown"
by the Everly Brothers 'cause it's really pretty, sometimes a purposely shambolic version of "Love Shack"
by the B-52s just to crack ourselves up and because it
was really big at the time, and sometimes we bowed to
the pressure and the begging and just played "Let's Go
Steady Debbie" again...and again. It was our "hit.")

Debbie seemed relieved when it was over. Nobody'd discussed it with any of us, but we could tell that their savings were running seriously low. Harry'd accept Minna's mac and cheese, or franks and beans, or sugar cookie/jam surprise with more frequency. He had holes in his shoes, and the left temple on his glasses was attached to the frame with a small safety pin. Sometimes, in midsong, the specs would fly across the room. Debbie adopted a little tabby cat to keep her company while Harry was rehearsing. They'd named it Neil in honor of Neil from the Young Ones. I noticed how Harry would lug a 10-pound sack of dry food back to the garage whenever it was his turn to run for beer. Young couple in love gets a new kitty, they wanna spoil it with that fancy wet shit that looks like chopped liver, not nuggets in bulk, right? Debbie even switched from the American Spirits, which you sometimes had to go to the city to get, to filtered Pall Malls, which were discounted at every gas station. She loved those American Spirits too, always talked about how clean they burned. If you're gonna kill yourself with cigs, you wanna kill yourself with your own brand. But she made do. So did Harry. All I can say is that under the circumstances, it was good that we didn't suck.

"That was so cool." She smiled, genuinely.

"Really?"

"I mean it. You guys sound great."

Archie beamed at her, flashing the gunked-up steel of his braces.

"Do you have any notes?" Harry asked.

"It'd be great if you guys had a light show," Debbie lamented. "I know that's not possible, but one day . . ."

"We can get Ma in here to flick that switch on and off real fast," I cracked. I wasn't trying to be mean. I just wasn't accustomed to my lead singer asking his girl-friend for notes on my band, even if she had shot some killer snaps of us on her own dime.

But Debbie gave as good as she got. I always re-spected her for that. "That's okay. I can just close my eyes and imagine it. And while I'm at it, I'll picture you as good-looking."

She winked at me. She was sexy sometimes. Then she shrugged and went on, "Well, if you can't have lights or a smoke machine, maybe you need, like, a theme song. And that'll be the first thing you play."

"A . . . a . . . a rave-up," Archie sputtered helpfully.

"Yeah. Like 'We are . . . we are the Jane Ashers,' " she hummed to the tune of "We Will Rock You" by Queen, or sort of—tone deaf, that gal. Seriously.

I looked over at Harry. He was smiling. I let it go. It wasn't a bad idea. I could tell the gears were whirling and he was already stringing together some phrases in his head.

"The Stones didn't need a Rolling Stones theme," Rudy reminded us. " 'Howdy do, we're the Rolling Stones.' "

"Well, it doesn't need to be a fucking name tag song," Harry said, cooling Rudy out instantly. Harry didn't curse as freely as the rest of us, so whenever he used the *f*-word it was pretty grave and we all hushed. "But it could be something like . . . uh . . . 'Hello There.' You know, Cheap Trick? 'Hello there, ladies and gentlemen.

Are you ready to rock?' I could write something like that for us. Kind of announce that we've . . . arrived."

Within a day and a half, we had a show announcing our quasi–theme song, called "Come In, Stand Up," although we only ever really referred to it as "the theme" or "the Jane Ashers' theme." It was basically a rave-up. Opened with a roll, then a two-chord riff.

> Don't sit on your hindquarters,
> Grab your sons and grab your daughters.
> We're going to play a song for you
> And we think dancing is in order...

It was a fun song to play, and Debbie was right. We had no dimming lights. Nothing to announce that we were about to take the stage. We didn't even have a stage. But we had a rave-up, and it completed our set. We were all convinced that the gigs would come. We even had flyers ready. I found an old photo of McCartney with Jane Asher. Paul's wearing a really nice dark suit (before the flower power stuff, that band had the best fucking clothes—they just looked so sharp). Jane Asher is wearing this cool dress, and they're posing with Paul's big sheepdog, Martha, who he wrote the song "Martha My Dear" for. I drew a little thought bubble coming out of the top of Martha's head. Martha was thinking, "Woof woof. I'm a Beatle's dog and I eat good. I say Jane Ashers rule, all right!" I showed it to Debbie: "You're the artist, what do you think?" She assured me it was "really cute." I think she was sincere.

"We're the best band in Ohio, Jeb! You know what, uh . . . Jeb . . . I love my band so much. . . . I would take a bullet for any of these guys. You know, in the leg. Or the fleshy part of the ass. Not the arm. Gotta drum, Jeb."

Jeb Crane was a freelance writer for the *Dean Beacon*. On the urging of Rudy's mother, he'd come to sit in on one of our rehearsals. Middle-aged guy, full beard, work shirt, khaki trousers, Hush Puppies, yellow teeth, smelled vaguely of BO and the kind of aftershave that glows blue in the bottle. Nice guy, though. He knew who Jane Asher the actress was. I'd read some of his reviews in the *Beacon* before and agreed with a lot of them. Probably put ships in bottles at night, or something more sinister. But we welcomed him into our space. He wanted to talk to Harry pretty exclusively, but Harry was still really shy with strangers unless he was singing to them. He sulked in the corner, doing the whole brooding, mysterious poet thing. Each time he put his hand on his head in a help-me-I'm-going-to-swoon pose, Crane would scribble in his chocolate-stained pad, then chew the end of his pen cap. Rudy, Archie, and I picked up the media-savvy slack . . . except none of us was too savvy.

"It's like things are different now. There's a new feeling of a climate of hope, right? Like with Clinton stopping the war and reuniting Fleetwood Mac? I feel like people like us have a chance now," Rudy opined. "To make some real money."

"I'm gonna kill Mark David Chapman," Archie blurted. "Don't print that. I kinda don't want him to know."

"Hey, you wanna see our van, Jeb? You wanna get high in the van? No? That's cool."

We were drunk. Knuckleheads. Giddy. We were starting to make a living at this. The piece appeared the day of Egg Fest. Front page of the Culture section, with Debbie's promo shot splayed across the top of the fold. We looked cool. Sounded ridiculous, but in a really appropriate, rock'n'roll kinda way. I bought five copies. Gave Minna one, distributed the rest to the other guys. I later found out Debbie pasted hers to the fridge and circled Harry's face with a big red Sharpie heart. Drew a big gay biker 'stache on me, antennae on Rudy, and dreadlocks on Archie with black ink. You couldn't fuck with the headline: "Local Band Starts to Make Real Noise."

We might have eluded the imminent attack with a bit more success had we not been so full of boiled eggs. We had 40 minutes of downtime before our big set. We'd drawn a record crowd for Eggfest '92: nearly 400, mostly kids . . . some from as far as Canton, we were told. We'd dubbed a bunch of copies of *Songs from the Deep End* onto any free cassettes we could find. When we ran out of blank tape, we'd cover the punched-out holes at the top of thrift-store Johnny Mathis tapes or how-to-quit-smoking-for-good cassettes with Scotch tape and dub our songs over that. People bought up all those without complaint. They were crazy for Jane Asher merch.

Nobody came for the clown. Most of the kids came for the music, some for the pony, others for the food.

Three came to murder us.

Robert E. Lee "Stagger" Wilkie wore a black executioner's hood most of the time, and if I had a face like Stagger did, I would hood it too. As I remember him, he was plug ugly. Low, bushy brows. Cheeks covered with zits. Lump of a nose. Watery eyes. Cleft chin, also covered with zits. Massive muscles, though, covered with tattoos and zits. With a face and body like that, you have to go into show business, either as a wrestler or a film noir heavy or the lead singer of a metal band named Unkillable. Wilkie opted for the latter, of course. He was about six foot two, but I suspect his boot heels added a few inches. With the hood and the plastic drugstore vampire cape (racked each year around October second), he was certainly menacing. I don't listen to that spooky metal shit. I like the Misfits and the Cramps and the psycho-horror end of punk rock, but I never liked the growly howly shit. Except maybe Slayer. I thought it was all a big heap of witchy jive. When I first saw Stagger and his two bandmates, Boz Leprosy and Chimp in Pain, I laughed. Boz was Chinese, and his real name was Wen. His parents ran the Jade Inn resturaunt over in Wagner, about 15 miles east. Good velvet corn soup. Like any proper Ohioan of the Jewish persuasion, I went there one Christmas with my ma and dad. I actually remember Boz Leprosy running around in the kitchen in his Underoos, playing with his Stretch Monster. He was about 5 then. Now he was 25, clad head to toe in black wool and holding a plastic walking stick with an imitation silver death's head at the tip and a very real metal sword concealed inside. Chimp in Pain, the drummer, was fresh from perusing some dusty dungeon master's guide. He held a home-fashioned mace—basically a nail-studded block of hardwood on a chain. He was chubby. His tits jiggled beneath his white turtleneck sweater and leather pants. I mean, what the fuck? Is that scary? It was a mock turtleneck!

We sensed no danger at first. We were just nervous about the gig. Harry drank and smoked away his nerves like we all did. He'd been sitting on an old wicker chair in the "artists' area" (basically a roped-off section of the park lawn with a picnic table and a couple of coolers).

"This is too much," he kept saying. He'd had a pair of prescription sunglasses made—horn-rims, geek style. They looked real queer since his lenses were so thick.

"Too much."

"This isn't enough, man. This is just the begining," I cracked. I was playing out a pattern on the picnic table and enjoying a cold beer. It was a great day. Three clouds in the sky. Perfect blue. Rudy was sneaking a joint with Archie behind the big cement toilets.

"Where's Funz?" Stagger growled in his stupid Muppet voice.

"Who wants to know?"

"Unkillable."

"Ooooh." I laughed. He stepped toward me. I rushed him to let him know that I wasn't gonna hesitate to engage in whatever he was bringing. It's a good strategy—he actually stepped back. Chimp in Pain raised his mace and swung it clumsily. He seemed worried that he'd accidentally impale himself on the spikes. He was out of practice, I guess.

"You scratch your mom's ass with that when she's itchy?" I snarled at Chimp in Pain.

too much, too late

"You're not playing with Funz," he said. "We've come to take him back."

"Oh, you have? Well, good luck with that." I looked over at Harry. He was just blinking, shocked.

"Come on, man," I mouthed.

Harry looked over at Debbie. She seemed seriously concerned.

"Don't," she whispered. Harry stayed put.

Great, I thought. *Here we go.*

I figured I should drop the Chimp first. He looked weak, hence the weapon, but he didn't want to use it. Just felt like he needed it. I made it seem like I was gonna take down Stagger first, the lead goon. I did a half step in his direction, like I was gonna rip off his hood, drag him down, and make him chew some earth. Then I switched my footing and tackled fatboy before he could raise the mace again. I punched him hard in the gut. It worked. He coughed and gurgled and cried. I grabbed the mace and threw it to Harry, who picked it up and held it defensively. As I gave the Chimp another gut massage Boz grabbed me from behind and pulled me back, exposing my own underbelly for Stagger to whale on. He commenced whaling.

"You stole our bass guitar player," he grunted as he took a shot.

"What the fuck are you talking about? He answered an ad!"

"He's ours."

"We haven't had a gig in months," Chimp in Pain moaned weakly. He wasn't getting back up, but I was hurting. Boz tightened his grip on my neck, and Stagger kept battering my ribs in.

"Dude, man . . . stop!" I pleaded with Boz. "Wen! Wen! I know you! I know your mom."

"My name is Boz Leprosy!"

"Shit!" I wheezed. I was starting to cough up blood.

My eyes pleaded with Harry. He looked over at Debbie again.

"No," she urged.

Harry dropped the mace. He actually looked relieved.

"Motherfucker . . . Help? Please?" I moaned.

Harry grabbed Boz around the neck and jerked him toward the ground. I actually heard a snap. Boz shrieked like a little girl. Harry jammed a knee down into Boz's breastbone as he hit the dirt backward, then elbowed him across the chin and started strangling him. It was brutal. Stagger actually stopped pummeling me. We both took five and watched it go down.

"Hey!" I called. "Don't kill him! We have a fucking show!"

"I'm sorry," Harry said sheepishly to Boz, who was ready for a stretcher. "Really. I've never been in a fight before." Harry got up. He looked at his bloody hands, then over at Debbie. She was wiping away tears.

"I'm sorry," he said to her.

"So, what now?" I asked Stagger. "We're on in 20 minutes. You wanna start this up again or what?"

I lit a cigarette and handed him one. He took it. I lit it. We sat on the grass and smoked as angels hovered over Unkillable's felled rhythm section.

"You can't play this show."

"Oh, we're playing it, Happyface. We're playing it." I balled my fists again to let him know I was ready for another go-round.

"If you insist on playing, I will curse your houses."

I chuckled.

"Don't!" Debbie shouted, then seemed embarrassed. We all turned toward her. She held an unlit cigarette in her mouth. It occurred to me at that very moment that it seemed odd. She'd been sucking on it all day, not lighting the thing. This was the same girl who smoked two at a time sometimes.

"Huh?"

"I'm pregnant," she choked out. "No curses, okay? No fucking curses, please."

I punched Stagger Lee hard across the jaw without warning. A sucker punch. His smoke was still in his mouth as he went down. Harry and I both ran to Debbie at the same time. I don't even know why I did, actually. It wasn't my kid. I was a nervous nelly. A mother hen. But I think putting an entire death metal band in the hospital is enough proof of manhood for you, isn't it? They might have been Unkillable, but they were definitely not Un-Kickassable.

Harry blocked my rush and wordlessly hugged her. She pulled away and stared at the blood on his hands.

"Hey," I intervened, "I begged Harry to help me. I didn't know. None of us knew. How could we know?"

"Why didn't you tell me?" Harry whispered.

"I was going to. After the gig. You were so nervous. I wanted you to be able to focus."

"When did you find out?"

"This morning."

I started to feel awkward, so I backed away a little. Sat down on the picnic table, where I'd been before Unkillable showed up. I could see Rudy and Archie in the distance, stalking back across the lawn, high as hell and oblivious to what they'd missed—and to the king hell beating they were gonna get from me. Once my fists healed up, anyway. I grabbed a beer from the cooler and held it against my mashed ribs. Wondered if I should see a doctor.

"I was feeling nauseous," she explained to Harry. Her expression was warm but blank. I think she was in shock. I tried not to look too closely, but just kind of kept my ears open to make sure everything was okay.

"So I got a test," she continued, "and it was positive."

There's no way this kid was planned. No way. Harry was obsessed with making this band work. Everything depended on it. You don't put a kid in the middle of that road. But maybe they'd fantasized about it secretly when they were snuggled in bed.

"Why didn't you tell me? I would have brought you some ginger ale." He hugged her tightly, then suddenly backed away, like maybe a hug wasn't gonna fix this. "Are you okay now?" he asked.

She nodded. "I had a few weird hours this morning, but I'm fine."

He stared at her belly and smiled. Then the smile failed and he put his hand over his chest.

"I can't smoke anymore, so please don't do anything that's going to stress me out, Harry." She placed the un-lit cigarette in her mouth. Harry's eyes began to flutter. His legs buckled. He found his balance and walked off toward the trees, staring at the sky like he was looking for some kind of guidance. It wasn't coming. I watched him and thought of the old Gun Club song, where Jeffrey Lee Pierce sings, *"I'm looking up and God is say-*

ing, 'What are you gonna do?' I'm looking up and I'm crying, 'I thought it was up to you!' "

I turned to Debbie. She was watching him with a mix of concern and affection. I could tell she was a little annoyed too.

"Uh . . . congratulations."

"Thank you, Sandy."

"You think he's gonna faint?"

"I hope not."

"It's a hell of a day for him to get into his first fight."

"I guess so."

"We gotta play in about ten minutes."

"I know."

"For a lot of people."

"I know."

"I hope he's got some adrenaline left."

"I wasn't going to say anything."

"Yeah. I appreciate that. That's very cool of you."

Harry fell over. We all ran to his side. My chest cavity felt like it was filled with heavy ball bearings. Drumming was gonna be . . . interesting. I smacked him in the face lightly a few times and called his name. He came to.

"What happened?"

"You fainted."

He looked at Debbie and me and smiled sheepishly. Then broadly.

"Sandy . . ."

"Yeah, Harry?"

"I'm gonna be a dad."

"It appears that way."

"It's gonna be so cool."

"If you say so."

He squeezed Debbie's left hand. She stared unblinkingly into his eyes, and I felt awkward yet again.

"Uh . . . are you ready to sing?"

Harry pulled himself up.

"I'm ready to sing."

"Are you sure?"

"I'm ready to destroy Eggfest, Sandy."

I grinned.

"Really?"

"Oh, fuck yes!"

Like I said, Harry didn't really curse unless something special was going down.

That night at Eggfest we played the same set we always did, but it still seemed like it was all over too quickly. I could have played for three or four hours, like Springsteen did. I would have beat the drums up there by myself so long as I had an audience. Harry was more commanding and confident than I'd ever seen him, and the band fell in behind his lead. Each of our songs seemed to graduate that day. They'd sounded good before, but now there wasn't one kink to isolate, criticize, and repair. Each song resonated so perfectly. As we broke down our gear and marched back to our area, Eggfesters pointed at us and sang our hooks and choruses. It was as perfect a live show as any rock'n'roll band ever played anywhere. And it would be our last for thirteen years.

4

Harry had been in the Olfactory about three or four minutes, nervously staring at the little amber- and-rose colored bottles tucked into velvet nests beneath the glass-top showcase. Mrs. Vance didn't recognize him from the back as she approached.

"Can I help you?" she asked.

Harry turned around, and she took a step back. It had been over a year since she'd seen her son. And rock'n'roll had changed him, obviously. He was lean. He was almost handsome.

"Hello, Mother."

She stared at him. Blinked wildly. "Harry?"

"How are you, Mother?"

She turned away and walked around the showcase, putting the glass between them. He reached across the glass and touched her arm gently. As he did he noticed his reflection in the impossibly shiny top, and for a minute he felt like he was on television. Foolish. Melodramatic. "I thought about you a lot. I was hoping you were okay."

"I'm fine," she said coolly. "I'm okay."

She picked up a half-full bottle of glass cleaner and began slicking down the table, wiping it with a tightly clenched paper towel.

"Someone told me you were in the newspaper. That's very impressive," she said absently.

He felt a little angry that she didn't seem to have changed, like he had.

"Mother, I'm sorry. I was wrong to leave you that way."

She looked up from her polishing.

"Well . . ." She smiled crookedly. "You've come back now." Harry was hoping to feel relief, a sense of conclusion, but he felt nothing. They gazed at each other blankly, as if on a bad blind date.

"Mother . . . *Mom* . . . can we go for a walk?"

"I have to keep the store open."

"Can't you close it up for ten minutes?"

"I really can't."

"Please?"

Harry grabbed her hand and guided her to the other side of the showcase, then toward the door. He felt the bones in her hand, which looked thinner than he'd remembered. A couple of brown spots had appeared along the knuckles. Harry decided that she had changed a bit after all. She was drying up.

"Mom, I'm going to have a baby. I'm going to be a father . . . and I'm going to get married."

Harry heaved a sigh. It felt good to say it.

It was fact. He pulled out a cigarette and jammed it into the corner of his mouth, then cracked the door and stuck half his body outside. He lit up and politely blew the smoke outside.

"You've developed bad habits."

"Did you hear me?"

"I heard you, Harry. What do you want me to say about all . . . that?"

"Tell me you're happy for me. Give me your blessing. I don't know."

"Is it the same . . . girl?"

"Debbie."

"Did she teach you to smoke?"

"No."

"You don't think she's strange? She wears black from head to toe. Like a witch." She took the cigarette away from him, and for a minute she was in command again. "Smoking is a very unattractive habit."

"I'm not trying to attract anyone. I'm just smoking."

"And what happens when it doesn't work out? Then you're stuck with an . . . addiction."

"We're in love. We're like a family now. Nobody's leaving."

"Hmmm."

"Mom, please take a walk with me. I want to buy a ring. I don't know what girls like. I need some help.

I need some . . . I don't know . . . advice from my mother?"

She stared at him again, looking a bit shamed this time.

Harry threw the cigarette into the gutter and allowed himself to regret coming. He told himself that if he never saw his mother again, he'd always know that he'd apologized. He knew she wouldn't be helping him pick out rings or anything else. He knew that he had his own family now.

She punched some keys on the electronic cash register, and the till slid open without any noise. He watched as she counted out a stack of twenty-dollar bills and neatly straightened them with her shaking, stiff old-lady hands.

"What are you doing?" he asked.

She walked over to Harry and handed him the money, like she was stopping a perfume customer who'd forgotten their change.

"Please don't spend this on cigarettes. Buy something nice. For your wife."

Harry stared at the money and shook his head. "I don't want your money."

"That's fine. But please take it anyway. You're going to need it."

"I'm not gonna need it, Mother."

"You'll find that this is all more complicated than you think. And very expensive. Raising a family."

"We're already a family," he snapped indignantly. "I have a woman and a cat and a band—a family. We do what we do . . . and it's okay. Besides, we're going to be big rock stars."

too much, too late

Harry felt foolish as soon as he said it. But he believed it.

Harry could not get home fast enough. He slipped on some wet leaves and nearly cracked his head open as he rushed back to Debbie, away from his mother. Debbie was in the kitchenette, covered with cat scratches. She'd been attempting to administer a pill to Neil, their new cat, who had a kitty cough.

"This is not easy," she sighed. "I need you, Harry." Harry kissed her and went to the bathroom to fetch some peroxide.

"We don't have any Band-Aids," he fretted. "I think we need to keep some around the house at all times. Maybe a whole first-aid kit. And . . . batteries? Cans of beans and stuff? Just in case."

"In case of what? I'm trying to give the cat a pill. That's all. Don't make me paranoid, please."

Harry handed her the peroxide, but she ignored it. She picked up a Bic pen and began chewing on the end. Debbie'd become something of a doodler after giving up her artistic aspirations for Harry and their coming family. She'd walk around with one of those Bic pens with the black, blue, green, and red ink cartridges all embedded. She'd been through about five of them already, after absentmindedly attempting to light the end.

"This being-a-grown-up thing? It's hard. Taking care of sick cats . . . stocking beans."

Harry whispered encouraging messages to himself along the lines of "You're all right," or "It's going so great," as he searched out Neil, who most certainly did not want to be found. But the cough was giving the cat away.

"Aha! He can't hide." Debbie put down the pen and joined Harry on the other side of the room. Harry reached under their orange hotel lobby chair and grabbed the kitty, taking some cuts himself. He held Neil firmly as Debbie ran and grabbed the pill.

"It's for your own good, you bastard. Swallow it!"

The cat let out a wail worthy of Iron Maiden's *Number of the Beast* and hissed at them.

"That's some cat," Harry observed. "Ungrateful and mean."

"Please."

"I saw my mother this morning."

Debbie sat down at the table and placed the Bic in her mouth. She picked up the peroxide, dabbed a napkin into the bottle end, and began swabbing Harry's arms, ignoring hers.

Harry took the napkin away and started wiping the dried blood off her arms.

"She's from outer space, Debbie." He paused. "I think we should invite Sandy and the band for Thanksgiving dinner. I think we should get a turkey and, uh . . . cook it."

"Stuff it."

"Yeah. What do you think, Deb?"

"I think that if that's something that would make you happy, I'll check out some cookbooks."

"We're a family."

"We have a sick cat."

"And a baby."

Harry put a cigarette in his mouth. She glared.

"I'm going to go outside. Don't worry."

"Motherfucker."

"Outside! You won't even smell it."

She was quiet for a moment, then said suddenly, "I think the baby's a girl. I don't know why I think that— I just do."

Harry got up and wrapped his arms around her.

"Why don't you get a beer? You're all tense."

He nodded, they opened the fridge and surveyed the contents. Beer. Cheese. Pickles. Yogurt. *This is my refrigerator,* he thought. *This is the food in my refrigerator. This is mine.*

He grabbed a Bud and some hamburger meat that had taken on a blue tint. Chucked the latter. Sat down and opened the bottle.

"That's right. Drink it for us girls."

He gulped the beer.

"You know, in the third trimester a glass of wine is considered okay," she informed him. "It's actually good for you."

Sometimes a new artist will tour on buzz alone—no serious budget, a modicum of label support, but enough media exposure to fill clubs and small theaters across the country. Since more often than not these artists have only one record, maybe a couple of EPs or something, they'll turn to the booker to pull together a local support act. This guy Conrad—I forget his last name or where exactly I met him (some blurry party), but I'll never forget his multiple facial piercings and trippy hairstyle (white-guy cornrows). It seemed like in a post-

Lollapalooza pop universe there were certain people who couldn't cram enough metal into their flesh. It wasn't my thing, but I tolerated Conrad, mostly because he claimed to be tight with the booker at the Agora in Cleveland, probably the biggest modern rock venue in the whole state, and hinted that he might be able to throw us a break.

99

Conrad and I were killing a case of beer one night after a gig at Wiffles, a sports bar in Cincinnati, where he lived and where we were getting a bit of a genuine following. Harry'd gone home to Debbie, and Rudy was probably getting blown by a Bengals fan. Archie was probably passed out in the back of his vehicle. Which left me and Con.

"She's so hot!"

"Who?"

"Liz Phair, man. Liz Phair. She's . . . Liz Phair! She's hot. She sings about sex. And she's hot. She's got this . . . mouth. It's hot." I was listening to him drop names. Even though I paid for the beer, I was convinced that my sort-of friend was one well-connected pincushion motherfucker. He talked about "Courtney" and "Billy" and "Kim" and "Perry," looking over at me to make sure he didn't have to slow down and add surnames or anything.

"Liz is an Ohio girl, man. From Cincinnati. Went to Oberlin. She'll love you guys."

"Well, can you give her a copy of the tape?"

"Yeah. Absolutely. Gimme a couple of them. I'll give one to Ed too."

"Eddie Vedder?"

"Don't call him Eddie. Call him Ed."

too much, too late

I found out pretty quickly after that that Liz Phair was indeed a big deal, one of the two dozen or so artists who would have remained on the fringe had it not been for Nirvana. Thanks to the success of *Nevermind,* provocateurs like her became contenders. And when Phair's tour manager inquired with the Agora's booker about an opening act for her sold-out date there in mid-February, the booker asked Conrad, and we got the gig.

Turns out Minna already owned a copy of Phair's debut, *Exile in Guyville.* She had most of the Matador Records catalog. I felt a little square stealing the CD from my mother, swiping the disc and leaving the jewel box untouched, but I didn't have time to track the thing down in the city, and this was a good five years before I would be able to buy it with a mouse click.

The Jane Ashers thought *Exile in Guyville* was one of the best records that we'd ever heard. Phair had moved to Chicago after college and wrote some of her songs about the insular and chauvinistic indie rock scene. I felt guilty hearing that. We could have been the subjects of some of those songs—marauding rock boys having postgig one-night stands and maybe making promises before leaving town, then blinking and shrugging when we saw the girl again, laughing too. We were assholes. And someone was calling us out.

Like most great indie rock, *Guyville* transcended its budgetary and technological limitations. It sounded raw and intimate, but thanks to all that rich melody it had a lush quality too. I was impressed. A little jealous. But mostly very, very excited, not least of all because Phair had nailed her Matador Records deal on the basis of a mailed-in demo called *Girly Sound.* I'm sure it was no better or worse than *Songs from the Deep End*. If these labels were signing people cold in the wake of Kurt, surely they could take a chance on us. I was fine living on hot dogs and mac and cheese. I had no rent. And there was enough gig money left after gas for cigarettes and beer. I was just impatient when it came to the recognition. I knew we could make it, and I didn't want to wait much longer to prove that to myself and to everybody else. Matador was the shit-hot label at the time thanks to Pavement's *Slanted and Enchanted* album, which we also loved. We figured there'd be someone connected with the label at the Cleveland show, if not Phair herself. And oh yeah, we also liked her mouth.

Liz Phair became an obsession for Rudy. I forgot to mention that the record was supposedly a song-by-song reply to the Rolling Stones' 1972 double album *Exile on Main Street* (widely considered their best because . . . it's their best).

Rudy bought the album and played it end to end with *Main Street* about twelve thousand times. Many of those hours were spent with Minna at his side taking copious notes in a marble journal, drawing diagrams, flowcharts, and elaborate maps while sharing Phair fan-boy (and fan-old-lady) trivia.

"You know her father's a scientist, Rudy?"

"Really?"

"And her middle name is Clark."

"Whoa."

Then Rudy'd cue up "Rocks Off," and Minna would select "6' 1"."

"I get it," he'd share. "I do, man. It's deep."

"I'll fuck you till your dick is blue," Minna sang one

day while bringing us a tray of Ritz crackers, Cheez Whiz, and Tab. I recognized the verse from the song "Flower." It was still . . . weird.

Our VW bus was loaded with our amps and cases. We were in my kitchen making sandwiches for the trip, piling bologna and American cheese assembly-line-style onto slices of whole-wheat bread, slicking it down with mustard, and slapping on a pickle slice. One after the other.

"This must be what working in McDonald's feels like," I quipped, relieved that I would never, ever have to do anything but play my drums for a living. "What a racket."

"I used to work at Hardee's," Archie volunteered. "It was all right. You could stick things in the fryer and see what they looked like fried. The manager once dared me to stick my thing in there. To see what it'd look like fried."

"Did you do it?"

"No. I'm not stupid, Sandy."

"It's good to know my bass player has the sense not to fry his penis in deep fat." I sighed. Scintillating stuff. Whenever Harry was gone, it was hard to participate in the conversations with the other guys in the band. I loved Rudy, but he didn't even try to use his intellect. And Archie . . . I bet Archie *did* try to fry his own dick.

"If you had a restaurant that served nothing but lamb, what would you charge for it?" Archie asked.

"Oh, that's a good question." Rudy nodded. "Maybe . . . ten bucks?"

The telephone rang. As soon as I heard it, I knew

something was up. But maybe this is hindsight again. Maybe it was just a ring like any other—wrong number, bill collector.

"I can't go, Sandy. I'm sorry." Harry's voice was thin and quavering, like he'd swallowed broken glass and couldn't use his throat muscles withouth lacerating them.

"What?"

"It's Debbie. She's in the hospital."

"Shit . . . what's . . . what . . ." The *I can't go* was still hanging there, but I told myself that whatever it was, I could convince him it was going to be all right. Like I always did.

"I don't know, Sandy. She was complaining about . . . pain. She was in pain. I called the doctor. I don't know, Sand. I don't know."

"Relax. Please."

"Okay. Okay. The . . . uh . . . the doctors are still in with her. They haven't told me shit."

"Okay, well, we'll be here, man. Call back as soon as you know anything. Don't worry about us. Worse comes to worst, we can split tomorrow."

"Sandy, that's not worse comes to worst."

"It's a figure of speech, man. Calm down. Who's there with you?"

"Nobody."

"Do you want me to come down there?"

"No. Maybe . . ."

"All right, listen. Call me back if you want me to come down there. Otherwise I'll be here waiting by the phone. Okay? It's gonna be all right, Harry. This is probably just morning sickness or whatever. Seriously. You need to keep it together. Smoke a cigarette. Take a

too much, too late

walk. She's in good hands. The doctors'll take care of her. Okay?"

"I knew something would go wrong, Sandy."

"Shut up with that shit."

"I'm sorry, Sandy. I'm fucking everything up."

He *was* fucking everything up. But what could I do about it? Without him there'd be nothing to fuck up. I broke the news to Rudy and Archie, who stared at each other in stoned confusion.

By noon we still hadn't heard from Harry. We started eating the road sandwiches nervously. By one, all the beer was gone.

"I think we need to go down there. This can't be good."

"Can't be good," Minna agreed. She was nursing a beer.

Rudy, Archie, and I unloaded the back of the van. The amps felt three times as heavy. I got behind the wheel and sped toward the hospital. Rudy sat in the passenger seat. Archie crouched in the cargo area. We were all joyless.

When we got there Debbie was sitting on the curb in the hospital parking lot, smoking a cigarette. Harry was rubbing her shoulders. Both of them had red and puffy eyes.

They'd lost the baby. I'm told this happens more frequently than you'd think but not so often in the third trimester. One minute you're pregnant, and the next you're not and you're smoking again. And it's pretty much the only relief you're gonna get. Happily, Debbie was okay—physically, at least. Mentally, she was shattered.

"They put a curse on us," she sobbed. "That band . . . Unkillable . . . they cursed us."

All we could do was stare at them. Nobody spoke for the longest time. Finally I suggested we drive them home. Nobody seemed to understand—it was like I was speaking in tongues. I repeated myself, and they finally nodded in agreement. I helped Harry get her up and into the car.

"I want to get drunk," she said. "Sandy, I wanna get fucked up."

"Okay," I allowed. "Might as well. We got nothing else to do now."

She nodded. I drove slowly, defeatedly back toward their apartment. I looked at the odometer as I maneuvered the painfully light van past miles of sprawling tract that seemed increasingly like prison grounds. The digits were unchanged.

It was in that moment on the curb in the hospital parking lot that music ceased to be a job or even a calling for Harry. It was there, as ambulances idled and the dead and dying were carried in and bundled babies were carried out, that Debbie Andrews became his only concern. It was there, fumbling for matches in the cold, that the Jane Ashers became a hobby. A weekend getaway.

We didn't know it then. But within half a week, it was obvious that Harry and Debbie had bunkered themselves. We weren't even invited to the wedding. Dean, Ohio, is a one-grocery-store, no-book-or-record-store, small-ass town, but if you want to badly enough, you can still hide from someone. Especially if you disguise yourself.

5

"Oh, bullshit!"

Rudy kept insisting what he saw was what he saw. And I held on to my incredulity all afternoon as we tried to jam or write or do anything to stave off the sudden and escalating sense of uselessness.

"Bullshit, bullshit, bullshit."

"Sandy, man, it was Harry."

"That doesn't mean he was working there. Harry can't work. He's too . . . Harry. The guy couldn't even sell shampoo over the phone."

"He was wearing an apron with a hammer sticking

out of it. It said Perry's Hardware on it. It was a Perry's Hardware apron and he was selling hooks."

"What kind of hooks?"

"Bronze hooks. The kind you use to hang up bathrobes and towels and shit."

"You saw him selling hooks?"

"I saw him selling hooks."

Through all the dread, part of me believed it. I knew he sure wasn't *writing* hooks. The only way to find out if Rudy had actually outed Harry as a 9-to-5er was obvious, but I was afraid. I preferred, for the day anyway, to tell myself that my guitar player was high and seeing things.

I couldn't sleep that night. I closed my eyes once or twice, but it only made me angrier. I watched the clock instead. At 7:30 a.m. I decided that I would rise in an hour and end this. At exactly 8:30 I snapped up and hit the floor. Pulled on my jeans, grabbed my ski hat and leather coat, and tiptoed down the hall so I wouldn't wake up Minna. Poured myself a thermos full of coffee and spent the next hour trying to start the old man's Le Sabre. The car had pretty much died with my dad. Occasionally it'd start, but so infrequently that I'd moved it out of the garage to rust. I figured it was more important for us to have the practice room—to invest hope in the band and not the Buick's gimpy engine.

I refilled the thermos and committed to the three-mile hike downtown. When I got to Perry's I pushed open the door and the bell rang, announcing another customer.

Harry began to turn around slowly, but I reached him in two swift strides and pushed him. Some two-inch nails fell out of his apron and scattered on the floor with a tinkle.

"Nice to see you weren't eaten by wild dogs, asshole," I snarled.

Harry stared at his feet sheepishly.

My anger softened a little. "Look . . . where the hell have you been? I'm worried about you. I haven't seen you in almost three months. I walk by the apartment and it's like nobody lives there."

"I know." He smiled, but his eyes were dead. Joyless. It made me mad again.

"So you work here now?"

"Yeah."

We stared at each other in silence for what seemed like an hour but was actually about three seconds. It was just me and him in the store. Someone trusted him with master keys. You're not supposed to trust the lead singer of a rock'n'roll band with master keys.

"Why do you work here now?" I screamed. I tried to keep my voice low and as manly as possible, but it came out as a scream.

"Shhh. Sandy. Please. Calm down."

"Are you telling me what to do? I don't work here. You can't tell me what to do. I'm a customer." I picked up a hinge and waved it at him. "I'm buying this."

"Please. Calm down."

"Are you still in the band or what?"

"Sandy . . . I'm sorry . . . let me explain . . ."

"Yeah. Okay. Good. Let's go to Dil's, man. Get some breakfast and figure this shit out," I suggested.

"I can't leave the store, Sandy."

"Huh? Oh, man. Listen to yourself." I sat down on a rickety plastic chair, lit a cig, and looked him over. "You look like a retard in that apron."

"I know."

He sat down next to me.

"So, what? We're not friends anymore? We're not in a band anymore? You just disappear?"

"I had to."

"Nah, don't gimme that shit. I want answers. Specific answers."

"Debbie's pregnant. Again."

"Oh . . ." That was specific, all right. "Well, that's . . . great. *Mazel tov.* That's great."

"I'm working here because we're going to need money for the baby."

"Yeah . . . well . . . we can get gigs, Harry. Steady gigs. And probably a deal. We lost some momentum there, but we can get it back like that."

"I need a more dependable source of income, Sandy."

"We were gonna get signed to Matador Records. Or Sub Pop."

"Maybe."

I handed him a cigarette to drag off. He shook his head.

"No. I quit."

"How?"

"Secondhand smoke is bad for the kid."

"Did you quit drinking too?"

"For now."

"You still eat, I see." I gestured to his gut, which bulged underneath that hellish apron. He grimaced.

too much, too late

"I'm fucking with you. I'm sorry. This is all just . . . I'm hurt, you know?"

"It was really hard, Sandy. I didn't want to close you guys out, but it was . . . it was bad."

"Yeah, well, I can understand that." In fact I didn't understand. Nothing like that had happened to me. "So what are you saying, like we're a bad influence on you? Like rock'n'roll is gonna give her another miscarriage?"

"No." He laughed. "Well, maybe for a minute I thought that I was being punished for having my values fucked up or something, but that's not important. Nothing is important except this baby. And Debbie. And I decided that I'm going to make sure that nothing happens to them, that they're stable and safe and healthy. I'm going to do that however I can."

"Come on . . ."

"No, Sandy, you don't understand. I can't risk anything happening. At all. Not anymore." He was growing a little exasperated.

"Do they let you use the radio in here?"

He shrugged. "They like the ball game on."

"You don't like baseball."

"It's kind of growing on me. The Reds are having a good year. I think."

I snorted, then rose and grabbed his shoulders. "Are you seriously telling me you can't play with us anymore, Harry?"

"I can't, Sandy. We need . . . stability."

I felt like crying.

"I think you're fucked in the head."

"How're Rudy and Arch?"

"Fuck you! What do you care?"

"Sandy, please . . ."

"You know what? We'll just replace you. That's all. You think you can't be replaced? I've got two words for you—Sammy Hagar."

"You know how bad Van Halen sucked with Sammy Hagar singing instead of David Lee Roth."

"Brian Johnson."

"Not as good as Bon Scott."

"Bullshit."

"It's a better argument, but you still lose, Sandy."

"What do you know about it? You sell hardware."

"I sell hardware so I can feed my family."

"Oh, yeah. Look at you. Tom Joad. You're a lead singer in a band, man. We could be selling out the Agora by the time the kid is born. When did you stop believing in this, man? Seriously?"

"I didn't stop believing. I swear, I didn't. Please . . . listen. I just have to do this."

"Fine. Do it. Disappear up your own ass. I'll go find us another singer, and I'm keeping the name too."

"You're really gonna find another singer?"

"Oh, so now you're concerned?"

He looked out the window and frowned.

"No."

Harry and Debbie had a healthy baby in July of '94, just before the fourth. They named him Matthew Allen Vance and sent around those photo postcards announcing his arrival: *Please share our joy . . .* I drew a Hitler mustache on the kid and added my own addendum: *which we refuse to share with anyone else.* Cute kid, though. Got Debbie's looks.

Rudy, Archie, and I continued to get together every day, just to have something to do. We'd play stuff like "19th Nervous Breakdown," and I'd sing. We never played Ashers songs. They were forbidden.

After a while, though, every day became every other day, and then that became the weekends and sometimes every other weekend. Things got worse when Rudy caved. He was in his mid-20s and started feeling it. He decided that he wanted to go to film school. I don't think he was particularly interested in making films. He was lazy, and the notion of getting college credit for watching and gabbing about movies seemed okay with him. His parents agreed to pay his tuition and living expenses. At least it was a degree, they reasoned.

I went back to tutoring at Harrison High. Gave some halfhearted drum lessons here and there. I wasn't about to get a real job, and unlike Rudy, I still didn't feel like it was time for college, even though I was past the age where most people have finished graduate school. I still wanted to play. Rock'n'roll was still the only thing that meant anything to me. I didn't care that now it was just me and Archie Funz sitting in the garage all day. But one night in the early summer of 1998, Archie lost it bad.

I don't know what Archie was smoking. His pot intake had increased to a bong hit every ten minutes. He was clearly trying to achieve a distorted sense of reality with no time or space for perspective. That's the way he wanted it, and I wasn't gonna pull the pipe out of his hand. He was a big boy. Besides, he was Archie Funz.

I was used to the weirdness. Maybe I should have been alarmed, but I guess I didn't confront him because deep down I was afraid that if we fought about it, I'd lose him too. So I let him schiz out. I regret it.

I played with him the day it happened. When we decided we'd had enough, I did the fake yawn and told him I was going to go in and take a nap. He packed up his bass. I told him he could leave it, maybe we'd jam later. He could go in and watch TV, make some food, so long as Minna was in her room.

"Nah, I gotta go," he told me.

"Where you going, Archie?"

"I gotta check something out."

"All right, man. I'll call you tomorrow."

I went to bed. Archie Funz got in his Fiesta, drove to a spot near the highway, parked, climbed to the top of an 85-foot-tall water tower, and took a headfirst dive onto the concrete. According to the cops, his face was taped up with duct tape when they found him four days later, broken and rotting in the dried-out weeds. This made the police initially suspicious that Archie's death was a homicide. But it turned out that Archie had affixed a pair of Walkman headphones to his ears with the tape so they'd remain on as he fell. The volume was turned up all the way to 10. The music must have been blasting in his ears as the earth rose up to take him.

The newspapers didn't say what was playing. When Rudy and I went to the funeral, it took me a few shots of bourbon to work up the courage to approach his uncle, Stanley Funz (who looked nothing like Archie, but then nobody really did), and ask if he knew. "I don't like music," was all Stanley said in response. It still haunts me. For a while I'd even lie awake handicapping various selections and wondering what I would have placed in the Walkman myself.

After that it was just me in the garage, beating my drum.

The Jane Ashers had had our requisite death, our myth-building Brian Jones. But not enough sex, not enough drugs, and certainly not enough rock'n'roll.

I started reading the want ads only after Minna took me aside one night after some chicken à la king from the can. She handed me a joint. I knew this wasn't gonna be good news.

"Sandy, we're broke."

"Ma?"

"Yeah. Yeah. We got no money."

"What about the insurance? Dad's life insurance?"

"The bank sent a letter. It's all gone."

"You spent Dad's insurance on weed?" I asked, then lit the joint and sucked in the smoke. I didn't care that my indignation was instantly compromised.

Minna shrugged. "Not just weed. Records too."

"What are we gonna do now, Ma? Do you have any stocks?"

"No stocks."

"Bonds? Jewelry?"

"Nah."

I got up and hugged her. She smiled.

"I'm sorry, Sandy."

"It's all right, Ma. I'll figure something out."

She pulled the joint from my fingers and put it to her lips.

As the millennium lurched to an end, I found myself

rising at 6 a.m. and taking the bus out to Wurst and Son's Lumber. I spent my mornings stacking pallets of industrial glue and Sheetrock to keep my mother in marijuana and mint-condition collectibles wrapped in cellophane, some with Japanese lettering or secret messages in the run out grooves. There was a transistor radio in the lumberyard, but it was broken. I never even attempted to fix or replace it, and I could have done both easily. And when I got home from work, I slept. I didn't even go out to the garage anymore. The dust on my kit grew thick while my hair grew thin.

PART TWO

in since sunrise for five or six cold beers or a few rounds of numbing rail cocktails. It was a cheap and dirty place, but the shared hopelessness was almost comforting.

Back in the day, when we'd see him at parties, Rudy and I had called Ben "Ben Jim Morrison" because from a distance he resembled Jim post–Miami arrest: a little puffed up with booze, disoriented but still surly, a happily lumbering badass. Ben had a quick wit when sober. He knew a couple hundred dirty jokes. When drunk, he was ready for anything. Plus he'd met the spirit of Mr. Mojo Risin. Ben had been to Paris in the early '80s and visited the famous grave at Père Lachaise cemetery. According to the story, which he recounted constantly, Ben took a picnic basket full of baguette, wine, and good cheese to the plot and stretched out to ponder . . . Fate? Snakes? Who knows. Anyway, he claimed that shortly thereafter he was approached by a solemn-looking old man with leathery red skin and unruly white shoulder-length hair. The man offered Ben a lump of brown hash. He accepted, and pulled out a pink marble pipe and began to cook and smoke it. The man watched silently. Finally he asked if Ben wanted him to take Ben's picture in front of the headstone, a bust of Jim. Ben gave the man his cheap camera. The man snapped, then handed the camera back. Ben turned to place it in the picnic basket. He planned to offer the strange man some wine as a gesture of gratitude and fraternity, but when he turned around, the old man was gone. When Ben returned to the States and took the photos in to be developed, he was told that something had gone wrong and the entire roll was messed up. He asked the Foto Shack clerk to go on and develop them anyway, to "see what colors come out." When he picked up the photos and flipped to the one that the old man had taken, he swore he could see the shape of a lizard creeping across the bleeding, melting, ruined print. The Lizard King, of course.

"Sandy, man. What's going on with you? I haven't seen you in a dog's age. Didn't you used to be in that band? What happened to you? I figured for sure I'd see you guys on *Bandstand*," Ben said to me the first day I walked in, sat down, and hooked the chain around my ankle to the brass rail on the bar.

"The Jane Ashers."

"Yeah. The Jane Ashers."

"We're history."

"Ah. Well, you know, that's not a good name for a band anyway. You know what a good name for a band is?"

"What Ben?"

"Basil Rathbone."

"Please gimme a beer, Ben."

Without acknowledging my order, Ben pulled a bottle of cheap tequila off the rail shelf. Poured two.

"To reuniting with old friends. Never say goodbye . . . always say ciao." We raised our glasses and belted down the tequila, which tasted like bait water and gasoline.

"You know who said that?"

"Huh?"

"Liberace. That'll be 10 bucks."

"Oh." I shifted. "I thought you were buying the round 'cause of . . . you know . . . we're old friends."

"It's okay, you can owe me. You want another?"

"No, man. Thanks."

Ben poured himself another.

"I don't know. Rock'n'roll is over, isn't it?" Ben laughed.

"Over?" I could already feel a headache coming on from the piss tequila. I wanted to go outside and lie down on the highway.

"It's just . . . I don't know . . . what's the word I'm looking for?"

"Great?" I offered hopefully.

"Trains. That's what I'm into now. You like trains?"

"No. I don't like trains."

"You see this?" Ben pulled his front tooth out. "You weren't there when I lost this. You haven't been there for me, man."

"How did you lose your tooth?" I offered, feigning concern.

"I dunno, man." He poured another shot.

After that, I hit Ben Jim Morrison's every day after work too. I decided I was going to get old and fat there. It was as good a place as any. Ben had good stories, and every third round was free. Being there took the sting out of the long day. I felt like Sandy James again. My paychecks said "Klein." The foreman called me "Klein," even when I politely asked him to stop. He seemed to get a kick out of it: "Lunch, Klein. Thirty-five minutes, Klein. There's a phone order, Klein, get it from the office and pull it."

The night before the accident, I'd hit on a girl and she wasn't interested. And I'd been certain that she would be. Maybe I hadn't looked in the mirror in a while. I wasn't young anymore, even though I still felt young in my mind. So when I hit on her, the girl got annoyed. She giggled, but I could tell she wasn't charmed. And for some reason, I didn't stop. I begged. I even sang. With each strikeout I got drunker, until Ben finally pitched me. I didn't die on the ride home. I found my bed. And the alarm rang at 7 a.m. I went into work, found my punch card, turned my forklift keys, and drove into the big steel pull-down doors and flipped the lift. It sounded like an Airbus jet hitting the tarmac nose first.

"What in fuck?" the foreman, Danny, shouted, and came running, his coffee still in his hands, spillin' over his fingers. My body was pretty twisted, but I was fairly sure I wasn't paralyzed or anything. Looking back now—and I do sometimes, whenever the lingering bone and muscle aches flare up—I think it was probably a turning point for me. If that redheaded girl at Ben's had taken me out behind the Dumpster and done stuff to me, I might never have crashed the lift, and if I'd never crashed the lift, I might still be driving it. God bless her for not fucking me. And think about this: I usually smoked fiendishly behind the wheel of the forklift. But that morning I wasn't smoking. And considering the fact that all the stuff in those drums I was moving across the floor was highly flammable, if I'd had a cig in my mouth the whole yard and probably half of the great state of Ohio would have gone up. If that's not a sign that I was fated for something else, then I don't know what is.

Still, I destroyed about $20,000 worth of merchandise and equipment. It could have been my ass. But when the insurance inspector showed up a few weeks later to examine the machinery, they found that the steering components in the lift were faulty. Now, I know

that accident had everything to do with me being hungover and shamed and pissed off and not a thing to do
with faulty steering components, but I held my tongue.
Who was I to argue with fate? I'm just a drummer.

Not only did I get workman's comp, but I made some
noise like I was gonna sue the company and soon it actually looked like I was gonna see some settlement cash,
maybe a lot. But in the meantime I found myself house-
bound and strangely terrified by this sudden and dangerous amount of free time I'd given myself. The job
had become something of a Zen trip for me—I hated it,
but it kept me regular.

So I spent even more time in Ben's tavern. I could
have lingered there forever—a bad boy turned bad man
turned old man, bourbon in my coffee, bourbon in my
ham sandwich, bourbon in my toothpaste. But it wasn't
my destiny. Four years after the accident, almost to the
day, everything changed.

"They offered you a settlement, Sand," Minna informed me absently one morning just after the new
year. "Why don't you take a shower?"

Minna hadn't told me what to do with my life since I
was a kid. It threw me a bit.

"Take a shower, Sand. And a shave too, huh?"

"Do I stink, Ma?"

"You stink real bad."

"Sorry, Ma."

"Here."

She handed me the letter. Insulting bastards that they
were, they presumed that I would accept their offer.
Maybe they finally checked me out. Found out that I
was just an ex-drummer who could be silenced for

$7,291.16. How they came up with that particular number is best left unexplored.

I gave Ma five grand for letting me live at home for the last 38 years (it was the right thing to do). With the rest I bought a laptop and an MP3 player and became something of a born-again gearhead. I put all my CDs on the player and sometimes took it to the bar with me and listened to that instead of Ben's Roger Miller– and Charlie Pride–fortified jukebox. I indulged in a little more positivity and revisited a few dreams. I thought about the possibility of actually making it to 40. Maybe the yard would take me back if I promised not to destroy anything. Maybe I could get a job at Ben's—I had won some favor with a booze upgrade and suddenly generous tipping. Maybe I would pack a bag and go elephant riding, or shooting, or saving, or whatever the fuck they do with elepants in Sri Lanka. I would find enlightenment and deliver my old ass from the material world. I figured I had about a month or two's worth of food, gas, and booze money. I intended to make it last until I figured out what I was going to do with my future. It was something I'd been figuring out since I was 18.

Rudy and I had started e-mailing each other. Reconnecting, I guess. Politely and tentatively at first, more out of respect for our past than for any real interest (on his part at least) in having any kind of meaningful future together. I hadn't seen him more than four or five times since he split the band for college—once at Archie Funz's funeral, a couple of dinners or beers here and there when he was back in Dean, but not at all for the last few years. I'd heard he'd gotten engaged to an Asian woman he met out in California but that ended too. I never found out the circumstances, and he didn't want to volunteer them. I just assumed Rudy wasn't an easy guy to live with. By the time Rudy'd moved back to Ohio, settling in Cincinnati, I was drowning over at Ben's and didn't want to see anyone. I was too ashamed. And vain. But my upswing and the Internet brought us back together. In many ways, the Web erases the notion of a "small town" like Dean. With one click, I knew everything going on in Cincinnati. Movie times. Bands coming through town. New restaurants opening. As I fell in love with popular culture again, I realized that I could be a virtual urbanite. And Rudy could reconnect with his roots without actually going home or picking up a phone and actually having a conversation, with all the pauses and discomfort.

I don't even want to tell you how I found him, but I will. I'd registered with Mopester, a social networking site that allowed you to become "mopes" with anybody in the world. Before you became a mope, you were asked to input your vital stats and fave/raves: sign, marital status, favorite books, records, movies, food. Most people used Mopester to hook up, spending hours scrolling through the members, then electronically inviting ones who maybe shared a love of frozen pizza and Public Image Limited's sophomore release. A lot of people did that. Not me.

There were others, including me, who used the Mopester site to track down those they'd lost track of. I was curious whether Rudy or Harry were mopes themselves, since for a while there it really did seem like everyone in the universe was registered. One night, after a few beers, I combed the community by searching each Mopester profile for buzzwords like "Keith Richards" or "hardware store." I felt positively ridiculous, but nobody was watching, you know? Harry was not a mope. Rudy was, and so I invited him to be one of *my* mopes. And there, in little boxes stuffed with text and delivered with a click, the seeds of a Jane Ashers reunion began.

Have you seen Vance much? he'd write.

Not at all, actually. Once. From a distance. Across a parking lot. And Debbie at the bank but she left before I could say hello.

They avoiding you? Is that even possible in Dean?

Don't know. I follow my path every day and don't run across him on it. That's all.

You don't need much hardware, I guess.

Well, the weird thing is, now I do. I've started tinkering again.

Computer stuff?

No. Recording equipment. Speaking of, have you played the Deep End *songs at all recently?*

No. Why? Do they sound like shit? I have it in my head that they sound great. I prefer to keep that memory.

They sound like shit.

What a bummer.

I know. I always figured someone would find it one day, decide it's great, and put it out.

Like Anne Frank's diary.

Shut the fuck up.

I'm kidding, man. I always felt the same.

But if they discovered that, they'd just be like, " 'Neptune's Pizza Kitchen'? What the fuck?"

Good pizza.

Shitty demo. We should really remix that shit. For posterity.

too much, too late

We should get together and rerecord the entire demo. Just to have it. For the kids.

You have kids?

No. Not my *kids.*

So who are all these other mopes on your account?

Stones fans.

Good to know you still love the Stones.

Till I die. I still have Keith's gum, by the way.

You know it was never Keith's gum, right?

No. It's his, Sandy. I still believe.

Also good to know.

After considering these happy exchanges with my old friend and guitarist, I decided that if nothing else, our old songs had to be rerecorded properly. I'd been reading manuals. Home recording texts. Real geek shit. And although I hadn't touched my kit in years, I'd never broken it down. It was still fully assembled out there under the poster of Winona Ryder in *Beetlejuice* we'd hung up after we found out she was dating the guy in Soul Asylum.

Everyone needs a project. Not a hobby, a project. Hobbies are trivial. Projects are serious. Nobody needs projects more than the elderly or the infirm or the otherwise forgotten who are still sharp in mind and energetic in spirit but somehow and often cruelly inconsequential to anyone beyond their private world. In a larger sense it's a way to reclaim some dignity, but it's also really fun. For me, drinking and thinking about death were hobbies. Preparing to record our songs for future generations was a motherfucking *project*.

"Is Harry there?"

"Who's this?" The voice on the end of the line was high. A kid.

"Who's *this*?"

"Matt."

"Are you the kid?"

"Who *is* this?"

"This is your Uncle Sandy. You heard about me?"

"No."

"What the fuck! Where's your pops?"

"He's at work."

"Where's Mom?"

"She's at work."

"You're there alone?"

"Mister, you're scaring me."

"You don't have to be scared, kid. I'm not a creep. I was your dad's drummer. His best friend. He never told you about me? About the Jane Ashers?"

"Nuh."

"Serious?"

"Nuh."

"What the fuck!"

"Do you want me to take a message?"

"A message? Yeah, I do have a message. Tell him . . ." I didn't know what to say. My brain shut down. It occured to me that it had been 12, almost 13 years. How do you build some kind of bridge from 1993 to the present with something that'll fit on a notepad? How do you condense 50 different feelings, 48 of them negative, into a brief message delivered via snot-nosed kid?

"Are you still there, mister?"

"Yeah. Sorry. Listen . . . Matt. Do they call you Matty?"

"Sometimes."

"Do you like rock'n'roll, Matty?"

"No."

"What the fuck! What do you like? You like the fucking . . . rap. Right? Hip-hop?"

"Yeah."

"I figured. What the hell can that stuff possibly be saying to you? What are you, 10? You're a 10-year-old white kid from fucking Ohio. Get it?"

"I'm almost 12."

"Are you a smart kid? Do you, like, get good grades?"

"Yeah."

"Yeah? You got a girlfriend?"

"No."

"You got a girl you like?"

"Yeah."

"Does she know you like her?"

"Um . . . do you have a message for my dad?"

"Tell him that Sandy called and that I need to talk to him about something very important."

"Okay. Does he have your number?"

"He's got my fucking number."

"Okay."

"Matty?"

"Yeah."

"This girl you like? She already knows you like her."

"Nuh."

"Oh, yeah, she does. They all do."

"I didn't tell anyone."

"Doesn't matter. She knows. Believe me. But it's

good to act like you know she already knows and not make a big thing about it. Be cool. Do you get that? You understand that?"

"I don't know."

"Yeah. You know what I'm talking about. You gotta go up to her and tell her that you dig her and you know that she knows it. She'll respect you. She'll put you above all those other guys who try to play it cool."

"Really?"

"Oh, fuck, yeah. You know how many of those manly man guys there are out there, ignoring her or being mean to her instead of just letting her know they're sweet on her? You'll blow her mind. Your dad, he never knew shit about girls. He married the eighth or ninth girl he ever fucked. That's your mom, by the way."

"Uh . . ."

"How is your mom? How's Debbie? She still pretty?"

"Uh . . ."

"All right. Fuck it. Listen, Matty, it's been good talking to you, my man."

Harry got the message. I was sure of it. But he never returned the call. I didn't get angry or hurt. Those were old emotions. I got that much more determined.

"Ma."

"Sandy?"

"Come out to the garage."

"I'm making peanut butter squares."

"Forget about that. I need an audience."

"What are you gonna do?"

"I'm gonna sing for you."

Minna followed me out to the garage and took a seat. "Wow, you got quite a setup, huh?" she said.

"Yeah . . . Hit the record button when I tell you. You see it?"

She examined the four-track like it was covered with beetles.

"It's okay to touch it, Ma. Just hit record."

She remained wary. Stoned.

"Ma!"

I came out from around the kit and hit record myself, then kissed her on the top of her head and laughed.

"Sorry, Sand. I don't wanna ruin anything."

"It's already ruined, Ma."

"Oh, okay."

"Don't worry. Testing, one two one two. These are songs written by Harry Vance and originally performed by myself and the Jane Ashers. Since Harry has made it clear to me that he has no interest in rerecording them for posterity, I am taking it upon myself to lay down the only studio-recorded versions of them. I feel, in my heart, that my versions do justice to his creative vision and are, to date, the definitive renditions for drum and vocal. If anyone hears this in the future, please note that the vocal melodies are arranged exactly the way Harry intended and my singing voice is more or less identical to his. Now, enough of this bullshit. Let's rock out! Woo hoo!" I almost let a giggle go as I counted off. I could picture Harry's chubby face as he listened to it. The pale, freckled skin deepening red. A slow burn, like in the cartoons. I counted off and laid down the beat for "I Mean You're Mean," then opened my mouth and took the lead vocals. Minna was polite at first—she kept her upbeat smile, nodded, and tapped her toe. But by the second verse she was showing discomfort, shifting in her seat. I ruined one song after another. Everything off *Deep End,* sung by me, the tone-deaf drummer. Pick any pompous sitcom or movie actor who ever inflicted his vanity record on an adoring public. I was worse. Minna finally cracked after about 15 minutes.

"Sand, I can't do this anymore. I can't. I got squares in the oven, Sand. I got my peanut butter squares."

"Okay, Ma. Go deal with your peanut butter squares." I laughed. "I'm gonna keep on rockin'."

I didn't need to play back the tape. I knew it was awful. Whether or not it was sufficiently horrible to convince Harry to rerecord them with me remained to be seen, but I had a pretty good feeling that I was playing the right angle.

I was still in my underwear and bathrobe when the doorbell rang. I'd been up late the night before, reading about the new portable digital studios that were coming out on the market. (Used to be I'd read porn at that hour.) I was tired, but I knew there was no way that Minna would even hear it, much less get it herself.

I wrapped the cloth robe around my belly and trudged down the stairs and across the cold tiles in my bare feet. I knew it was Harry even before I could make out his face through the beveled glass. For a second I had my doubts about opening the door. His eyes were unlined. Their expressiveness and intensity had not dimmed with age. His face was wider. Fuller. Not plump, just older. He'd been eating well. His hair was still high, thick, and unruly, but there was gray in his sideburns, stiff white strands that seemed to belong to someone else. Me, I'd pluck them. He was wearing a powder-blue button-down shirt with short sleeves, a wristwatch with a worn brown leather band, a navy tie with gold stripes, khakis, and lace-up shoes. He looked like an inspector. He was holding a bag from the donut shop. I opened the door and squinted in the sun. He reached into the bag and pulled out a cup of coffee.

"You still take it black?" he said. The voice was deeper.

I nodded and grabbed the coffee. Sniffed it.

"Don't worry, there's no poison in there," he cracked. "The poison's in the donuts."

"Great."

"I have an hour and a half before I have to open the store. Would you like me to review this?" He pulled out my tape and waved it. I shook my head and motioned for him to come in.

"You remember the couch," I quipped. "Have a seat. I'll throw on some clothes."

I watched him look around the house and smile. It hadn't changed at all. I'm sure there were still pretzels lying around from when he lived on the couch. Harry seemed to breathe in the stasis. I assumed he found it somewhat comforting.

We were sitting in the diner together for the first time since we were kids. I'd suggested we take a ride over to Dil's and talk a bit more. I hadn't been there in years, afraid that I might run into Harry. It was good to see that nothing had changed except the jukebox—some numskull had had the bright idea to rip out the excellent individual chrome boxes and install a high-tech, freestanding box by the toilets. "On the Road Again," by Willie Nelson, was still there, probably by some kind of mandate. But during a cursory inspection on my way to piss, I noticed the live version of "Do You Feel Like We Do" by Peter Frampton had been retired, replaced by Britney Spears's cover of "I Love Rock 'N' Roll," which was a cover version when Joan Jett and the Blackhearts did it. Not that Britney would know this. The Arrows did it first. The Arrows.

"That's a shame about the jukeboxes," Harry agreed. "Those things'll probably be worth something."

"I wish they'd told me. I would have bid on them. Set them up in the garage or something."

"First you're a relic. Then you're kitsch. Then you're a serious collectible." Harry laughed.

"So what are we?"

"I think we're relics, Sand." He picked up the tape and twirled it in his fingers. "Although this . . . this is definitely kitsch."

"So help me make it a collectible. Huh?"

He shook his head.

"You look more like Captain Kangaroo than I remembered," I accused. "What happened to you?"

"I don't know. I'm happy, I guess."

"Too happy, I think. You look soft."

"You look the same. Kinda."

We ordered. Harry had a bowl of oatmeal and a glass of freshly squeezed orange juice. I had two eggs over medium, bacon, sausage, ham, grits, and a small box of Frosted Flakes. "Look, Harry, I don't wanna play the catch-up game with you. I don't wanna know what you've been doing. I don't wanna tell you what I've been doing. As if you'd care."

"I care, Sandy," Harry insisted.

"Bullshit. You totally abandoned us."

"Here we go."

"You didn't even go to Archie's funeral, man."

"I wasn't invited."

"Neither were we. But we went. Me and Rudy. We stood there with his weird uncle and the undertaker, and it was fucking depressing."

"Shit."

"Did he ever mention to you, like, what he would play if he knew he was about to die? Like, what song he wanted to go out listening to? Anything like that?"

"No."

"Shit."

"Look, Sandy . . . I feel really bad. About Archie. About everything. I was a little selfish."

"A little, huh?"

"I was very scared. I felt like I had to protect my family."

"You should have protected us! We needed protecting. That thing you had with Debbie, that was strong. Anyone could see it."

"Not me. I worried."

"You were an idiot."

"I was insecure. I didn't have any paradigm like you did. Your dad died. Mine split."

"Well, you're still an idiot. You messed up a good thing. You left a great band."

"I guess I did."

"Well, I want you to know that I accept your apology."

"Really?"

"Fuck, why not? We're almost dead."

"Sandy, what about you? Do you have a . . . you know, someone?"

"I do not."

"Okay."

"It is okay. I've got big plans, Harry."

"Well . . . I'd like to hear them."

We paid the check and I offered to walk Harry to work. He'd been made manager of the hardware store and even owned a percentage of it now, in addition to the drawerful of navy ties and the cheap wristwatch.

"I talked to the kid," I confessed.

"I know. You cursed. We're trying to teach him to express himself without using profanity, Sandy."

"It's nothing he's not gonna hear on the playground. Shit. He doesn't know anything about music, that kid."

"Deb and I didn't want to force our tastes on him. We wanted him to develop his own identity. Our own parents were . . . destructive."

"I know. I was there, remember?"

"Yeah. I do."

"A couple of days after he talked to you something happened—he brought home a girl. I think she's his tutor. I hope she's his tutor."

"Ha ha. She cute?"

"She's 16."

"Yeah? She cute?"

"Sandy, she's 16!"

"I might have given him some advice. I don't remember. Good for him. Older women'll teach him shit he needs to know, I guess."

"That's what I'm afraid of."

He unlocked the store. I shifted from one foot to the other, my hands in my pockets, wondering if I should come in.

"I've got some stuff to do, but if you wanna hang out . . ."

"Yeah. Sure. Why not?" I had nothing else to do.

Harry began unpacking boxes of thick canvas work gloves. I offered to help.

"You know I had a job?"

"Really?"

"Yeah, after Archie died and Rudy split for college."

"I heard something about that."

"Minna started complaining she was going broke, so I did what I had to do."

"You're a good son, Sandy."

"Yeah. Whatever."

"My kid—"

"He's got an attitude problem. It's all the rap."

"He doesn't even like me anymore."

"He *doesn't* know what you gave up to raise him, right? I mean, why don't you ever shove that back in his fucking face when he mouths off?"

"No, Sandy."

"I would."

"I didn't do it to get some kind of reward. I don't expect to be unconditionally loved. It'd be nice. I just want to be appreciated for being a good father. For being . . . *there*. But that's not enough anymore."

"I told you."

"He's angry."

"Rap."

"Debbie and I have done everything to make him feel loved. And he *is* loved. I mean . . . my dad . . . her dad . . . they . . ." He wandered off toward the stock-room in the back. I followed.

"And he still hates you."

"I didn't say 'hate,' Sand. He doesn't hate me. He's my kid."

"He hates you."

Harry slumped.

"Yeah. He does. What the fuck?" Harry laughed bitterly. "Debbie doesn't tolerate it. She gives him the attitude right back."

"Course she does."

"But man, it kills me."

"And he doesn't even know about the Ashers?"

"Nope."

"Why the fuck not?"

Harry shrugged.

"Does he know about your . . . talent?"

Harry chuckled.

"He doesn't know his old man's a fucking genius, huh?"

"He thinks I co-own a hardware store."

"*I* think you co-own a hardware store too."

I stayed in the store for most of the day, smoking and glaring at each customer. Harry allowed it. During lunch, he turned the store over to some sporto-lookin' kid with a crew cut.

"That's Nash," he told me. "He's part time. Good kid."

"Looks like a wrestler."

"I guess."

"You relate to Nash?"

"Not really."

"You're like 150 years old, man."

"I guess."

"Don't you feel creaky?"

"Yeah, I do feel a little creaky."

We walked back to the diner. It was easier this time. We maligned the new juke selections with increased volume and outrage. Harry ate fried clams even though they were bad for him.

"Archie, man. That was something, huh?" he marveled sadly.

"I guess Mark Chapman's resting easier in his prison cell."

"We can't do justice to some of these songs without him, you know. He was a mental case, but he was really talented."

I poured milk into my coffee and passed the creamer across the table to him. He took it, nodded thanks, and lightened his cup. He sipped some and looked around at all the Deaners eating their specials.

"I don't regret anything, Sandy. I have a great kid. You gotta meet him. On a good day. He's the best. And I was there, you know? For his first snowstorm. His first ball game. I held his hand when he was scared. Everything . . ."

"Everything but the music."

"Maybe I deserve this."

"Play him the music. Show him this side of you. Who you really are. He'll forgive you for anything. I'm sure of it."

7

"Goddamn it, Rudy. Where's your hair?"

Getting Rudy on board was easy: it took one e-mail. But getting used to the baldness was difficult. The last time I'd seen him, he'd had a full head of black hair.

"It started thinning, man, so I just let it go. I set it free. It still hasn't come back." He giggled. "And you wanna know something weird?"

"Always."

"Once I went bald, I could really feel the music when I was playing. I wasn't so caught up in posing. Nothing else was competing for my attention. I wasn't such a punk. I wasn't trying to be Keith. I'm much happier just connecting with the noise."

"Well, you don't look a thing like him anymore, so I guess that's fortunate."

Rudy truly no longer resembled Keith Richards, but rather looked like what he was—a highly intelligent, middle-aged bald Jewish man—with two exceptions. One was that Rudy still kept a cigarette behind his left ear. It looked odd, especially with the naked pate.

"I quit," he told me and Harry as we stared in amazement.

"How long has it been there?"

"Five months."

The other was his chiseled physique.

"Christ, Rudy. You're buff," Harry said, and stared down a little shamefaced at his own increasingly pear-shaped physique.

"Yeah, I know. Weird, right? I go to the gym." He saw our looks and laughed. "I know . . . but it's good, man. When I first started, I was out of shape. I was convinced that everyone was staring. All these fitness freaks, right?"

"Right."

"I used to program my desired heart rate on the treadmill. You know, for cardio. I told it I was 77 years old. I could barely take a step without wheezing."

"We're old and decrepit!" I laughed.

"I'm in the best shape of my life. I'm not decrepit. I'm just old, man," Rudy cackled.

"And bald," I reminded him.

"And sad," Harry put in.

"Very sad," I agreed.

"Yeah. Kind of sad. But hey, let's rock the heck out," Rudy offered in a mock old man's voice.

He plugged in his new Telecaster. I set the tape rolling, then hurried behind the kit. Harry took Archie's space under Winona Ryder (who had not aged a day since we placed her poster on the garage wall) and picked up Archie's red and white Dan Electro. He strummed out the chords to "I Mean You're Mean."

"This is for Archie," he announced. "One . . . two . . . three . . ."

We sounded terrible, like three guys playing in three isolation booths with no headphones.

But the volume . . . the volume felt so great. Rudy insisted that we all wear earplugs. "It's the smart way to go," he warned. "Can't play in tune if you're deaf, right?"

We all agreed but compensated for our nod to physical decay by cranking the volume to car-alarm-triggering levels. The noise melted away 11 years of bad memories. We were older. We were not famous. We were not rich. We had baldness and furrowed brows and fatness. But the furrowed brows were no longer sources of shame when we played. They were proof that we'd lived. Celebrate the furrow!

Basically Matty Vance didn't want to hang out with his dad on Saturdays anymore, so the Jane Ashers got Harry. In the early fall of 2005, the reunited band were still "Dad's hobby," a weekend thing, second prize after the affections of his kid, which had almost completely dried up sometime after the onset of puberty. This was to be expected, but if anyone should have been able to understand the confusion and anger and urgency of those years, it was Harry. But never once did Harry tap his pouting kid on the back and say, *Hey, schmuck, you think you're frustrated? Listen to this.* I would have. I know that's easy to say because I don't have any kids, but I would have. I'm sure of it. And there'd be spankings. Withheld allowances. Anything to keep my kid from making me feel square and out of touch.

It occurred to me that maybe Harry had just forgotten. He surely remembered the melodies to those angst-fests, because the guy never wrote a forgettable tune, but what with the shared sweaters and lighted Christmas wreaths and ordering in once a week and "the shows we like to watch" and the puppies and kittens and preschool and Little League and grade school and gray hair and more puppies, he had no room for those unsatisfied lyrics. Storage, that's where they were, and it was a shame. They might have helped.

Harry sat back down on the milk crate after running through what we could remember from our old set. He hadn't written anything new since the early '90s, but those old songs were still fun to bash out, if a little exhausting. Harry seemed winded. He stared up at Winona.

"I thought about you guys when she got arrested," he confessed.

"I would have taken the rap for Winona if I'd been with her," Rudy declared.

"I'd do time for Winona," I agreed. "Wouldn't you?"

"Minimum security, maybe," Rudy joked. "How about you, Har?"

"Maybe. Yeah. If . . . you know . . ."

"Winona can't vote." I belched. "Do you believe that? Winona Ryder can't fucking vote. Who wants more beer?"

"I better not." Harry worried. "I gotta drive home."

"You drive a Volvo. You can crash it," I protested. It was true. Harry Vance drove a used Volvo, a forest green 1983 station wagon. Safest car in existence.

"Debbie's making spaghetti and meatballs," he admitted.

"Sounds seriously delicious," I said. "Make sure you don't put too much of that Kraft grated cheese on it, man. Cholesterol, you know?" I shotgunned a beer and lit a smoke.

"Cheese is fine," Rudy corrected me as he fiddled with his tuner. "It's the carbs you need to be wary of at your age, Harry. Once you pass 35, it's hard to drop any weight. The body settles in for the rest of the night. I'm speaking metaphorically. You know?"

"I knew that." Harry smiled. He stared longingly at the sixer of beer on the floor next to my bass drum. I picked one up and waggled it like I was gonna throw it at him. He nodded. I tossed.

"I know I need to exercise," Harry blurted out, sounding sad, "but I'm really, really tired."

"Listen, man. You should bring the kid here. Let him hang out with us a little. We'll help you put him straight," I suggested.

"Yeah," Rudy agreed. He was nibbling on an energy bar. I looked at him cockeyed.

"Rudy, man . . ."

"Huh?"

"You're bald! I can't get over it."

too much, too late

"Get over it." He chomped on the bar and flashed me a wide grin full of granola and raisins. "Harry, your kid's not afraid of bald people, is he?"

"He likes Tupac a lot. Tupac was bald."

"All these rappers shave their heads. It's the shiznit!" Rudy said proudly. I tossed an empty beer can at his shiny skull.

"You think I should bring him next weekend?" Harry asked.

"Fuck, yes."

"Well . . . I'll ask him."

"Don't ask him. Tell him. Punish him if he refuses to come."

"We don't punish Matty. We have conversations, Sandy. We used to, anyway. We don't talk much anymore."

"Well, yeah, it's hard." I shrugged. "I guess. You and Debbie are okay?"

Harry popped open his beer.

"Until I come home drunk."

"It's just a beer," I pointed out.

"Carbs," Rudy warned. "Right there. Carbs."

"We're fine. It's not the same anymore, but it's fine. It's . . . reflexive. You know? I touch her in her sleep and she knows it's me. Who else would it be?" Harry eyed my pack of cigarettes. "Do you have an extra one of those?"

"Sure." I tossed him the pack.

"You guys are killing me," Rudy pleaded.

"Sorry." Harry lit up. "I quit a couple of years ago, but I sneak one or two sometimes. Debbie knows, but we don't talk about it. She lets it slide, I guess."

Rudy stared at us. We were considerate, blowing our smoke into the concrete floor.

"Oh, fuck it." Rudy pulled the cigarette from beind his ear. I tossed him the pack of matches. "If you can sneak, I can sneak."

"I'm not sneaking, I'm smoking," I proudly corrected him. "Doesn't anybody commit to shit anymore?"

"I've committed to a lot, Sandy." Harry laughed and stared lovingly at his cigarette. "Man, these are good."

"He doesn't wanna come," Harry said the next Saturday afternoon when I asked where the kid was. "He told me I was a fat loser."

"Aw, man. Let's go get him."

"No. Let's just play."

"Nah. Come on. That's bullshit."

I grabbed Harry and pushed him, shoulders first, toward the green Volvo.

"Ma, tell Rudy we'll be back in twenty minutes. Ma? Ma!"

"Okay," Minna called. I'm sure she didn't hear what the hell I was saying—probably had headphones on. But I could always rely on Rudy to amuse himself somehow.

"Get in," I commanded. He got in the passenger seat. I grabbed the key, inserted it, and started the engine up.

"This is bad," he fretted.

"Look at me. I'm driving a Volvo! How fast can this thing go?"

"Not very."

I floored the Volvo toward the Vance house.

too much, too late

"**Matty! Where are** you, you little a-hole?"

We marched upstairs, and Harry nodded toward a closed door. I closed my eyes as I turned the knob. My balls are big, but they're not that big—I knew that if I made eye contact with anyone inside, I probably wouldn't say what I'd sped all the way there to say.

"Get your shit. We're leaving. Now!"

As soon as I'd said it, I opened my eyes. He was a strange-looking kid. Maybe a year or two before, he'd been really cute. Now he was being elongated by nature, and probably resisting it. It flushed his face and gave him an air of pain or poor health. Worse, he wore a baggy Adidas sweat suit, sneakers, and a do-rag on his head. He looked more like Debbie than Harry, but more like Vanilla Ice than either of them. I didn't like him from the first spark. He had snob eyes and chewed-up nails and chocolate crumbs in the corner of his lips.

"Get out!" he squealed.

"Shut up."

I looked the room over. Posters of Master P and Tupac were hung on the walls.

"What the fuck is this?" I rushed the Master P poster, pulled it down, crumpled it, and stomped on it with my boots. "Master P? You think he's a genius? Huh? Fuck that. Get your shit. Come on. Up!"

I heard something like a harrumph, and it jarred me out of my theatrics. I looked around. Two glasses of milk sat on the night table along with some Oreo cookies and a purse with Hello Kitty on it. Matty wasn't alone. He'd been hanging with the tutor. I scowled at this 16-year-old cherub-cheeked little thing too. Only unlike Matty, she was glaring right back.

"What are you, like a total racist or something?" she trilled.

"Huh?"

"That's not Master P. That's Jay-Z. And he *is* so much a genius? Duh!"

I took a step back. She had big breasts she'd harnessed up, making some cleavage that probably kept the boy up late. Dyed blue-black hair with straight bangs. She wore black Converse low-tops, fishnets, a red plaid skirt, and a faded gray Siouxsie and the Banshees T-shirt covered with yellow Joy Division badges.

"Who the fuck are you?"

"Who the fuck are *you*?"

"I'm Uncle Sandy. Sandy James."

She got up, picked up the poster of Jay-Z, and straightened it out. She seemed fearless.

"I'm Motorrrju."

"Huh?"

She drew closer and pronounced the name condescendingly. "Mo-torrr-ju."

Her standing me down emboldened Matty, who joined her on the floor across from me. He looked odd next to her. He might have had Debbie's looks, but he dressed like young Harry—mad scientist prep.

"Where's my father?"

"He's downstairs."

"Oh."

"Get your shit. We're going now," I ordered.

"Where?"

"My place."

"Are you some kind of kidnapper?" Motorrrju interrogated me.

"No. I'm a drummer."

She looked confused.

"Well, I have to study," Matty protested. "I have a history test."

"I've got a history lesson for you. Come on."

"I'm not going anywhere with you," Motorrrju announced.

"You don't have to come. He does."

She looked at me sideways.

"Don't give me that look, little girly." I pointed at her boobs. "Name one Joy Division song that's not 'Love Will Tear Us Apart.' "

She didn't flinch.

" 'Disorder.' "

"That's one."

" 'Transmission,' 'Digital,' 'Atmosphere,' 'Atrocity Exhibition,' 'Passover,' 'She's Lost Control,' 'Dead Souls,' 'Isolation,' ummmm . . ."

"All right."

" 'Incubation'!"

"All right!"

" 'From Safety to Where . . . ?' "

"To where?" Matty wondered.

"Shut up." I had to hand it to her. She put Archie Funz to shame, R.I.P. I lit a cigarette.

"Don't smoke in my room," Matty begged. "Please?"

"You should really think about quitting," Motorrrju warned. "At your age."

Then she grabbed the pack out of my hand and put

a cigarette in her mouth. I lit it, calling her bluff. She smoked it, calling mine.

"Please don't smoke in my room!" He was staring at her now.

"Downstairs," I shouted.

I pushed them toward the kitchen. Harry sat at the table, staring into a heart-shaped sky-blue ashtray smudged with black.

"Dad? You smoke?"

He looked up at Matty and quickly stubbed it out.

"No."

The kid looked at him suspiciously.

"Sometimes. Almost never."

"Dad, he was in my room!"

"I know."

"Is he really my uncle?"

"Well . . . yeah. Kind of."

Matty arched his eyebrows and frowned. It was hardly fearsome, but Harry returned his gaze to the dirty ashtray.

"Dad, I need to study. I told you."

"I know. I'm sorry."

"No, he's not. He's not sorry. Bullshit," I hissed at Matty. "Get your coat and get in the fucking Volvo. You can study later."

He looked over at Harry, who shrugged. He looked back at me with the same sneer he'd developed to vex Dad, but it didn't work on me. He gave up.

"What are you going to do to me?"

"Play you some music."

Harry stood up, put his hand on his boy's shoulder,

and squeezed it. "It'll only take a few minutes," he apologized. "I promise."

"Unless we jam," I warned.

"Unless we jam," he agreed. "But we almost never jam. We're a power pop band."

Matty looked alarmed. "You are?"

"Yes, son. We're called the Jane Ashers."

"Does Mom know?"

"Uh-huh."

"Oh."

Rudy and Minna were smoking pot when we all walked in. Minna instinctively covered up her stash at the sight of a couple of children.

"Who are the kids, Sand?"

"This is Harry's son, Matthew. You can call him Matty. And this is Motorrrju."

"Motor who?"

Motorrrju extended her hand to Minna. Minna looked at it queerly, probably wondering if it was some kind of headfuck.

"Can I have some of that pot?" Motorrrju asked.

"Are you a cop?"

"I'm 16."

"Answer the question."

"No. I'm not a cop."

Minna uncovered her stash.

"Sandy . . . please don't get my son's math tutor stoned," Harry whispered. "I don't wanna go to jail."

"I forgot how good Minna's weed is," Rudy said, slit-eyed, goat-faced, a goofy red, yellow, and green Ras-tourist cap on his bald-ass head.

"Whose hat is that?" I pointed.

"Mine."

"It's stupid. Take it off. We're gonna play."

Rudy scanned the room for approval.

"Stupid," Motorrrju agreed, packing Minna's green glass pipe. She picked up the lighter, sucked a long, freaky string of weed smoke into her lungs, and exhaled through her button nose. "All right. Let's hear it."

We started with the Jane Ashers' theme, and we rocked it. Technically speaking, it wasn't the best performance we'd ever done, but it was easily the best we'd ever done in the 21st century. Nobody seemed too impressed. Harry looked at Matty for approval. Matty stared at his feet. Motorrrju sat next to her non-boyfriend on the spare amp and watched us play "Who Told You You Knew Shit About Love." Still nothing.

"Uh, okay, Matty, this next song is about . . . Mom," Harry said through the mike. He looked over at me and shook his head. It was ridiculous, but it felt right somehow. Something was encouraging this. Wasn't just me anymore. We went into "Let's Go Steady Debbie." I counted, Rudy chimed, Harry belted. Harry treated that song right, like he hadn't done since back in the early '90s, when Debbie first started watching our sets. By the second verse (different from the first) Motorrrju's eyes were glazed over. Her cheeks were a bit flushed.

When it was over, Harry threw down the mike and lit a cigarette. Matty just stared at him, then looked at my old bike in the corner, a Bridgestone, 90cc's of belching, farting, stalling glory. He was probably contemplating how quickly he could do us all in with the right dose of carbon monoxide. Motorrrju was sweating. She looked at Harry—with his potbelly and graying hair, sweatshirt, khaki shorts, and sneakers—like he was Elvis. P, not even C. Then she turned to Matty. "Oh, my God, your dad just put babies in me," she said in her high, squeaky, absurdly declarative voice. "My vagina just exploded."

It was the best review we'd ever had.

I figured the girl was just gonna drink up all our beer (she did), smoke all Minna's pot (she tried), and leave. I'd never see her again . . . unless it was in a courtroom. Turns out she went home and posted the following on her blog.

> Okay, for realz, you guys. Holy shit! I just heard the best fucking band like ever in my life. They're called the Jane Ashers and if they don't make you blow your load too, then whatevs cause I swear the lead singer impregnated me. They don't look hot like Joy Division but if you close your eyes, it's like everything makes sense. It's like doing heroin (I bet) or eating really yumz macaroni and cheese. Like comfort food but so so rockin'. I can't stop thinking about them. They're so good, yo. So so good! I can't even describe it. They make me want to be in love. They're my new faves band and I don't even want to fuck them. But I do. Or my brain does. So weirdz! Why does nobody know about this band? Why why why do they not have like a deal? Can I really be the only one who knows about this? I want to

burn all my other records and delete everything from my iPod! I also want a Coke and something with mayonnaise on it!

Natalie Levine was her real name. She called herself Motorrrju because of the chorus to "Sister Christian" by Night Ranger. And because it sounded like Motorhead. And because she was a Jew. That was her handle on the Web. She was a blogger. She had a thing for posting photos of baby animals—"Look at this hippo!" ran one caption—but mostly she wrote about rock'n'roll.

I was still relatively new to the whole information age phenomenon, so she was my very first real blogger. (I used to play *Frogger* in the '80s.) My initial impulse was to roll my eyes at this trend, but I soon realized that little Natalie Levine had the ear of a huge number of teenage boys and girls. They hit her blog every day to find out what she was into at the moment. Now you might be asking yourself right now, *Who really cares what this little girl from Dean, Ohio, is into?* But Motorrrju had a preternatural ability to anticipate trends, and that translates into money and power pretty quickly in the info age. Cool has become currency. But Natalie was just writing about what she liked. When major movie studios contacted her about placing banner ads for opening blockbusters across the top of her page, she was initially as shocked as anyone else would be. What she did wasn't calculated or mercenary. It was a world party. A bash-and-mash fest. Adults with movies to open and units to sell weren't invited, but they were welcome. Everyone was. But she was just too good. She wrote about the Olsen twins, and suddenly they were fashion icons. She wrote about getting her period, and suddenly she was Judy Blume. She wrote about what she bought at the Hot Topic outlet, and everybody else bought it at the Hot Topic outlet. And so, like Ace Rothstein in *Casino,* she could not help but let the dark forces in after a while. When I met Natalie she was hanging in the balance between innocence and corruption. She'd already separated herself from Motorrrju because Motorrrju was starting to stink. I had no idea how famous she was. I was still gassed that another Jewish family had moved to Dean. It never occurred to me to work her. I just thought she was really cute. Besides, when I was a kid, Elton John was famous. Richard Dawson was famous. Pelé the soccer star was famous. Now you didn't even have to be famous to be famous. You didn't have to do anything anyway. You just had to like the right shit.

Her posting on the Jane Ashers drew over a thousand comments within the first hour. By the end of the day, it was up to two hundred thousand. Everything from *Whoaz, we have to hear this band like now!* to *Oh, man, I saw them play in Philly last year. They're so over!* (we'd never played Philadelphia or anywhere else in the last year, of course) and even *Mayonnaise is the best!*

She posted again the next night:

> I can't get these songs out of my head and I
> don't want to. I wanna like, do something de-
> structive and constructive all at the same time. I
> wanna scream and shout and kiss someone too.

Please, for the love of God, please listen to these
songs. I will figure out a way to beam them to
you if you ask. I will fucking sing them for you.
I want to listen to these songs, and nothing but
these songs, for the next 18 hours. I'm drunk
right now, but I feel this way when I'm sober
too. It's like I'm listening to Mozart for the first
time and witnessing genius firsthand. And I've
never even listened to Mozart. Everything makes
sense to me and life is so so so good.

That drunken post got half a million hits. The following weekend, Motorrrju came down again. No Matty
this time—apparently he'd broken up with her because
she wanted to have babies with his dad. Not a bad
reason.

But clearly Harry's plan to win his kid's respect had
backfired. He was miserable. And an hour late for
rehearsal.

"I blew it," he told me over the phone when I called
him, laboring to keep my temper down. "I don't know
what happened, Sand. Everything's a bit messy over
here. Debbie's pissed. I don't think I should play. I
should take him to a Reds game or something."

I tried to convince Harry that playing with us would
be good for him. "Leave Matty alone!"

"You don't know anything about being a dad, Sand.
You can't just give up."

"Is he gonna go anywhere at all with you now? Even
if you had box seats?"

"No."

"So come here. Get over here. There are girls here."

"Jesus. Don't say that."

"Young girls."

"Debbie is . . . she's . . ."

"Chill out. It's just Motorrrju and some friends."

"She's there? What's she doing there?"

"She wants a tape. I'm showing her my studio."

"Don't give them drugs."

"Relax. I'm just hanging out."

"Oh, Jesus."

"Get in the Volvo and come see this, man. It's trippy."

"I'll come down there if you promise no beer and no drugs. They're minors. Get rid of it all or I don't play."

"Fine."

I hung up the phone and grabbed the beer out of Motorrrju's hand.

"Fuck you," she shouted, and pushed me.

"He's not gonna play if you're drinking."

She poured out her beer.

Harry showed up for our weekly weekend jam that Saturday to find twenty-five teenage girls and boys waiting for him. When they first walked into the garage, man, the look on all their pretty young faces was priceless. They recongized Winona. But when they saw me and Rudy, it was like a giant, communal *Huh?* One by one, they'd turn to Motorrrju with an expression that seemed to ask, *What the hell is this? These guys are old!*

"Just wait," she said. They weren't immediately eased when Harry sheepishly walked in either. But when we started playing . . . man, we had those little fuckers in the pocket of our dirty khaki shorts. Harry did his killer cover of "This Is Where I Belong," by the Kinks, and one by one they melted. We told them we'd written that one.

"You did not," Motorrrju screamed. "Don't lie." She was good.

Then we went into "Roots." They all started dancing. Right there in the garage, like it was the fucking Peach Pit. It felt great! Even Harry was swayed. We closed our set with "Debbie." I really felt like a rock star there in the garage, but as soon as we stopped playing, I felt like a creepy old guy again. Where the hell had these kids been fifteen years ago? In the womb, I guess. And what the hell was in our music that made them act like this? Weren't there any idols their age who could articulate it better than we could? I guess not, because whatever romantic sentiment their generation was needing, we were giving it to them in Dean, Ohio. And this time we preserved it for them. I made Motorrrju a pretty-good-quality DAT off my home-assembled sound board. She asked if it was okay to put it on her blog. I wasn't 100 percent sure what that even meant, really. I figured, you know, let her dance around her bedroom to the shit if it knocks her out so much. So I said, "Yeah, sure."

Harry got all shy and split right after the jam. He went home to hide from the world with his wife and his hateful b-boy kid and his stupid job. He wouldn't be able to hide for long.

"I've been in *Billboard*," Natalie boasted between bites of her small garden salad. "*Hits* magazine. *CMJ*. I've been in *Variety* twice. I wish I could have been in *Sassy* but it's gone now."

"Right."

"Oh, and I'm failing French. *Je suis échoue français.*"

"Uh, you want like a cheeseburger or something? I'm buying."

"Can't. It's trayf."

"Oh, right. You're kosher, huh?"

"I don't eat swine."

"How does it feel to be the only other Jew in Dean, Ohio?"

"My parents are Jewish."

"Oh, yeah. Mine too. My ma. My dad's dead."

"My dad sells eyeglasses."

The waitress came to take our order after avoiding it as long as possible.

"I'll have some ice cream. Chocolate, please. I don't usually eat ice cream. I like frozen yogurt from TCBY but they don't have it here, obviously."

"I know what you eat for dessert. I read your blog."

"The whole country knows what I eat for dessert, I guess."

"England too."

"You know, I once got an e-mail from a boy in Moscow with a heart defect."

The truckers and office ladies were staring at us. Maybe they were wondering if she was my daughter or if they should phone the sheriff. Or maybe it was the hair. Natalie'd taken a razor to her sides and given herself a little Mohawk. Piled the spared tufts of hair about 18 inches into the air. She was a tiny thing, and I suppose she was craving some height. She wore a lime green angora sweater and a tight black skirt. Fifteen or 16 silver chains danged into her cleavage, each one carrying a chintzy little charm or trinket: razor blade, mini brass knuckles, Norfin troll, shrunken heads, rabbits' feet, star of David, crucifix. In my day, this was like sending an invitation to a good beating, but Kurt Cobain had died for her hairstyle, and these days even the Target over in Bailey, Ohio, sold faux vintage Black Flag T-shirts.

I didn't bring that up. I was there to pick Natalie's brain. See, something had happened that morning, and it'd kind of knocked me out. More so than the little garage party, which was a trip in itself. I'd gotten a phone call from a reporter . . . in London. Asking about the Jane Ashers. The much-bootlegged MP3 file of "Let's Go Steady Debbie" (which was quickly becoming our unofficial debut single) was set to be their Track of the Week the following issue, and he was requesting a mini-interview for a sidebar to run along with it. I thought it must have been bullshit. Surely it was a prank, some high school dickbag having a laugh at my expense. The accent wasn't half bad, but I told the reporter that I couldn't possibly talk until the following morning and asked him to call back. He agreed, and I ran right over to Harry's store to try to purchase one of those caller ID boxes. If the number came up with a country code, I would spill.

Harry was back in that apron full of nails, holding a stupid mop.

"The *NME*?"

"It has to be legit, right? I mean, the guy called me 'mate.' "

"Wow. What are you gonna tell him?"

"I don't know. What should I tell him?"

"Well . . . don't tell him anything about me. I mean, don't talk about me."

"How am I gonna talk about the Jane Ashers to the fucking *NME* and not talk about you?"

"I don't want to worry the kid, Sandy. He's really freaked out by all this. If he thinks it's gonna continue . . ."

"It's not? We have a hit song."

"On the Internet."

"That's where the business is these days, man. It's not like back in the fucking '90s. The Internet is the radio. The Net *is* what MTV was. MTV doesn't even play videos anymore."

"They don't?"

"No, they show rich people's homes. Cribs, they call them. Nice homes. Nice cars too. Rides, they call them. They *pimp* them. We could be those people now. With cribs and rides."

"Jesus, Sandy. This is all so weird."

"Look, he thought you were a big loser, right? And now he sees that you're not. It's gonna take him some time to adjust. This is a good thing."

"He won't even come to the dinner table. He eats in his room."

"He's processing it. You want me to talk to him, I'll talk to him."

"You're not allowed to talk to him, actually. Ever again. Debbie's rule."

"Oh, yeah?" I picked up a toilet brush and gestured with it. "Well, maybe I should explain everything to her."

"You don't wanna do that."

"I don't fear her. She's not my ball and chain."

"Sandy, I talked to her already. This is the best it's gonna get, believe me. She didn't even want me going over to play anymore. Now she's okay with it. I told her . . . I told her I needed it. She's cool."

"You talked to her?"

"Yeah."

"You defended us?"

"I did."

"Wow. It only took you 13 years."

A gruff man in a flannel shirt entered the store, triggering that annoying *ding-dong* that Harry probably couldn't even hear anymore.

"Sandy, I've got a customer."

"You've got fans."

"Please. We're not going to be rich and famous. Don't get carried away with this. It's really fun and I love it. I do. I'm so happy to be playing with you guys again, but it's not real life. My kid won't talk to me. My wife is pissed. And I have about 600 lightbulbs downstairs that I have to stack by wattage."

"Fuck that. We're big in England. Do you know where you get big first? You get big in England first. Motorrrju told me. It's like industry dogma. London makes the taste for the whole world when it comes to rock'n'roll."

"She's 16, Sandy."

"She's brilliant. You should hear the wisdom coming out of this little girl's mouth. She's—"

I realized I was grinning broadly just thinking about her. I picked up a key ring off the counter. Fiddled with it. Put it back.

"We may already be big in Japan. I bet we're huge in Japan already and don't even know it."

"We're not big in Japan."

"Don't you wanna see the world before you die? Get out of Ohio?"

"I like Ohio."

"Whatever the fuck! Lookit, I need one of those caller ID boxes. You sell those?"

"No."

"I was hoping you'd treat me a little better if I was a customer or something." I punched him in the arm and smiled. "It's gonna be all right, man. Trust me. I got a good feeling about all this. The tide is turning or something."

"Okay, Sandy. I'll see you on Saturday."

"You think maybe we ought to add like a Wednesday night too?"

"I'll think about it."

"Yeah. You think about it. Ask your wife. See what she says."

I found a caller ID box at Radio Shack in Bailey, drove home, and hooked it up, then realized I had fuck-all to do between that afternoon and the following morning, when I would talk to England . . . maybe. I signed on to the Web, found Motorrrju loitering in the computer room of Harrison High, and invited her to lunch. I figured the best way to safeguard myself against some kind of fall was to attempt to understand exactly what was going on here. Plus I thought she was appealing, even if she was 16. She suggested we meet in a bar. I told her that it was the diner or nothing. She agreed. Maybe she thought I was cute too. Or she wanted to show off her new hairdo to any takers.

"Basically, I guess my blog's initial raison d'être was to provide my family with proof that I wasn't drinking and miserable and really was trying to do something right."

"Who says *raison d'être*?"

"Someone trying to pass French."

"It's a Buzzcocks song."

"I know that. They're on the list."

"What list?"

"Old bands that are important to know about, I guess."

"Right. Go on."

"So I sent the link out to my sisters and friends and stuff."

"How many sisters?"

"Two. Both older. One's a teacher. The other has a baby. I'm an aunt."

"Right."

"I wanted them to see that I was actually trying to clean up my act. Which I felt had gotten a bit messy."

"Oh, yeah?"

"I like alcohol."

"Me too."

"Anyway, since then it's turned into an outlet for my thoughts. That's all. I'm the youngest child and was constantly competing with my sisters for attention from my parents. Even to this day I could be telling a story or talking about something that means a lot to me, and the moment anyone else starts talking they get the spotlight. And I've been written about in the *Wall Street Journal*. They don't even care."

"Some people aren't impressed by rock'n'roll the way they should be. I think that's amazing. You're only 16 . . . What the hell did the *Wall Street Journal* write?"

"They wrote about the A&R people that call me and the major corporate sponsors that want space on my blog. Nobody's allowed to call me until I finish my homework. I'm failing trig."

"So you said."

"Oh, yeah. I forget. I smoke a lot of pot."

"What do they want from you?"

"They want me to come to New York and run their imprints. Make them cooler—I don't know. They offer me all kinds of money."

"What kind of money?"

"Mid–six figures."

"Fuck. You should take it."

"Nah."

"What, you holding out for a mill? You're 16!"

"Believe me, I have this conversation with myself every day. But I can't. I didn't start the blog to make money. I turn down ad banners all the time too. I have to screen and actually like the movie. Or drink the energy drink. It has to cure my hangover or I will not endorse it."

"Jesus."

"I'm not a prophet, Sandy. I'm a space case. I started it to keep tabs on my own life. I've got a really bad memory."

"Pot."

"Pot."

"Yeah. My mom's a total stoner. She leaves the oven on just about every night. I don't even wonder when I come in. I just reflexively turn the thing off."

"Word."

It was scary how well I was relating to this kid.

"I decided to add a counter when people I'd link to on my site would write me and say, 'I got three hundred hits from you linking me.' When I added a counter and found out that about 4,000 were reading it every day, I was shocked. Then it went to ten thousand. Then a hundred thousand. I get really scared. You have to be careful. One minute you're telling people what to listen to and the next you're telling them who to vote for. Or who to kill. I just like *The Family Guy*. You know that show?"

"Yeah."

"I didn't *ask* Fox to put it back on the air. But they did."

"Natalie, you're gonna really need that money one day. You don't know about the world. Things don't turn out the way you plan. It's good to have savings. Don't you wanna go to college or something?"

"I just wanna be inspired." She blushed, then picked the cherry off the top of her chocolate ice cream and ate it with a big chomp. "I love your band. You guys are like Christmas every day."

"And Chanukah."

"You guys are like Kwaanza every day. You're going to be very big, Sandy."

"No."

too much, too late

"I'm really never wrong about these things."

A shudder went through me.

"Don't you think we're too old?"

"I don't know. What's too old?"

She burped and asked if it was okay to order another bowl of ice cream. I nodded slowly. She ate her chocolate and bummed a smoke, then I drove her home. She had trigonometry homework.

"When do cigarettes taste better than they do after some chocolate?"

"Well, after—" I cut myself off.

"Sex? Yeah, but . . ."

"Wait . . . you've had sex?"

"I meant making out."

"Right."

She ashed out the window.

"Keep that down. People'll think I'm letting you smoke."

She pitched the butt and blew smoke into the car. She wasn't as pro as she wanted to be. Who blows smoke *into* a car?

"I want you to talk to Matty," I told her. "Put him straight."

"He won't talk to me."

"Yeah, well, if you really love the Jane Ashers, you have to do this. Make him chill out on the old man. 'Cause it's really screwing with our good thing here. I waited years to play with that guy again. You were a kid when the band split up."

"Sandy . . . I can't talk to that boy anymore."

"Why not?"

"I knew he had a crush on me and that was hard enough. But he has *bad* taste in music."

When we pulled up in front of her house she kissed me on the cheek, then asked for a couple of smokes for study hour.

"No. Your mom and dad'll smell it. Then they'll come looking for me. With a rope."

"Please."

"No. Come on. Git. I gotta figure out what I'm gonna say to England."

"Play up the Ohio thing," she advised with a wink. "They love that over there. Any Americana."

"They're gonna ask me about being old, aren't they?"

"You *are* old, Sandy."

"I know, but I don't wanna, like, fucking dwell on that."

"Then stop dwelling on it."

She got out and walked up the stoop. I tried not to look at her ass as she moved. The house was modest. Nicer than Harry's, not as nice as Minna's. Toyota Tercel in the driveway with a dented left fender and cardboard on the windshield. The whole spread looked like it could use some repair. A six-figure salary would do a lot to jack up the value all around.

"Do you reckon your boy's a super-genius then, mate? Eccentric white middle-aged American working-class husband and father, creating teenage symphonies to love buzzes in the wood-paneled basement . . . on a four-track."

"Well . . . he's . . . white."

"Brilliant!"

That was the line of questioning the guy from *NME* took: another American freak/genius explodes out of nowhere—sensational, do you reckon? What was supposed to be a capsule review was bumped up to a cover feature. Somehow they got hold of Harry's driver's license photo, Photoshopped on some extra gray hair, arched his eyebrows, and shadowed the bags under his eyes to give the effect of a prisoner who just had his yard exercise privileges reinstated after a year in solitary.

Made him look five years older than he was and a hundred times more sinister. The headline was priceless: "Your Children Love This Old Man More Than They Love You! World Exclusive! Mad! Mundane! Middle-aged! Inside the World of the Jane Ashers."

When Harry saw the issue, he blanched. But he couldn't dwell on it. Not with all the A&R men in the trees outside his home, in front of his store, in the cupboard, under the sink, waving pens and promising world travel. They'd shove notes under the door: *What do I have to do to get you? Anything. Anything.* They'd leave stacks of money on the stoop like milk. Video game players for the kid. Fur-lined boots that nobody should wear, anywhere. His-and-her schwag for the taking. They'd disguise themselves as UPS men. Harry nearly signed away all his publishing rights before catching a glint of the gold tooth embedded in one imposter's mouth. Then they'd run—not like men, like bugs. I wanted them there, but I hated these people too. It didn't help that nobody was leaving cool shit at my house.

There had to be a better way. . . .

"Let's Go Steady Debbie" had been downloaded so many times, it froze Natalie's Web site. The bootleg was being played on mainstream radio in Los Angeles and New York and Chicago and even Cleveland, topping the radio play charts in the trades. The solo was used as a bumper for talk radio programs. They even played it at Riverfront Stadium on the big PA. And since it was all unlicensed, we weren't seeing a cent from any of it. So Natalie and I invested some time and money into revving up the blog and creating a 99-cent official download. I put a few days into cleaning up the sound quality, and we threw in "Who Told You You Knew Shit About Love" as a free B-side. More than a quarter of a million people bought the thing, sending it to the top of the Internet sales charts too.

"Okay, you're buying me something nice," Natalie told me a few days later.

"Why?"

"Well, the bad news is my site is frozen again. Which pisses me off 'cause I really wanted to write about how much I hate Weird Eyebrow Girl."

"Who?"

"From *America's Next Top Model*."

"Ah. So what's the good news?"

"Oh, uh . . . you just made a little over $300,000."

I lit a cigarette.

"Uh-huh." I was silent for a long time. "So . . . what do you want? A car?"

"Sure."

"Okay."

"Thank you."

"Thank *you*."

The following week the single was number 22 on the hot 100, the actual charts. A heat-seeker bookended by Avril Lavigne and someone named Ludacris. Natalie and I went to the bank and deposited my earnings in a savings account. "To start collecting serious interest," she observed. I got two cashier's checks for a hundred grand apiece made out to Harry and Rudy. Those checks looked heavy . . . dangerous. Like notices from some other world. I sealed them in envelopes and instantly envisioned losing both somehow. That is, whenever I wasn't glancing and reglancing at the pop charts.

"Ludacris. *This* is fucking ludicrous," I cracked, waving that week's issue. "We're on the actual charts. We don't belong here."

"Sure you do. Lisa Loeb topped the singles chart in 1994 and she didn't have a deal either. You're only at number 22."

"How old were you in 1994?"

"I was like five, Sandy."

"So how the fuck do you know all this shit?"

"If I feel like I don't know something about pop culture, I start to get headaches."

"You're a cute little weirdo, you know that?"

"Nuh-uh. Some girls like horses. This fascinates me. That's all. Let's get some champagne."

"You have expensive tastes."

"I like being drunk a lot."

"You'll like the money too."

We pulled into the liquor store and bought a couple of bottles of Cristal.

"Mom'll like this." I winked, desperately. "We'll put

some ginger ale in a glass for you so you can toast like the big folks, okay?"

She rolled her eyes, lit a cigarette, and burped loudly. I paid the bill. Four hundred dollars.

"Listen," she told me, "you know you can sign with an indie even though you'll be offered deals with majors too. In this day and age, there's really no difference in terms of distribution, and you've already got the promotion momentum. It's grass roots. You can't buy that. The hard sell—billboards and stuff—it'll only corrupt things, cheapen it all. They'll tell you you need to suck up to all these program directors, but you're already on the radio. Everything's different now, but nobody wants to accept it. It's like, why are we still depending on fossil fuel, you know? It's over. Let's admit that the rules have changed."

"Are you stoned?"

"Yes. Chips. We need chips. Let's go to the gas station."

It was hard to keep my eyes on the road as I drove my old man's car toward the convenience store. I kept staring at Natalie's skull.

"You should be our manager. Really."

"I can't."

"I know. You don't want to corrupt this whole purity thing you're working on."

"I can't be your manager because I don't want to spend eight hours of my day, every day, proving to every person we encounter, all over the world, that I can be your manager at sixteen. What kind of life would that be for me? Plus I'm failing French. *Je suis* . . . oh, fuck it."

"Hey, dig it, Rudy, man. Get over here."

"I'm making supper."

"You won't regret it."

"I can't, Sandy. I've already defrosted chicken."

"It's just chicken."

"It's really expensive, free-range chicken, Sandy."

"I'll give you a hundred thousand dollars if you're here in twenty minutes."

"Sandy?"

"It's true. I've got a check made out to you for a hundred grand. I've got one for Harry too."

"I'll be right over."

It was true. And Rudy and I sat in the garage under Winona for at least an hour, staring at all the zeroes. She didn't seem impressed by it all. I guess she'd seen bigger paydays.

"This is more money than my dad saved in his lifetime," I sniffed. "Dang."

"Did you ever think you'd say 'dang' the moment you got rich?"

"No."

"You just said 'dang,' man."

"I did say 'dang.' I might say it again."

" 'Dang' is pretty appropriate. Are we gonna be famous, Sandy?" Rudy whispered.

I opened a beer.

"Maybe."

"Which company do you think I should endorse? You know, 'Rudy Tunick only plays with Silvertone electric guitar strings.' "

"And uses Propecia for his male pattern baldness."

"I don't mind you making fun of me. It's inevitable. People age. When are you gonna grow up?"

"Shut up. You're bumming me out."

"Man, you better check that. Get right with nature."

"Fuck nature."

"You haven't changed at all."

"Yeah, well, you went bald. Come on. Let's go drop this on Harry."

"Okay. Lemme finish my beer."

"Leave it."

"It's a waste."

"We can buy more. A lot more."

"I guess."

Rudy put his half-drunk beer down.

Debbie was chilly. I got no hug. No "Oh, my God. How are you? How have you been? I'm very happy you survived the nineties." I mean, this was an old friend, and a dozen or so years had passed since we'd last seen each other.

I don't really hold it against Deb. She was stressed. The telephone was ringing every 30 seconds. But you'd think, what with a stranger on the line every time, wanting something, promising something, she would be relieved to see a familiar face. I was certainly ready to give her a big squeeze. Had my arms wide open and everything. Said a big, long "Hey" as she opened the kitchen door. And then she started to shut it.

"What the hell, Debbie?"

"Later, Sandy. We're eating."

The door closed.

Rudy climbed up behind me. "What just happened?"

"She won't let us in."

"No way."

"I don't believe it."

"How does she look? Is she still good-looking, Sandy?"

"I don't know."

I did know. I just couldn't get past the rejection. She was still a handsome woman. Time had been kind to her, but motherhood had made her hard somehow. Where Harry had kept a dewy complexion and a baby face, age had sharpened Debbie's features. It was also more than a little bit weird to see her in a color (red), since she'd always been the queen of undertaker chic.

Rudy and I carefully pushed our way into the kitchen. They were at the table. Matty got a load of us, pushed his plate of baked chicken and corn away, and stomped back up to his room.

"That was the first time the three of us have eaten together since you guys got back together." Debbie pulled out a pack of cigarettes and that blue ashtray. "And I'm smoking again."

"You quit?"

"Ten years ago, Sandy."

"Sorry."

I sat down and stared at the chicken. Rudy joined me.

"Is that organic?" he asked, but got no reply.

"They're coming to the store, Sandy. These major label A&R executives. In the hardware store. They followed Debbie to the supermarket."

I turned to Debbie.

"What do they say when they reach you?"

"They say they want to make us rich. They're so sleazy. It's like a pyramid scheme."

"Well . . . not really. I mean, they do want to make us rich. They just want to make themselves richer. I think we're going to have to sign with an indie. Keep the overhead low and hold on to more of the profits."

"Okay, thanks, Sandy," she hissed. "I'll be sure to tell them."

"Oh, and speaking of profits," I announced, "I wanted to deliver this." I pulled the check envelope from my pocket and laid it on the table next to the coleslaw, which wasn't homemade and just depressed me. Like that's what she wanted when she drove her shitty car into town to get accosted by record execs at the Foodway. Coleslaw.

"What's that?"

"That's a check. For you. I split it evenly for now, but you should probably get a lawyer and a publishing deal. When you figure all that shit out, you can hold my and Rudy's shares against our performing royalties and stuff. Oh . . . it's for a hundred thousand dollars."

I fixed my eyes on Debbie's face to see if she lost any tension in her muscles. The jaw stayed clenched but trembled a little. She tried not to stare down at the check. Harry picked it up and opened it.

"This isn't a joke?"

"No, actually."

Harry looked at Debbie pleadingly. She said nothing.

"This is a real check."

"Yeah, Harry. Put it in the bank. And call me tomorrow. We need to talk about management." I got up, picked a roll off the table, bit into it, and said with my mouth full, "Good to see you again, Deb. You're looking well."

Rudy nodded in agreement and touched her forearm warmly as he passed. She didn't recoil like she did when I passed, just nodded and smiled with those thin lips of hers.

As soon as we'd closed the door behind us, I dragged Rudy over under the window and whispered to him to hold still and shut up.

"Huh?"

"Listen."

We stood there and eavesdropped.

"Are you going to say something?" came Harry's voice. He sounded desperate.

"Rudy went bald," Debbie finally said.

He laughed, but it was mirthless.

"I should go look in on Matt," Harry offered.

"Go."

There was a minute or two of silence. Then we heard Harry again.

"Why does he hate me?"

"He doesn't hate you. He's just figuring out that he doesn't have to like you. It's natural. You're letting it get to you."

"We gave up so much. . . ."

"Well . . . maybe not. I mean, it seems to be coming back to you."

"I didn't ask for this. It just . . . happened."

"What kind of person would I be if I resented you, Harry?"

She didn't say she didn't resent him. She only asked,

as if she'd been wondering guiltily. "Besides, I was never a genius like you."

"Yes, you were. I thought you were." He paused, then added, "I guess I should probably give notice at the store?"

"Let's see if it clears," Debbie quipped.

"You know what's a good song? 'Call Me the Breeze.' You guys should cover that one."

We were drinking at Ben's. We'd come to ask him to be our manager. He had hustle, and we knew he was intimidating. He'd been successfully running a business for years, and he loved rock'n'roll, even if trains were his new thing. Plus Skynyrd's version of "Call Me the Breeze" *was* a killer song. Not really our style, but certainly a worthy boogie.

"Yeah. Okay. I believe that you good people have successfully demonstrated to me on this day that such a venture would be worth my time and efforts. As I see it, you will benefit from my expertise and I from your generosity and popularity with the adolescent community."

"That sounds good." I shrugged. "We just need help with all this craziness."

"And help you shall have. Let's toast our union with a shot of the very good stuff."

Ben brought down a bottle of scotch and poured out four shots.

"Now, this isn't the good stuff," he noted. "This is the very good stuff. Thirty-eight years old. About $2,500 a bottle."

I was almost 39. The liquid had been around as long

as I had. It had seasoned. And so had I. It was time to
be enjoyed. We raised a toast. It was the best thing I ever
tasted. I wanted another but held my tongue. We had

business to discuss.

"All right. The way I see it, the first thing you need to
do is set up an office. Field some of these calls. Stop 'em
from calling you at home, messing with the wife and kid."

"Thank you," Harry blurted out with genuine gratitude.

We all did another shot of the very good stuff.

The next day, Ben leased a storefront next to the ice
cream parlor and catty-corner to Harry's mom's old
store.

Ashers Incorporated headquarters was nondescript
and difficult to find if you'd just flown in from Los
Angeles.

Deliberately so. But we were a business. We had
phones and a water cooler and were ready to field serious offers.

"Diphthong. Have you heard of Diphthong?"

Ben was shuffling papers at his big metal desk. He'd
gotten a deal on some used office furniture and supplies
and set up shop quickly with the expense budget we'd
given him.

"Diphthong, huh?" But I got distracted by the suit
Ben had bought for himself: light purple with rhinestones all over it. A collector's item, handmade by
Nudie, the late "Rodeo Tailor," who'd famously made
custom outfits for Elvis and Graham Parsons. "Nice
suit," I complimented him.

marc spitz

"You like it? Used to belong to Buck Owens."

"It's very rock'n'roll," Harry said approvingly.

He'd expensed that to Ashers Inc. as well, but we let it go, as he'd spent nearly a full 48 hours tirelessly negotiating every offer. And because he'd beat us if we didn't.

"So, what about Diphthong?" Ben asked again. "Surely you've heard of Diphthong."

We'd heard of Diphthong. They were a big indie. Major label distribution but with cred up the bum thanks to the classic compilation *The Diphthong Remains the Same*, released in '94. It had been out of print until a recent reissue that was greeted like returning Jesus in the rock press. Diphthong Records was founded and co-run by Hillary and Tracey Marks, twin dudes with chick names. They had been born in London but schooled in America. They had no accents. Two pasty rich kids who dressed like working-class kids in torn jeans, cardigans, old merch T-shirts, and Converse All-Stars. Bullshit came naturally to them, and it was even charming. Tracey wore thick black-rimmed glasses but had perfect vision. Hillary was slightly chubbier but did more cocaine. It was enough to dizzy you.

"We are going to give you total creative freedom," Tracey promised over dinner at Finley's. Harry had left Debbie home with the kid. Ben had brought a baseball bat. Rudy had worn his ugly Rasta hat. I'd told him to. It was a test. If Diphthong Records wanted us with the hat, they really wanted us. "We're not even going to give you advice. You don't need it. You've built your own culture," Tracey enthused. "What are we gonna tell you that you don't already know, right?"

too much, too late

"For example," Hillary interjected, "we are not going to tell you that you need a bass player."

"Our bass player died," I replied. "Years ago."

"That's tragic," Hillary said. Then he ordered more boiled shrimp.

"We love that you're from the Midwest," Tracey gushed.

"What are your politics?"

"Well, you know . . . I vote," I replied.

"We don't discriminate, of course. We're just curious."

"I guess you could say we're into tolerance. Personal freedom. The right to choose. If you're a woman."

"Amen." Hillary grinned and raised a glass of expensive red. I clinked awkwardly.

"We aren't an overtly political band," Harry said with a shrug. "But I'm a registered Democrat. If that helps. So's my wife."

"Rivers Cuomo of Weezer," Tracey said out of nowhere. "Was one of his legs too short or was the other too long?"

"Huh?" Harry was clearly puzzled.

"Too long," I answered. "He had to have it shortened."

"Ah . . . you're an optimist." Hillary nodded approvingly.

"Why can't the Postal Service and Death Cab for Cutie tour on opposite coasts at the same time?"

"Can I get another stuffed artichoke?" Ben asked, oblivious to their oddly spontaneous trivia game.

"What television show did Rilo Kiley's Jenny Lewis have a role on when she was a child star?"

"Hillary, are you giving us, like, a test?"

"No. I'm just getting to know you."

"What is the secret ingredient in this salad dressing?" Tracey asked, as if to make light of their poorly received pop pop quiz.

"It's anise." Ben growled.

"Fair enough." Tracey nodded. "A gourmand."

Our manager stroked the edge of the bat grip.

"Honestly, gentlemen," Tracey went on, "we wouldn't have cared if you were a gaggle of inbred Nazi hog fuckers with warts and beards."

"This is Ohio, man. Do you even know where you are?"

"It's not important," Tracey assured us. "Do I know where I am? No. Do I care? No. We just love the music. We want to bring you to New York and record there. We'll try out some bass players. If you want to do the White Stripes, Yeah Yeah Yeahs, Doors, um . . . Jon Spencer Blues Explosion tired, rote, awful, dreary no-bass thing, that's cool. Completely up to you."

Ben snorted. "I'd like the cheese plate."

Hillary nodded. "That is totally up to you as well."

"The studio time is going to come out of our advance," I asked. "Right?"

"The advance will cover all recoupable expenses, yes," Tracey replied. "That's standard."

"Because I have a studio in my garage. I've been working on it for a year. It's professional-quality. And the acoustics in there—"

"Does it have glass walls and very shiny buffed floors?"

"No."

"Did John Lennon record there the night he was murdered?"

"No. He didn't."

"Is there a coffeemaker?"

"No. But . . ."

"If you wanna record here, record here. We love it here. We love this shrimp." Tracey plopped a bright pink prawn into his mouth with gusto.

"We have to mix in New York, of course," Hillary urged. "Or London. Can't mix here. This isn't lunacy. Right? Is this lunacy?"

"I don't know." Harry laughed. He was partially giddy, mostly fearful. He eased his nerves with wine so expensive it hurt to drink it.

"We'll think about New York," I promised.

"You must come visit either way," Hillary demanded. "Let us show you around. Maybe play a secret show? At the Bowery? For the media? We'll promote it heavily."

"As a secret," Tracey put in.

"Of course," Hillary agreed. "Show everyone you're not a novelty act. You're a real loud, evil fucking rock'n'roll band. What do you think? Shake up those jaded bastards."

"We hate those bastards," Tracey said.

"Hated bastards!" Hillary reiterated.

"They'll stand there with their arms crossed, judging, and you'll blow their heads apart, one by one by one," Tracey crowed, evidently imagining the bloodshed and relishing it. "It'll be a legendary show. I feel like I'm there already. Absolutely fucking legendary. The kind of show people will talk about for years."

Mad as they were, we believed the twins had what it

took to handle us. We wanted cred, but we also wanted the payday we'd been waiting for. We all knew what it was like to punch a clock and leave the bills on the table for another day when your stomach was a bit stronger. Diphthong was a good balance of both cash and credibility, and there were only a few like them to choose from.

"Now tell me, is there anything you want to ask us? We are an open book," Hillary promised.

"There are no secrets here," Tracey insisted. "In fact, I will confide in you that I am thinking about ordering the rum cake for dessert."

"I have a question," I replied. "What do you think of Rudy's hat?"

"I hate it," Tracey answered without pause. "I truly hate it. If it had a neck, I'd wring it."

"It's atrocious," Hillary agreed. "But if it's integral to your creative expression, then we want to be in business with the hat."

"We will not pull our offer because of the hat."

I gave Minna the good news as soon as I got home. I was buzzed on wine and champagne. She was stoned, crouched over her vinyl, lovingly cleaning a copy of *International Pop Overthrow* by Material Issue with an anti-static rag. Minna didn't believe in plastic sleeve covers, but she mothered her vinyl like you wouldn't believe. Not a mote on any of it. Plastic was not necessary.

"Hi, Ma."

"I heard you on the radio."

"Yeah? How'd it sound?"

"A little like a . . . like a bucket."

"Like we're playing in a bucket?"

"Yeah. Tinny."

"Well, we're gonna fix that. We're making a record.
It's official. Almost."

"You're gonna make a record." She smiled, wiping
some dry gunk from the corner of her eye and patting
her gray hair.

"Yeah, Ma. How freaky is that? Finally. A real record.
And a tour too. Don't worry, though. I'll make sure
you've got everything you need before I go. Maybe you
can even come to the show. If we play Cleveland or
whatever. Get out of the house. Yeah?"

"I'll listen to you on the radio."

"Okay, Ma. All right. I gotta make some calls."

"You want some pizza, Sand?"

"No, Ma. I'm fulla shrimp."

"Shrimps," she echoed, then picked up her pipe and
fired it up. She stared at me, her eyes wide and blinking.

I went out to the garage, signed on to the Web, and
found Natalie lingering there.

Going with Dip.

How much?

Mill.

LOL. Fake indies amuse me.

You said they'd give us cred.

No. Diphthong is good, she typed. *I sent you a link to a
legal advisory site especially for musicians. Well, all artists,
really. It's a flat rate for as much counseling as you need inside a 30-day period. Don't hesitate to use it. And tell Harry
he needs to get a publishing deal.*

Okay. Thank you.

No problem. Hey, dude, where's my car?

We'll go to the dealership in the morning. Bring your mom and dad. I'll buy them one too.

What did they say about the studio budget?

They said we can record here if we want. But I got the *feeling everyone wanted to go to New York.*

Go to New York. Just keep an eye on the clock. Don't lose your head.

PART THREE

8

Harry got the news over his half grapefruit and bran flakes. Seemed like every family meal was destined to be interrupted by some urgent rock'n'roll-related matter. Harry processed the info, made a few notes, finished his coffee, then went upstairs to talk to the kid.

Debbie already knew about the possibility of a last-minute trip to New York. She couldn't have been happy about being left behind—Debbie was a fun girl, morose but fun, and an art enthusiast, even if that had become something of a hobby too over the years, so why wouldn't she wanna go to New York City after years and years in Dean?—but given Matty's precarious emotional state, they'd decided it was best to preserve as much of the old normalcy as possible, so she would stay home with him.

"You know your mother and I love you very much, right?" Matty sat on the bed, wearing an oversized T-shirt with a graffiti-style portrait of the late rapper Big Pun, who weighed something like 500 pounds when he passed. Harry tried not to stare at it.

"This is a talk," Matty observed.

Harry nodded.

"You're getting a divorce, aren't you?"

"What? No. No. God. Never. No."

"But something's happening?"

"Yes. I'm going to New York City. With the band. For a while. Not long, but it's sort of open-ended. We're getting signed and we're going to make a record. And probably tour too. Things have changed, and I think they're going to change a bit more, and I just want you to know that your mother and I love you. No matter what. And that I won't be gone long, no matter what. And as far away as I go, and whatever I see, I will think about you every day."

"Okay."

"I mean it, Matt. If you don't see me for three weeks, I'll be thinking about you every day for three weeks."

"Fine."

"Will . . . you be thinking about me?"

"I don't know."

"Matt . . . what's going on here? You and I were pals. Weren't we?"

The kid turned away.

"Did I do something to upset you?"

He wouldn't answer.

"This is a good thing, what's happening. It's good for us financially. That's for sure. I'm looking into getting us a nicer place to live. And there'll be money for you to go to whatever college you want. Graduate school too. You can be anything. Matty, will you look at me, please? What's wrong? Do you not like my music?"

"No."

"No you don't like it, or no you don't dislike it?"

"It's okay."

"Then what is it?"

Matty fiddled with the laces on his sneakers. When he spoke his voice was high.

"I liked Natalie."

"Oh."

"I liked her. And when she heard you sing that song about Mom, she told me she couldn't hang around with me as much as she used to because she needed to look for her one true love and that I should go looking for mine. But . . . *she's* mine."

"Oh. Wow. Okay. Isn't she a little old for you?"

"Aren't you a little old for everyone? And I don't like hearing you sing about Mom. It's . . . weird."

"No, it's not."

"It's gross."

"Now you're just being mean. That's a really good song and you know it. It's the best thing I've ever written."

"When did you write it?"

"A long time ago. Before you were born. I was a little

older than you are now, actually." Matty looked his father over and seemed to focus on Harry's wrinkles and gray hair.

"Why can't you just be my dad?"

"I was still just your dad for the whole of last year and you acted like you hated me."

"Well, you should go back to that and I won't act like I hate you anymore."

"Look, this is silly. I just want you to know that I will never leave you. I'll always be there for you. I want you to be sure of that. It's important to me. That's never going to change, no matter what happens out there. And I'm going to come back to you as soon as I'm done. I promise. It'll be like nothing has changed. When I come back, I will be your dad again just like I am now. My dad left me. You knew that."

"Yeah."

"It was very painful. And confusing. I wondered what I did wrong. But now I know I didn't do anything wrong. Do you understand? I'd never put you through that. Do you believe me?"

"Yeah. Okay."

"Good."

Harry pulled off Matty's do-rag. Matty grabbed it back and fiddled with it.

"So . . . are you going to stop acting weird to me now?"

"Maybe."

"Maybe?"

"Okay."

"Thank you. I fucking hated it."

"Are you going to curse now that you're a rock star?"

marc spitz

"I always curse. Just not around you."

"Does Mom curse?"

"No. Mom never curses."

"Is that true?"

"Ask Mom."

As we left for New York City on a cold morning in November, with all the brown and orange leaves blowing up and the sky cloudless and vast, it hurt to say goodbye to Natalie. Knowing I couldn't do anything about it (for a hundred different reasons, chief of all that dating her was a felony) was kind of liberating. But I wondered, as we were in transit, why I wasn't 100 percent psyched to have my dream come true. I determined that it was because I didn't have anyone to really share the experience with. I tried to put it out of my mind. I told myself I had my band, music, money, and adventures just up the road, but my heart hurt. I would see amazing things, but I wouldn't see Natalie Levine for a long time, and I hated myself a little bit for dwelling on that. It wasn't like me.

I bought one of those slick, handheld 10-in-1 organizer jobs. The ones that surf the Net, pay your taxes, knead dough, and enable you to instant-message your underage crush while cruising down the street on your own two feet. Harry and I commiserated on the plane. It felt good. Like the old days, even if the subject matter had gotten adult and strange. He told me how he'd left Matty with his old Hohner harmonica, the one his own father had left behind when he split. It was some kind of private challenge. Unlike the wayward old man, he would come back for it. Harry was feeling weird knowing he wouldn't be sleeping with Debbie that night, or the next night, or the next. I told him he should think about her sleeping in her big, warm, new bed in her big, warm, new house. Old house, actually. The one he'd bought for her just before leaving for New York. The one he'd promised they'd live in someday. The one with lilac bushes on the wide lawn and safety behind its doors. Maybe it got him through those first few nights.

Do you know the song "Talk of the Town" by the Pretenders? I always loved that song. I consider it probably one of the ten best singles ever released. Over the years, when intoxicated a certain way, I'd insist it's the best ever, but then I've also insisted that about "Bad Case of Loving You" by Robert Palmer, which just isn't true. Still, "Talk of the Town" is perfect every time I hear it. Maybe it's because I know the band's leader, Chrissie Hynde, is an Ohioan. Maybe because it's beautiful. I was hearing "Talk of the Town" in my head as we began our flight to John F. Kennedy International. "*Oh, but it's hard to live by the rules. I never could and still never do,*" Chrissie sang.

I forced myself onto a bit of a high, and my walk had become a strut. *I'm signed to Diphthong Records,* I repeated to myself. *My little band is worth one million dollars to someone. We've been played in Topeka and Athens and Istanbul. We were banned in Iran. Big in Japan. Very famous in places I would probably never visit. I am now middle-aged. But I'm a professional musician and I will never have to work at anything else again. All you people who warned me to grow up? Fuck you. All you people who tried to grab me and take me down with them? You couldn't catch me, suckers. I am going to stay 18 for all time like Mr. Mick Jagger, and if you have a problem with that, you can kiss my arrested ass.*

Harry . . . he had no strut and a much different inter-
pretation of "Talk of the Town." He saw Chrissie Hynde's confession as a lament, whereas I was sure it was a boast.

"Hey, sad sack. Read some of this fan mail. It's trippy."

I threw a pile of letters into Harry's lap.

"You should really read them," Ben Jim Morrison agreed, " 'cause I just hired someone to do it professionally. This is probably the last sack of fan mail you'll ever see."

"They have people who do that?" Rudy marveled.

"Yeah," Ben informed him. "It's called a . . . what's the word? A *service*."

Harry ignored them. I opened one myself and began to recite. Or slur, as I'd been through a few little blue airplane bottles of Skyy vodka already.

" 'My name is Osco. Not that it really matters.' Dude, if you have a name like Osco, it really matters," I commented, then resumed my recital. " 'I need some advice and I think you might be the guys to ask since your song 'Let's Go Steady Debbie' makes me think of Samantha. She's not my girlfriend but I want her to be my girlfriend.' "

"Stop," Harry said.

"Why?"

"Sandy, stop reading that. Please."

"Jesus. Come on, Vance. This kid is like 18. It's harmless."

"It's not harmless. It's harming me. I can't give anyone advice."

"Harry, eat some peanuts. They're free. That's my advice. Lighten up."

"Do you think this is a mistake, Sandy?"

"Are you fucked? There are people waiting for us at that airport. We're like the Beatles."

"But we're not the Beatles. I work in a hardware store."

"You have to quit that job."

"I tried. It felt . . . wrong. I took a leave."

"You have a million-dollar record deal. You can buy that store and turn it into a head shop. Harry, let go. Enjoy this. This is it. You know?"

"Is it? It doesn't feel like *it*."

"You never think this feels like it, even when it *is* it. Something amazing is happening here. We get to play music. For people who wanna fucking hear it. How is that not it? How is that not the best thing ever?"

"That part is fine, but . . . you know, music is easy."

"Will you try to experience this? Will you promise me you'll try? Be the Beatles. For like a week?" Harry nodded. I could tell that part of him wanted to be a Beatle. At least be George.

Rudy and Tom came up the aisle and handed us all some gum.

"Chew this," Rudy advised. "It'll keep your ears from popping."

He'd flown plenty over the past decade. He'd even been to New York City once, and promised to be our guide should we need one.

"Yeah, we're gonna eat hot dogs and get mugged and uh, see *Cats,* right?"

"*Cats* closed, Sandy."

"No way!"

We landed at the airport and were immediately accosted by a throng of manic kids. They were all around 16 or 17, some a little younger, very few older. They wore torn jeans, Converse sneakers, and Hot Topic tees, and carried large black bags full of high-tech hardware. Band buttons ran up and down the straps of the bags—compulsively collected, dozens of them, for every band, but mostly our band. But we didn't look much like any band then. We looked like three tired old guys and a carny (Ben was wearing Ray Charles shades and a black pony-skin cowboy hat). Harry'd undone his belt midflight and his pants sagged. One of his cheap Buster Browns was untied. He'd been going grayer and grayer with stress, and in bright light his looked almost white. His glasses were crooked. He was cracking gum and yawning, and the kids just died.

"Harry! Harry! Where's Debbie?"

Rudy and I stared at each other.

"Sandy! Rudy!"

"Uh . . . hey."

"Howdy."

Ben dropped his carry-on. The sound of bottles rattling emanated from inside the canvas. He snorted as he tried to fend off the kids' desperate, invading hands. "Come on. Stop that shit. Quit it, kids. Come on. Yeah. It's good to see you too. Great. Hi. Hi. Oh . . . hi. Fucking cut it out!"

The airline employees couldn't believe what they were seeing either. Double, triple, quadruple takes. Like there was some boy band just behind us, lingering at the gate, afraid to show their faces for fear of being mobbed. But there were no heartthrobs. We were the heartthrobs. They didn't want to jump our bones—we just made their hearts, well, throb. Some of the kids were there with their parents. The kids who didn't drive, I guess. The parents' look of surprise was mixed with a little concern. Many of them appeared to be our age.

"Harry! Harry . . . talk to me! Harry! Help me!"

Harry shrank back and looked pleadingly at Ben.

"All right. Outtathaway, lil' babies."

We made our way to the waiting limo.

"Can you believe that?" I shouted. "They recognized us."

"From all the press?"

"I guess."

"That was terrifying," Ben groaned. "Children. Everywhere." He opened a fifth of Jack Daniel's and handed it to me. I took a swig and handed it to Rudy.

"What?" I shrugged as he stared at me like I was out of my head. "It's rock'n'roll."

"Clichéd, yeah."

"That's what makes it cool. Keith does it."

Rudy blushed. He'd lived beyond his obsession, but he'd never, ever live that shit down. He took the bottle.

"Keith," he echoed, then swigged and winced. "Has blood on his hands."

"Whatever, dudes! Check out this fucking limo," I enthused.

It was only a Town Car, but I didn't care. I was ready

to make myself at home in places like this, new-smelling and full of soft leather.

"Is this Manhattan now?"

"It's Queens," the driver flatly informed us.

"Hey, driver. Put on the radio. Let's see if we're on the radio."

"Don't," Harry requested.

The driver put on the radio. Classic rock station. The Who were on: "Slip Kid." Harry bobbed his head to Keith Moon's beat. His lips relaxed, and he seemed somewhat pacified by the tune.

"I can't believe we're in New York." He laughed. "Where are we playing again?"

"We are rocking the Bowery Ballroom," Rudy croaked.

"Is that near CBGB?" Harry wondered. "On the Bowery, right?"

"I don't know. I'll find out for ya, boss," Ben drawled.

Harry looked out the tinted window at the Empire State Building and some other tall buildings, still across the East River but drawing nearer. He nodded and raised the JD to his lips.

"Yes!" I giggled. "I know *that* building. We are here! Like motherfucking King Kong."

Autumn in New York was bittersweet for Harry Vance. It's a very romantic season. Almost constantly breathtaking. The air smells like love . . . and trash. In a good way. Harry was quickly smitten with his surroundings, but very clearly aching for his other half. I remember wishing he'd just commit to the moment. Some people recognized him. Hip kids mostly, with their rooster haircuts and skinny jeans and tight leather coats and scarves. They were too cool to point; they'd pretend they didn't know who we were, but as we passed we'd swivel our necks and catch them whispering to each other.

"A knish is a potato square," I told Harry. "It's good. I had one once. It's a Jewish thing."

We were standing in front of Yonah Schimmel's, a little storefront on Houston Street. We'd left our hotel, the Solita, to go looking for Ludlow Guitars, but the smell had brought us here.

"Get one. You'll have something to tell Debbie."

"Since 1910," Rudy pointed out. "So you know it's gonna be good."

We walked in and purchased a knish each. Harry got his with spinach.

"Not what I'd choose, but go ahead." I shrugged. "Eat it."

"It's delicious, Sandy." He handed it to me for a taste.

"Nah . . . indulge, man. Indulge."

We walked a ways up the street and passed a T-shirt store called Burkina. Harry peered in at all the silk screens of fallen hip-hop and R&B stars: Biggie, Tupac, Aaliyah, Big Pun.

"You think I should get Matty some stuff? He likes dead rappers."

"He doesn't like dead rappers. He just thinks he does."

"He's really into hip-hop, Sandy."

"Is Tupac West Coast or East Coast?" Rudy wondered.

"He's West Coast," Harry answered. "But he was born on the East Coast. I've read up on him."

"Why?"

" 'Cause my son admires him."

"For *what*?"

"I should buy Matty some presents."

"You're here 20 minutes and you wanna buy presents? You just bought your family a house."

Harry went in, slapped down his credit card, and bought up some oversized T-shirts.

"You know, the Shakur estate doesn't even see any profits from that," I commented.

"Who told you that?"

"Motorrrju."

"Your girlfriend," Rudy joked. I pushed him.

"Besides, Tupac is still fucking alive, man," I cracked. "If your kid would open his fucking eyes, he'd see that too. He's down in South America with Bruce Lee."

The showcase at the Bowery was not designed to build buzz. It was designed to justify hype. And probably show the world, or at least the print media, that Diphthong Records' new prize acquisition was a sound investment. We knew we were show ponies. We were from the Midwest, but we weren't naive about what these New Yorkers wanted from us.

"We've got a full house and a very desirable guest list. I thought you'd be pleased to know that Kate Moss is on it."

I smiled. "She's pretty."

We were sitting in a private booth at Milk and

Honey, an old-fashioned speakeasy on Eldridge Street on the Lower East Side. It was the kind of place with real linens in the toilet and chipped ice in your cocktails—cocktails you had to be patient for, since these were "mixologists" making them, not bartenders. There were real mint leaves in the mojitos, which is what I was drinking. I felt like it wasn't the kind of place where you'd just order a cold beer. Besides, I'd cracked enough beer tabs in my day. I was ready for some care. We were informed that you had to be invited to get lit there, so we already felt special. Then, after a half hour, we felt drunk and very special. Plus it was one of the only places in the entire city where you could light up.

"David Bowie RSVP'd," Hillary whispered before taking a sip of his blood-orange-flavored screwdriver.

"Bowie?"

"Yes."

"No."

"Actually, yes."

"*David* Bowie?"

"Sandy, please don't let it rattle you. David checks out everything. He's famous for it."

"Not in Ohio he isn't."

"But you should feel proud. Since his heart surgery he doesn't go out nearly as much. Maybe four times a week."

"What about Sarah Vowell?" Rudy asked.

"Who?" I shouted.

"Sarah Vowell. She lives in New York."

"Who the hell is Sarah Vowell? What about Winona?" I inquired. "Is she coming?"

"Winona Ryder is not coming." Tracey giggled. "She's terribly Gen X, anyway."

"So are we, Trace."

"Right. Well, which one of you wants to date her and ruin your band?"

"I do," I declared. Then I thought of Natalie and felt guilty. Why was I so hung up? I could never be with her, for so many reasons. I decided I needed to get laid. By someone over 18. Sometime soon.

"You want me to look into it?" Ben offered, scribbling Winona's name on the hotel notepad he'd been doodling on.

"Nah. If it's meant to be, it's meant to be, Benny," I told him.

"The Spurts will be there, or at least most of them. They usually travel in a pack, like wolfmen," Hillary offered as consolation. Not that lack of Winona is something consolable.

"The Spurts, huh? That's cool," Rudy said.

A year ago, the Spurts were the hottest band in the world. Today, they were number two. I guess they were coming to check out the aging fuckers who'd overthrown 'em. The Spurts had been on my pop culture radar for a while. I knew a lot about them because I was jealous. I'd done the research to fuel my rage, I guess. I'd envied them because they were rock stars and I wasn't. They'd gone to good schools and I hadn't. They had skinny blond girls and I had drunken old women with bar-snack breath. They made the clothes we'd been wearing since the late '80s, thrift-picked jackets and dirty Converses and skinny pants, into a worldwide fashion craze, and we could barely fit into our skinny pants anymore. But mostly I'd envied them because they were a really good band and I'd lost mine.

"Oh, yeah? The Spurts. Are they any good?" I asked, then sucked my sprig of mint against the roof of my mouth. I knew who produced their albums. I knew who they thanked on the inner sleeve. I even knew how many units they moved. And one of those units was shifted to me. But now that I was in a bigger band, all my animosity turned to warmth. They were the first band since Nirvana to get a good garage (or in their case basement-crafted) rock song on the radio amid the latest awful permutation of metal.

"Make sure they get backstage, Ben," I ordered. It was the first time I'd said anything like that. An order.

"Spurts. Backstage. Got it, Sandy. Now, speaking of Ryder . . ."

"Were we?"

"Winona Ryder. We were speaking of her."

"Fifteen minutes ago, man. We stopped."

"We gotta sort out this matter of the concert rider."

"Oh, I get it. That's clever, Ben." Rudy smiled.

"Thanks, man. I've been waiting to say it for, like, a minute. I knew it was good. What do you want in the dressing room?"

"Oh, shit." Rudy giggled. "Our first rider."

"What are our options?" Harry asked. He was drinking ginger ale. Didn't want to slur over the phone to Deb later that night, he said.

"Well, how about fish?" Ben suggested. "It's light, healthy. A nice Dover sole, maybe? With a curry leaf emulsion. Asparagus tips. Those are good."

"Really? We can order that?"

Hillary gently grabbed the pen out of Ben's hand.

"The show isn't until 11 p.m. I recommend you just do a buyout for dinner and eat early. Request a few coolers of beer, and a bottle of something nice. But that's just a recommendation—do what you like."

Shamed, Ben Jim Morrison grabbed his pen back and sucked it like a thumb.

"We'll just get the beer," he said.

Unbeknownst to us, Hillary and Tracey had invited guests to join us at the exclusive bar. The first visitor was a skinny blond guy with a red-and-black-striped sweater, ripped jeans, and black engineer boots. He was obviously in his very early 20s and wore a brown Members Only jacket with a lot of irony and a few badges pinned to it. The second was a clean-cut gentleman, slightly older. He wore a blue windbreaker, cords, and expensive-looking basketball sneakers. He had a thin silver cell phone permanently pressed to his ear, the lobe of which was much pinker than his free ear. The third and final guest was a full-on goth kid with perfectly applied black eyeliner and a high pompadour that was equal parts pre-army Elvis and Eraserhead. He wore a black sharkskin suit with a black-and-white-striped polo shirt underneath. And he was tiny. When they first sat down, I thought they were all fans.

"Hey, man, we're talking here," I said to the skinny blond dude.

He grinned. "I know. It's so great. Welcome to New York, man."

"Sandy, Rudy, Harry," Hillary intervened, "this is Crispin. He'll be looking after you on tour."

"We have Ben for that," Harry protested.

"Of course. Crispin will be at Ben's disposal 24 hours a day. Ben will delegate, and Crispin here will mind you. He's a road manager. A very good one. Years of experience."

"Oh, yeah? You look like someone should card you in here."

"I'm 24," he said with a cheerful air, not at all offended. "I just got off tour with the Spurts in September. Before that I did some East Coast dates with Dashboard Confessional. I'm really looking forward to showing you guys the ropes."

"We've toured," I snarled. Maybe mentioning the Spurts ticked me off. I don't know. I actually was happy to have Crispin. He wasn't getting a percentage like Ben Jim Morrison was. He was paid by Diphthong as part of our tour support budget. Definitely not a lot, but enough cash to keep a 24-year-old kid in attitude. It showed me that the label was protecting its investment, or so I thought, and again I allowed myself to feel special. I just felt bad for Benny. We all knew what was going on. They were indicating, without saying anything directly, that they considered him almost completely incompetent and unessential. This was very English, very fake indie.

"I'm James Pullman," the clean-cut gent introduced himself. "I'll be handling your press." He looked more like a golf pro than a rock'n'roller. I didn't trust him. "There's a lot of it lined up already. *Headphones* is talking about a cover. *Rolling Stone*'s very wait-and-see. Probably 'cause you don't have giant breasts. Right?"

"Right," Harry said, smiling, but it was clear he didn't get it.

"*Time* wants a quote. *The New Yorker* is sniffing around. *SNL* has put in an offer. Conan. Letterman. Ferguson. Kimmel. *Mad TV*, we don't wanna do that."

"Television?" I blurted out.

"You have a problem with television, Sandy?"

"Uh . . . no."

"Are you wanted by the law?"

"Not yet."

He ignored me and turned his attention to Harry. "Hiro wants to know if you'd be interested in being a guest DJ."

"Hiro?"

"Japanese restaurant in the Maritime Hotel."

"I don't DJ."

"Anyone can DJ. You press a button."

"I don't have any records here."

"I'll program a playlist for you. 'Deceptacon' by Le Tigre."

"DFA remix," Crispin amended.

"Some '80s kitsch," Pullman continued, like he was prescribing medication. "Maybe 'Bette Davis Eyes.' You show up and . . . that's it. I also need you to post a letter to fans for the message board."

"We have a message board?" Harry wondered aloud.

Pullman stared at Harry with quietly burning eyes until Harry had to turn away.

"Great." James stood up. "I just wanted to say hello

and let you guys know that I'm extremely excited to be working with all of you." He shook our hands, then ran right out of there.

"Jesus, where's he going?"

"It's his daughter's birthday."

"He's got a daughter?" Harry asked with a little disbelief.

"Two years old."

"Oh, he's in for it." Harry smiled. "Terrible twos."

"He's used to dealing with petulant children. He works in rock'n'roll," Hillary joked. "Who wants another round?"

"I'll take a Manhattan," the slick Nick Cave kid said.

We all stared at him.

"Who are you?" Rudy asked, a little suspicious but not quite rude.

"I'm Charlie Quickness." He smiled.

"And . . . ?" I said. Quite rude.

"I'm your new bass player."

"Says who?"

"Charlie's here for the free drinks, Sandy," Tracey assured me. "He's what they call a ligger."

"I'm a ligger with attitude," Charlie added.

"But," Tracey continued, "he does know *all* the songs. And look at that *punim*."

Tracey squeezed Charlie's cheeks as if they were fleshy. They were not. You could cut ham with his cheekbones.

"We really think Charlie will complete the equation," Hillary urged. "Now, hear me out. I want you to know that since we founded this label, we have seen . . . how many, 500?"

Tracey nodded. "Easy."

"Five hundred crap bands. It got to the point where I hired someone to figure out what was missing."

"A scientist," Hillary said, then removed a piece of paper from his wallet, unfolded it, and pushed it across the bar table toward me. It was full of equations, X's and O's, and illegible notes. "That is the key to a brilliant rock'n'roll band. And according to that, you are one element shy."

"I'm the shy elephant," Charlie Quickness put in. I wanted to slug him, but he took out a small digital camera and took a photo of me instead. The flash disoriented me.

I knew I was only hitting the posh rum, but I felt like I was on acid.

"It's like mixing nitroglycerin," Hillary slurred. He was a little drunk. I could tell he'd given this speech before. Maybe to the Spurts. Certainly to Charlie Quickness. "You need the right amount of insecurity and the right amount of swagger. The swagger doesn't work without the insecurity. You just look like a wanker. And too much insecurity and you're . . ."

"Cat Power," Tracey offered.

"You need tunes. That's a given. And you certainly have them. But bands with tunes can be dead boring too. Can't they? No, you need the whole package." Hillary gathered up his paper and shook it in my face. "It's inarguable. It's science."

Had I been in a different frame of mind I might have overturned the table right there. I had plenty of swagger, or at least I liked to think I did. The Jane Ashers, after all we'd survived, did not need a swagger transfusion in the form of this kid. But we were all warm and giddy with drink, so I let it slide, and so did Harry and Rudy. By the end of the night, I'd stolen Charlie's camera and found myself scrolling through the digital photo album. Nearly every photo was of a different overweight young woman.

Ben Jim Morrison was nursing his hurt pride with whiskey. He eventually insisted that there were hidden cameras in the wall sconces. Before passing out and gashing his forehead on the edge of the table, he informed us all we were a "gaggle of twats" with "weak, chewy centers."

Harry called Debbie before falling asleep. She assured him that everything was fine. This would become routine. He'd later find out that Matty had been suspended for punching a classmate and calling him a faggot. Debbie dealt with that on her own. When he was found with a bag of weed, she handled it. Maybe they had an unspoken agreement in terms of threat level—he wouldn't be notified unless it soared from orange to red. Debbie didn't want to distract him. She made sure that everything in Ohio was "fine," even when it was a gathering mess.

We rehearsed with Charlie Quickness on bass all weekend. The guy dressed up even when he was stuck in a room all day with nobody but us to check him out. Didn't even remove his jacket or break a sweat. His hair was perfectly high too. He didn't even seem to have to spray it. It just grew that way. We'd focus on one song until we had it coiled tight, then the next until that could kick the previous song in the ass and build us a little momentum. Diphthong recorded everything.

I don't know how many times I called poor Charlie "Archie," but he took it as flattery, or said he did anyway. By the end of the first night, we had a full set of strung-together hits, including the big hit that every 16-year-old with a computer already knew. Twice a day the crew would deliver these deep foil trays full of relatively exotic fare you wouldn't find next to the fried clams on the diner menu: sushi made out of eel and fluke and other sea creatures, falafel and hummus and baba ganoush, garlicky and filling. We'd sit in a circle like dogs, examining the food, checking with each other before tentatively raising each curious bit to our lips.

Rudy and I attempted to haze Charlie. Earlier I'd eaten a largish hunk of wasabi and nearly shat my melted skull. Needed three cold beers and a nap to recover. So I said to Charlie, "Hey, Charlie, man. Try some of this. It's delicious." I handed him a glob of the evil stuff.

But Charlie was a New Yorker. "Thanks, Sandy," he said, and cheerfully smeared a mote across his sticky rice with surgical precision.

"Careful not to eat too much of that," he warned. "It's really hot."

Once when we ducked out to grab some air, I watched him as he purposefully strode up the street toward a body. As he hovered over this fallen individual, I quickened my pace and shouted, "Shit! What happened? Should I call the police?" But Charlie knelt down and shoved a $50 bill in the guy's rotting brown suit jacket. He stood up and smiled at me.

"I always wanted to do that."

I realized that not only was this person not injured or deceased, but he was now the richest bum on the block.

"I wish I could be there when he finds it. But that's the beauty of it, huh?"

"Yeah. I guess."

I followed Charlie back to the studio, wondering where the fuck I really was.

I didn't understand New York. I was faking it. But faking it was fun.

Charlie Quickness fascinated me. That night I drank with him. Harry begged off, and Rudy went to some theater in Greenwich Village to catch a screening of the John Cassavetes film *Shadows*. Crispin, Ben Jim Morrison, Charlie, and I bar-hopped all over the Lower East Side—the Hole, Rothko, Motor City, the Delancey—but by three it was just me and him on a pair of cylindrical Naugahyde stools in some low-ceilinged, blue-lit basement bar called the Darkroom. Crispin had left first, to be fresh for tomorrow's big day, he said, and Ben followed. The thought crossed my mind that maybe Ben meant to drag Crispin into an alley and stab him in the teeth, but I wasn't about to come to the kid's aid. Even if I liked him, which I didn't, I really couldn't leave. I was too transfixed watching Quickness pull his ladies. It was a remarkable thing—he didn't have to move, and barely had to speak. They came straight over to him, mesmerized. He'd chat with them for a while, then they'd rise and walk away, a little hunched and dejected, one after another. I watched a brown-haired, almond-eyed dolly in a green wool dress and fishnets rise and float toward the door, light a cigarette in the alley, and pout.

"Is she a model?"

"She's a DJ."

"On the radio?"

"She spins records in bars and looks hot and bored."

"Damn."

"You can go after her if you want her, Sandy. She's not my type."

"What do you mean? She's gorgeous."

"I like 'em with a little more stuffing in the roaster."

"I can dig that. Yeah. But she's *gorgeous,* Charlie."

"Go get her. She loves the band. She's on the list tomorrow."

"She didn't say anything to me about loving my band."

"She's shy."

"Her boobs are hanging out of her dress, and I can see the good half of her ass from the back."

"She's overcompensating for being socially awkward and shy, Sandy."

"Yeah, well, she's a smoker. I don't kiss smokers." I pulled out a cigarette. "Charlie, can we smoke in here?"

"They can't." He smiled and lit me up, then himself. "But we can."

"Could you smoke in bars before you joined my band?"

"Not really. Just the basement of Lit." Charlie hugged me. "Thank you," he cried. "Thank you. Thank you. Thank you."

I pulled him off. "Fetch me another vodka tonic."

too much, too late

"Yes, sir." He rose and followed a plump gal in a pink New York Dolls T-shirt, voluminous black skirt, and high boots, with peachy flesh overflowing at neckline, hem, and sleeve. He dogged her all the way to the bar, then looked back at me, smiled, and winked. I lifted my empty glass and toasted him. I sucked some lime juice into my mouth. It was lonely at the top . . . temporarily.

"Hey there . . ."

"Hey."

"You're the Jane Asher."

She was a gorgeous, light-skinned black chick with long, straight hair and twitchy eyes. Reminded me of a postcard someone once sent me of Josephine Baker, or would have if it wasn't for the PVC trench coat, brown mohair miniskirt, spacey blue tights, and pink Reebok high tops. Not the toast of Paris, just somewhat toasted.

She smiled. "Isn't it cool? One minute you're on the television and the next you're here with me. I love New York. Do you love New York?"

"It's a great place to visit. That's for sure."

"So you know Charlie?"

"He's my bass player."

"Yeah. Everyone knows Charlie. Who else are you here with? Big, famous rock guy. Where's your entourage?"

Her breath smelled a little like Trident gum. "Where's Harry Vance?"

"He's home counting sheep."

"You form like Voltron and he da head," she drawled.

"Huh?"

"What?"

"Wu Tang."

"Who?"

"That shit's from the first Wu Tang. I'm paraphras-
ing . . . I think I'm drunk."

"How old are you?"

"I'm 19."

"Aren't you, like, not allowed to be here if you're
only 19?"

"Yeah, but I'm here with a rock star."

Whatever. At least she was legal. I took her into the
men's room and fucked her on the sink. There was only
a sliver of white light in the boxlike room, so it didn't
feel quite as exhibitionistic as it probably seemed. These
guys would stagger in with their Small Faces haircuts
and too-small jean jackets and try not to be thrown by
the scene. They'd piss in the urinal (or on the floor),
wash up, check their hair. Only one of them addressed
us directly, a fey kid in a gold wool suit, black shirt, and
red tie. He looked at her, looked at me, looked at me in
her, and chuckled.

"Lisa, you're such a starfucker," he said.

I limped back to the bar to find Charlie. The DJ was
playing "Heat of the Moment" by Asia, segueing out of
"Hounds of Love" by Kate Bush and into "Take
Ecstasy with Me," by a band with an unpronounceable
name that appeared in print as !!!. Then "To Hell with
Poverty" by Gang of Four into "Creep" by TLC.
Nobody reacted, despite such odd sonic juxtaposition.
Lisa the starfucker slinked out behind me, and I
watched her kibitz. Her friends pointed at me.
Laughed. Shook their heads. I knew what was going on:
I was being compared and contrasted. Deconstructed.
My endurance. My size. Did I bite? Did I whimper?

Did I call her "mum"? Fuck it, man. I told myself that gossip shit was about her self-worth. Not mine. I ordered a chilled Stoli shot and pounded it and decided I needed to get used to this. It was empty and soulless and impersonal and cheap. But at least it was fucking. *For the next three years, this will be what fucking is to me. People who like my band and want to say they fucked me after I'm gone. Or in this case, while I'm still right here.* I needed another. Ordered it.

"That's on us." The bartender smiled. "We're excited about tomorrow night."

"What's tomorrow night?"

He just laughed, then resumed serving cocktails to dead-eyed hipsters.

Charlie materialized. "Where were you?"

"I was—"

"Never mind, I know where you were. How was she?"

"She was—"

"Never mind, I know how she was. Everybody does."

"Jesus. It's a good thing I never have to show my face in this fucking place again, huh?"

"Well, Sandy, this is where the afterparty is, tomorrow night."

I told him I was feeling hungry and was gonna see if the Turkish restaurant on the corner had anything at all I could digest. He was waiting around for a coke delivery and seemed relieved that I didn't need him to accompany me. I waited on line, praying nobody would recognize me. *I'm just the drummer,* I repeated in my head. *Please.* Nobody did. After I ate I went back to the hotel and fell asleep wondering what diseases I'd just given myself, and resolved to send Ben Jim Morrison out for a gigantic box of rubbers in the morning. I was adapting.

When I woke up the morning of the show, I had no idea where I was. I don't know if you've felt that often, but it can be terrifying. It can also be exhilarating. You lie there and piece everything together. In my case, it was a slow smile. Like, *Okay, I understand. I remember last night and last year, and I know that tonight I will be playing New York City for the first time. I know I don't have to get up early today. I know what's in my bank account, and it's a big number. I know my breakfast will taste really good.*

At sound check we ran through the Jane Ashers theme, which would be our opening song, of course. Then we'd do "Another Girl, Another Planet," "I Mean You're Mean," "Roots," and "Debbie" for the encore. It was a secret show, so it wasn't like we had to play for two hours. We would keep it short, sweet, and sweaty. Crispin showed up with a batch of coke from somewhere, and we all had a line in the dressing room.

Harry walked around the stage and stared up at the balcony. "God. In five hours, that's gonna be full of people."

The Bowery Ballroom, if you've never been, is a beautiful venue. Three levels of brick and stone, dating back to the 1920s. It used to be a theater, and the brass and hardwood ornaments remain—fancy brass railings, vaulted plaster ceilings, and the like. Just about a decade ago, it was revamped as a rock venue, and thanks to the great acoustics and perfect size everyone had played there at least once. And now it was our turn. We felt at home. Didn't even bother to go back to the hotel. All the coke was with us, and nobody wanted to risk Harry coming down with a case of the butterfly flu.

The sound of people marching up and down the stairs and in and out of the little dressing room behind the stage was constant, and seemed louder and more and more intrusive with each line I did. We had pizza for dinner. A whole stack of great New York thin-crust pies. Not like the thick, doughy shit we had back home. I would only unclench my jaw for something like that . . . under the circumstances. I consumed plenty of JD too, alternating shots and lines in an attempt to mix up the perfect buzz in my brain: warm and cold, mental and mellow—the mellow was key. There was lots of chatter about religion, about the war and what we needed to do to fix it, about breasts, about cocks, about rock, about chattering while on coke.

None of these strangers interacted much with Harry. They kept a respectful distance, awestruck. Me, Rudy, and Charlie, it was safe to enter our personal space. I'd pull out a cigarette and someone would rush to light it. I'd make a stupid joke or say something to myself, and everyone around me would smile like they understood. Like it was the wisest, funniest, most Buddha-like statement ever uttered. "Pizza . . . good." Cue the stiff smiles and plastic empathy.

Without the whiskey, I might have been alarmed by Harry's behavior. He was hitting our coke hard. Granted, it was his medicine. One part coke, two parts liquor, and the butterflies lay down and died in the stomach. But for some reason he was dealing himself four parts coke and six parts whiskey and chain-smoking, ignoring the really good pizza.

"Sandy," he whispered to me. His eyes were demonic. Frightening. "Let's go tear this place up. Let's tear it all up."

"All right, man. I'm with ya."

"Sandy."

"Yeah?"

"We're gonna tear it up."

"We are."

"Tear it up."

"Yes. That."

"You were right, Sandy. You were right all along. This is *it*."

I grabbed his hand and squeezed it. His palms were damp. I could feel his pulse jumping, but I didn't worry. Whatever means it'd taken him to get there (and I knew what means they were), he was locked in now, like an astronaut before liftoff. Pod doors welded. No ejection. No deviation from the plan. We were ready to blast into orbit.

Crispin, who was also pretty ripped, sidled up to us. "Tell me not to worry."

"Don't worry."

He leaned in and whispered in my ear, "He looks pretty intense."

"You watch him closely," I warned. "One day you can tell your kids you saw a real rock'n'roll show."

"Okay, Sandy."

He walked back over to the couch, sat down, and started cutting out a line. I sat down next to him.

too much, too late

"You know," he said as he raised a rolled-up cigarette paper to his nose, "cocaine has never stopped being a socially acceptable drug in New York City. Nobody gives a shit. If this was heroin"—he gestured to the little pile on the table—"there'd be weeping and wailing." *Snort.* "But this . . . this is like smoking. It's nothing."

I inched myself over to him and cut myself a line.

"So . . ." He stared up, blankly. "What's Ohio like?"

James ducked back and wished us a good show. He was wearing a black leather jacket that seemed to me to be entirely too clean. Probably had vitamin C in the pockets.

"Everybody's here who should be here."

"Bowie?"

He nodded.

"Kate Moss too."

"Is she pretty?"

"Yes. She's Kate Moss. Oh, so, Trace and Hillary wanted me to let you know they're very proud of you guys. They're up at the table. We'll see you all after the show. Don't say anything controversial from the stage. You love the president. You love New York. You're glad to be here. You love every other band who may or may not be competing for the 18-to-35 demographic."

"All right, James. Rock on."

The music grew louder as the crowd noise increased. The sound guys must have dug our pre-show selections, which Crispin burned for us on his laptop and labeled "First NYC Show: Songs Predating My Birth."

"Helen Wheels" by Wings
"Uncontrollable Urge" by Devo

"Open My Eyes" by the Nazz
"Rock of All Ages" by Badfinger
"And So It Goes" by Nick Lowe

And then . . . lights out.

We went out there and tore it up. And for one full hour, it was . . . *it*.

I remember Harry saying, "Hello, New York City," which I found both hysterical and incredibly thrilling. I remember closing my eyes and just hitting the rifle shot that starts the theme, without counting it off. Rudy and Charlie giggled and fell in. Somewhere we just decided to wing it, and if you're already tight in your brain and muscle memory, that can produce the best energy. We had it. I remember at one point Harry introduced us as "the Bay City Rollers," tweaking our odd teeny-bopper appeal. I remember thinking, *I can't see anybody out there, but they sound pretty.*

I remember Charlie thrusting his fist in the air, arena-rock style, and me calling him back to the riser to ask him to please stop. He laughed and apologized. "I just can't believe I'm playing here," he said. "You don't know how many shows I've seen here. And the shows I couldn't even get into, fuck." He was playing well— better than me, his bass notes providing a decent guide whenever I fell off—so I let it slide.

I remember playing "Debbie" twice. We couldn't follow it. They wouldn't stop screaming. I watched Harry pace and Rudy and Charlie lay down their guitars. Harry walked back to the riser.

"Let's just fucking do it again?"

"Yeah?"

"Fuck it, man. Give 'em what they want."

I remember counting it off again, and New York reacting like we hadn't just played it. Turn it into a burger commercial, play it to death—you can't kill that number with coke or anything else. "Debbie" was steady.

Sure enough, our NYC fans were sleeker than any Eggfester or pool-shooting salt-of-the-earth fucker we'd played for in the distant past. They were not unlike the teenagers we rocked in my dad's garage, just stretched out, drunk, and with more money, I guess. Bowie didn't come backstage, but Kate Moss did. I had to stop looking at her. I didn't want to be rude. But she was glowing.

Mick Rock showed up too. Curly gray hair, super-tall, with sunglasses at night, he took my picture, and it flashed in my head: *The guy who shot the cover of* Raw Power *just took my picture*. I just grabbed a piece of the wall and braved it all. I was dizzy. Numb. Drained. Stinking. James chaperoned each honored guest, each somebody, making introductions.

"Thanks. Thanks. Thanks. Thanks a lot. Thanks. Thank you."

Everything else was just disembodied philosophy, floating into my ringing ears and competing with the little monkey-screech voice in my head begging for more blow.

"Look around. There are no kids here, man. It's all media. They're selling you back to the kids who already know the score."

"Thank God the party isn't at Pianos. I'm so sick of

Pianos. Pianos is so last year. Next year the Darkroom will be last year. Right now it's this year. Year year year."

I remember the girl I screwed less than 24 hours before coming up to me and asking if I remembered her. I remembered her.

I remember the Spurts. I only counted three of them. Billy Annanova, the lead singer, was there. Like Harry, he had that aura thing. Nobody crowded him. He walked freely through crowds, invisible G-men keeping the riffraff away. He had dirty brown hair and a black zip-up jacket that was either real expensive and Japanese or purchased at some army-navy outlet for $30. He wore it well, with shredded jeans and Converse sneakers. He looked older than his years. Worldly.

"What's up," he said.

"What's up," I echoed.

"Cool," he replied, as if that was some kind of answer.

"What's cool?" I said. It felt like high school.

"It's cool we're here. Talking."

"Oh. Yeah. It is."

"All right." He smiled, then hugged me. He smelled of smoke and stank of spilled beer. I hugged back. I don't know why.

Jeffrey Ballard III, the kinky-haired guitarist, seemed equally at home in such a tumult. Smoking. Drunk but able to handle it. If this was their world, these guys seemed more than happy to share it. Ballard paired off with Rudy, offering him a smoke.

Hillary and Tracey cornered Harry and began kissing his ass. He didn't seem to respond with any awkwardness or humility. He just nodded and consumed all the praise like it was merely another feeding. Something had changed. Even in my scrambled state, I made a mental note of it. He'd chewed through some bindings out there. He was digging the free movement.

"That was the best show this city's seen in six months," I heard Hillary say.

"Eight months," Tracey corrected him. "Eight and a half months."

"Did you meet those darling Spurts?" Tracey asked.

"No. I don't think so."

"Let me introduce you. We've been discussing the possibility of a co-headlining tour," Hillary began.

"You'll be headlining, of course." Tracey winked.

"Okay . . ."

Tracey tugged Harry toward the corner where Billy and I were upending bottles looking for anything full.

"I used to just drink them off the table," I confided. "Didn't care what was in 'em. As long as it was alcohol, you know?"

"No. I like to know what's in 'em."

"It's all alcohol, man." I found a watery J.D. and shrugged.

"Harry Vance, meet Billy Annanova."

Billy looked over Harry. Harry looked Billy up and down. Both looked around the room at the chattering, swaying, happy New York City VIPs.

"Alone at last," Billy cracked.

Harry laughed.

Some blond girl with a short vintage fur coat and horn-rimmed glasses, like a sexy librarian from 1955, approached them.

"So . . . uh . . . you don't know me. But I wrote you a letter, but I'm embarrassed to give it to you."

Harry's phone rang.

"Excuse me," he apologized, "I have to get this. It's my wife."

"The cat's sick."

"Debbie? I can't hear you. What are you saying?" Harry moved farther and farther away from the crowd in the dressing room, out the door, and back onstage. He stood there, alone, awkward, cheek pressed against his phone.

"Who's sick?"

"Neil. Our cat?"

"Oh, no. What's wrong?"

"I don't know. I'm with the vet now. He was seizing, and I drove him to the animal hospital."

"Jesus, Debbie. I'm sorry I wasn't around."

"It's okay. I didn't want to distract you from your show."

"You should have called me. Uh . . . the show's over now. It went really good."

"Are you okay? You sound weird."

"I'm a little out of breath."

Harry wiped his brow and closed his eyes. Inhaled deeply.

"Look, I'm sure the kitty's going to be fine. Maybe he ate something rank outside."

"Yeah. I'm sure. I just wanted to hear your voice."

"It's really good to hear yours too. I miss you so fucking much."

too much, too late

"You do?"

"Yes. Of course I do."

"I haven't heard from you all day."

"It's been really busy here. It's been . . . fucking surreal."

"What's with all the swearing?"

"I don't know. I'm . . . things are weird. I'm fine. Really. How are you?"

"I'm okay. It's a little weird here."

"What? Why?"

"Well, Harry, we're living in my grandma's old house now. Have you forgotten?"

"Oh, no. Of course not. Yeah. I bet that's kind of weird. Is it too weird?"

"No. It's fine. It just catches me every once in a while. I walk down the hall and look at a socket and say, 'I know that socket. Where do I know that socket from?' Ha."

"Socket. Ha."

Harry looked back at the revelers in the dressing room. His revelers. His dressing room. A party in his honor. He wanted to rejoin them.

"How's Matty?"

"He's fine."

"Really? No details?"

"No details. Come home, okay? Have a safe flight."

"Thanks. Yeah. We'll be back tomorrow, I think. Is it tomorrow? I'll ask Ben."

"It's tomorrow. I have it marked down."

"Okay. Good. I can't wait. I love you."

"I love you too."

"Okay, baby. Bye."

"Bye."

He put his phone in his pocket, looked up at the ceiling and said a quick prayer for his ill kitty, then walked back into the smoke and heat.

After the Bowery closed down, the party moved to the Darkroom and then to someone's apartment up on Second Avenue and 18th or 19th Street. Me, Harry, Rudy, Ben Jim Morrison, Crispin, the Spurts, and a half dozen odd hipster girls were drinking and falling about four leather couches, which had been arranged in a square formation, so you had to climb over them to get in or out of the confab. In the middle there was a coffee table, dusted with substances and holding five or six full ashtrays. I remember an American flag hanging on the wall. A few acoustic guitars, many of them valuable. Someone went to the corner for a beer run.

"What do you call it? Where are you going?"

"The bodega."

"Bodega?"

"Bodega."

"Bodega?"

"Bodega, yeah."

"What the fuck is that?"

"Deli."

"Deli?"

"Deli, yeah."

"Deli?"

"Grocery store."

"Fuck. Okay! Thank you!"

There was much giggling and drug snorting and camaraderie and trying to get the volume on the TV to go as loud as possible. VH1 Classic. "Wheel in the Sky," by Journey. Don't remember why it absolutely had to be ear-swelling at the time.

"Hey . . . hey . . . uh . . . Billy . . . what's the coolest place you guys have played?" Rudy asked.

"I don't know. Scotland was pretty cool. Japan."

"Oh, man. We're gonna get to see the world." He rubbed his palms together like a little kid.

"When you're in Tokyo, you wanna go to Tsukiji Sushi," Ballard insisted to me. "Write that down," he commanded. "T-s-u-k-i-j-i."

I shrugged awkwardly. "I don't have a pen."

"Tsukiji sushi. You like sushi?"

"Yeah. I like eel." What was with these young New York kids and sushi? Did they all wanna be Japanese or something? When I was a kid, we all wanted to be black.

"Oh, if you like eel, you'll fucking die for Tsukiji."

"I like fluke too. Fluke sushi."

He ignored me and turned his attention to the girls. I felt very high school, trying to impress these 23-year-old kids and make sure they knew that I was a rock star too, just like the Spurts. Marco Salinger, their bass player, was fast becoming my favorite Spurt. He sat in the corner and said nothing.

Charlie Quickness reclined like a tomcat and surveyed the asses of the six or seven women with us. He sniffed derisively, as if to say, *Too skinny,* then excused himself and went out into the night, chubby chasing.

Unlike us, he didn't have to fly back to Dean, Ohio, in the morning.

"You don't wanna play *SNL*," Billy advised.

"Why not?" Crispin asked eagerly, taking mental notes. I bet he knew how to spell the name of that sushi joint in Japan too. He was loving this shit. Moving up in the social ranks, climbing high.

"They force you to play the hit. They'll pull you if you don't. We'll play the radio festivals 'cause we have to, but nobody's gonna tell us what the fuck to play, right?"

"Right," I replied, not knowing what the fuck he was talking about, only that he was waiting for agreement before moving on, and it was becoming painful.

"You wanna do Conan," he said. "Conan is great. Who's producing your album?"

"I think we're gonna try to do it ourselves, Billy," Rudy said earnestly.

Billy laughed. "Whoa. Good luck, man. That's fucking great." He rose up and hugged Rudy tightly. Patted him on the back. Hugged me next. Then Harry. Kissed him on the cheek too. We didn't get one of those.

"So, when we go out on the road, I think we need to bring you guys just so we know what the fuck we're doing." Harry laughed. He had no problem admitting that he was green. Why would he? He had the whole wide-eyed innocent genius thing to fall back on. He looked like a baby too. I looked like I'd been around, but I'd been nowhere. I wanted to see the world and eat weird fish in Japan and take a boat trip through wherever the fuck, but I didn't want some city kid to

too much, too late

be my tour guide. I medicated my shame with more liquor.

At around 5 a.m. some of the Spurts decided they were hungry and jetted off to some all-night brasserie in Soho for oysters and Bloody Marys. Rudy went with them. So did Crispin. Ben was passed out. So were most of the girls, except Harry's librarian and my Wu Tang Clan chick from the previous night. Harry rose wordlessly and walked toward the door. The librarian chick followed.

"Where you going?" I croaked.

He didn't answer. Didn't look back. Just split. And she followed. I'm not saying anything happened in his room that night. I didn't see anything. All I'm relating is that the guy didn't answer me or make eye contact. I let it slide. It was late.

I found myself in front of a big window with Ballard, who was weaving a bit. I looked back at the party scene.

"Boy, I feel sorry for whoever owns this place. It's trashed."

He stared at me and smiled. "This is my place."

"Oh . . ."

He turned his attention back to the window.

"Sandy, look down there."

I stared through the glass down at the side of a building. There were ugly, greenish yellow fluorescent lights illuminating each little room. The edifice looked industrial and horrid.

"What is that?"

"That's Beth Israel Hospital, man."

We continued to stare at the rows and rows of windows below us. Some had shades pulled. Others didn't. Each one seemed like a little void.

"There are people dying in there," Ballard whispered.

"Right now."

I turned away and shook my fading Wu Tang girl awake.

9

I'd lived in Dean all my life. I knew every squirrel. Every blade of grass. Every mailbox. Every horsefly. The place never looked strange to me, even when I was high and my own ears looked strange to me, but as we were driving home from the airport, the town felt off somehow. Home hadn't changed. The same plate of half-eaten Steak-umm sandwiches and Ore-Ida fries was out on the kitchen table. Minna had fixed it for us the day I left for New York. There was a different record on the turntable, "Pale Blue Eyes" by the Velvet Underground. Other than that, it was static. I used to find that comforting; now I found it kind of unnerving.

The house was freezing. I pulled my scarf tightly around my neck to ward off the draft. Minna walked in, wrapped in a yellow afghan. She was barefoot, and her toes looked bluish.

"Ma, it's freezing in here!" I shouted as I hugged her.

"Oh. Yeah. I meant to turn up the thermostat."

"Are you okay?"

"Huh? Oh, yeah. I got the Capitol versions of the old Beatles albums on CD. They just came out."

"Uh-huh."

"I was playing them against the English versions. Wanted to see which ones I liked better."

"You bought them all?"

"Yeah."

" 'Cause I can get you whatever you're missing."

"I bought them all."

"Which one do you like better?"

"Oh, Sand. I can't decide."

I hugged her a second time, then went over to the thermostat and amped it about 15 degrees. I walked up to my bed and flopped down backward onto my broken-in mattress. I lay there and counted all the aches in my 38-year-old body.

Harry initially instructed the taxi driver to take him to his old place before reminding himself that nobody lived there anymore. He redirected the guy to the lilac house. Harry bounded up the long walk, past the now-dormant lilac bushes. He searched his pockets and realized that he didn't have a key. Sheepishly, he knocked on the door. Debbie opened it. He didn't even look at her, just grabbed her and hugged her. Smelled her neck. Buried his face in her soft hair.

She pulled him back and stared at him. He tried to look away.

"Well," she said with a comforting smile, "you look like you've been . . . active."

"I've been hyperactive, Deb."

"We'll take care of you."

He embraced her again. "I missed you."

"I missed you too."

"No, I really missed you. This is not much good without you."

"I know. But that's not what the papers are saying."

"Huh?"

She smiled and tried to cheer him.

"A packet of clippings came today, from someone named James something. I read a few of them. Rave reviews, Harry."

"Really?" He couldn't temper his interest or pride. It was an odd side of him. He knew she hadn't seen it so close to the surface in years.

"I can read them to you while you're in the bath. We have a nice big bathtub."

"We do?"

"Oh, yeah. Sunken."

"Wow. Sunken."

"You want the tour now or later?"

"Later."

"You sure?"

"I need a nap. Will you come with me?"

"I just woke up. I have some errands to run."

"Okay. Well, tell me where the bedroom is."

"Upstairs, down the hall on the left. Second door. I taped all our shows. We have TiVo now. They're all saved."

"Did you watch them already?"

"Yes."

"Okay . . . that's okay. Where's Matty?"

"He's at school."

"Oh . . . right." He traipsed away in a fog, staring at the unfamiliar moldings and wallpaper and furniture.

"Is this ours?" he said, holding up an orange vase.

"It's ours."

"Oh, good. It's pretty."

Harry slept all day. At 4 p.m. Debbie woke him with a kiss. He grabbed her and pulled her into the bed with him.

"I thought I might be home. It doesn't smell like home, but I opened my eyes and I saw our stuff and I wondered if I was dreaming."

"Are you rested?"

"Yes."

"Are you hungry?"

"A little."

"Okay, come down to the kitchen."

Harry dragged himself out of bed, pulled on his bathrobe, and walked with her hand in hand down to the kitchen. He sat at the table. It was new as well. Their old card table, at which they'd planned their entire adult lives together, was gone. Maybe it was at the dump. He didn't ask. He picked at a plate of cheese and crackers. She handed him a beer.

"Maybe some tea instead?"

"You're gonna need the beer."

A chill went through him. It started in his balls, then ran up through his belly and over his shoulders like scurrying roaches.

"Why?"

"Well, for a start, the cat's dead."

"I was going to ask about the cat."

"Yeah, I know. You were tired." She held his hand. "He died last night. The vet said it was quick at the end."

"Jesus. Neil."

"He was 13. That's good for a cat."

"You seem so calm about it. Neil's dead."

"I cried last night. Alone."

"I'm sorry, Deb. I should have been here. I'm so sorry. Shit."

"There's more."

Harry pulled out a pack of cigarettes and reflexively lit one up.

"You're hooked on those again, aren't you?"

"No."

"Aren't you?"

"Yes."

"Gimme one."

He pushed the pack across the table past the sweating cheese, and pulled on his beer.

"Worse than Neil dying?"

"Matty's not home yet. It's nearly five and he's not here. Did you notice that too?"

"Deb . . . what happened."

"He's in detention."

She lit a cigarette. He saw that it chilled her out a little too much, giving her a major head rush. He watched as she let it flow into her bloodstream, enjoying every toxic bit.

"What did he do?"

"Well, they found an eighth of marijuana in his locker. Do you know how much an eighth of marijuana costs?"

"No."

"A lot. Two hundred dollars or something. That's what he tells me. Do you know how he got the marijuana?"

"Debbie, please. Just tell me."

"He traded your harmonica for it. To a fan. Of yours."

"Jesus. I thought he was playing it."

"Well . . . no. Obviously."

"My harmonica . . . ?"

"I'm sorry. I'll try to find out who's got it. We'll get it back. But when he comes home, I need you to talk to him. I can't anymore."

"Why?"

"Because I keep wanting to hit him. I'm so furious, Harry. Our son is doing drugs!"

Harry felt flushed with guilt. Ever since he'd boarded the airplane for the trip home, he'd found himself fiending for more cocaine.

"Debbie, it's just pot. It's not like it's . . . you know . . . other stuff."

"Well, maybe he can get hold of one of your leather jackets and score some heroin."

"You're really mad."

"I'm really mad."

"I can't remember the last time I've seen you this mad. Maybe when I refused to talk to my mother. Remember?"

"I'm glad you brought that up."

"My mother. Is she okay?"

"She's fine. She sent us flowers. Over there by the window."

"For what?"

"As a housewarming gift. We moved in while you were gone."

"Deb, I'm sorry. I'm out of it."

She rose. Put out her cigarette on the plate edge. Rubbed his shoulders. Kissed his neck. Grabbed another from the pack.

"Drink the beer," she whispered.

Harry took another pull off the beer.

"Also—" She cleared her throat. "Someone claiming to be your father has been calling the office line. Ben will tell you tonight, I'm sure."

"My father?"

Debbie nodded.

"I'm sorry. I knew you'd want to know. I didn't tell you any of this while you were gone because I knew you had to do this all the way, Harry. But now that you're back . . . well, I can't take all this weirdness myself."

"My father."

"Yeah."

"Does Mom know?"

"Nobody knows."

"How did he find me?"

Debbie handed him the Federal Express package full

marc spitz

of press clippings. Harry weakly grabbed it and stared in at the half-inch-thick stack of photocopied paper.

"They're dancing out of the woodwork."

Harry raised himself unsteadily and walked down the hall.

"Is that a porch?" he inquired. Debbie smiled and nodded.

"I'll be on the porch."

"Benny."

"Harry. I was just thinking about you."

"Yeah. I know why."

"You do?"

"Yeah."

"Oh, thank Christ. I've been sitting here for an hour wondering how the hell I should break this to you. I've started drinking. Again."

"Ben, you never quit drinking."

"Yeah, but I was gonna."

"Look, who took the call?"

"Steve. He's an intern."

"We have an intern?"

"Steve."

Harry was silent. Just overwhelmed.

"He's a bartender back at the old place. I gave him 200 bucks to answer the phone, open the mail, feed the fish."

"Fish."

"Saltwater. It's beautiful. You didn't get the bill?"

"No."

"Starfish. We got coral."

"Okay, well, that's great. Tell me about my dad."

"We have squids."

"Ben, did Steve seem to think this guy was for real?"

"You know, I asked him that. Actually. I did."

"And . . . ?"

"He said the guy didn't sound crazy. He wasn't stuttering or spitting."

"Oh, God. Did he sound nice? Like a nice old man?"

"I guess. Yeah."

"Did he sound like he could be my dad? Like, really? My father?"

"Harry, how he sounded doesn't mean shit. You're famous now. All the nut jobs are going to come calling. I want to talk to you about security. I know a guy who can get you an Uzi."

"I don't want an Uzi, Ben."

"If you do, tell me. He can get Uzis. Glocks. Hand grenades."

"I'm gonna throw a hand grenade at a stalker?"

"Nah. It's just for peace of mind."

"Ben, I'm fine. I'm sitting on my new porch right now. I don't feel like a target."

"Good. Hey, that's great!"

"Listen, man. If my father . . . if that guy, whoever he is, calls back, you tell him that I'm not even gonna consider taking his call unless he goes and sees my fucking mother. Immediately. No. Fuck. What if he *is* a psycho? I mean, how do I make sure he's not?"

"There's only one way, I guess. You check him out."

"I can't."

"You want me to check him out?"

"You'd do that?"

"Absolutely. I'll check him out real good. I'll get DNA analyzed and everything."

"Really?"

"Just say the word."

"Will he volunteer DNA?"

"We'll get it."

"Okay. Do it."

"Yeah?"

"Yes. Please. Take care of this. I can't think about it. My head is going to explode."

"Listen, don't worry about this. It's done. You have an album to write. Just keep the hits coming, chief."

"Ben."

"Yeah, chief?"

"Thanks."

"Yeah, no problem. Hey, you ever wonder what Natalie Merchant's like in bed?"

"No."

"I'm sitting here watching VH1 Classic. We had the dish put on the roof while I was gone. Amazing clarity. High definition. I can get the soccer matches from Quito on this fucking thing."

"We have a dish there?"

"You didn't get the bill?"

"No. Not yet."

"Yeah. I've always had a thing for her. You think she's got hair on her pits? She looks like she might, right?"

"Ben, I gotta go."

"You sure you don't need anything else? You get the washer and dryer?"

"I don't know. Probably. I haven't really spent much time in the kitchen."

"Housewarming gift."

"Oh, thanks."

"You get the bill for it?"

"I don't know."

"You will."

"Oh . . . a cat. I need a new cat."

"You want a mouser? Or one of them poofy things?"

"Just a normal cat. A house cat."

"What color?"

"Tabby."

"Nice. I'll have one sent over in the morning. First thing."

"Really?"

"Oh, yeah. All you have to do is sign for it. They'll bill you."

"Great."

"Isn't it?"

I had been waiting for Motorrrju to contact me. I decided I would swallow some pride. It was weird. While I was gone, I totally considered her my girlfriend in my head, where it was perfectly legal to do so. But something was up here in the real world. She was ducking me.

"Why haven't you called me? You knew I was back."

"I can't talk, Sandy. I was asleep."

"Can I see you? I can't sleep."

"I have school in the morning."

I almost wanted to say, *Quit! And while you're at it, be 18!*

I knew she knew when we were set to return, because I'd been reading her blog and she'd posted our itinerary.

I'd been reading it every day, obviously, and knew something was eating her, but I didn't have time to focus on it until I was back in Ohio.

> 8:14 p.m. I'm supposed to update the blog and discuss what's been going on with me lately, but I'm feeling totally uninspired and sad and I think it might be too deep to share with the entire Internerd. Plus it could get some people in trouble. Thinking about it is making my head dizzy, so I'm gonna just sit in my room tonight and watch television and eat.
>
> 10:19 p.m. I honestly can't believe how much I love Jane Ashers sometimes. I couldn't watch TV. It was boring reruns. I played "Go Steady Debbie" really loud and felt better like Vedder in an instant. I'm not going to let what's happening in New York City put the mockers on that. It's about the music, and that band makes me wanna never stop dancing. They make me so happy I wanna run down the street hugging people.
>
> 10:35 P.S. This puppy is so cute, I wanna punch it in the nose.

"Can I come over?"

"No, Sandy."

"Well, can you talk?"

"I'm half asleep. And stoned."

"You fell asleep stoned?"

"Yeah. Matty Vance had this really excellent pot. He sold me two joints. I smoked one. I'm saving the other for third period. Just before philosophy."

"Can I see you after school?"

too much, too late

"You don't wanna see me. You're a big rock star now. It's weird, isn't it?"

"No."

"It was weird seeing you on TV. I felt like . . . I don't know."

"Felt like what?"

"Like I didn't know you anymore. Like you didn't belong to me."

"I still belong to you. I wanna belong to you. That's why I'm calling here. I can't sleep. At least let me come over and smoke some weed."

"No. My parents would disapprove."

"I'll write them a check or something."

"See? You're a decadent rock star now. I can't relate. I'm just a true fan."

"No, you're not. You're my friend. I miss you. You don't miss me?"

"I do. But even if I saw you, Sandy . . . I'd still miss you."

"Jesus. Sometimes you're such a teenager. Will you call me tomorrow?"

"Yes."

"You promise?"

"I promise."

I hung up and felt a little better. I had something to look forward to: a phone call from a 16-year-old girl.

Harry and the kid only spent a few minutes together, as Debbie insisted that Matty stay confined to his room. But the father-son conversation was eventful.

"Matty?"

"What?"

"Can I come in?"

"I guess."

Harry sat on the bed. "Why'd you sell my harmonica for weed? I thought you were gonna learn to play it."

"I can't play it."

"Did you try?"

He nodded.

"Well, was it good weed at least?"

"Don't try to be cool."

"Seriously, was it?"

"Yes."

"So you smoked it before you got caught?"

"Yeah."

"How did you get caught?"

"I left my locker unlocked."

"Why?"

"I was stoned."

"Ha. Okay. Well, that was pretty dumb."

"What do you want? You didn't even bring me anything from New York."

"I got you a lot. Your mom won't let me give it to you. She's pretty upset. I don't know what to do with her."

"Why don't you write a *song* about it?" Matty got up and stared out the window.

"The window's a lot bigger in here than in the other house, huh? Must have a lot of nice light during the day."

"I guess."

"This house is weird."

He turned around and stared at his father, interested.

"Isn't it? It's fucking weird."

"Are you cursing to impress me?"

too much, too late

"I'm pointing out that living in this place is fucking weird. That's all. Did you know that when your mother and I first moved in together, I pointed at this house and said, 'One day we will live here'? And now we do. And that's weird. Isn't it?"

"Fucking weird."

"I used to think things could be perfect if I just lived a certain way. It had to be black or white. Good or bad. Safe or dangerous. Now I kind of realize none of that matters. This dream of a perfect family is just as bad as any other fantasy. There's no guarantee that your mom and I are gonna be those people walking the street hand in hand in the coats, looking all charming."

"What people?"

"I saw them in New York. Old people. In coats. They were charming."

"Oh."

"Life is messy! It's messy, man. And it doesn't matter if you run away from what you want or hold on to that dream for so long people think you're pathetic. Either way, what happens to you in the end is never going to look like what you need it to look like. It's going to look . . . messy. You know?"

"No."

"These days I think life is all about the moment, Matty," Harry said, staring out the new big window. "So . . . you fucked up. In a moment. You sold my harmonica for drugs. That's all. My dad messed up in the moment. He split for San Francisco with some secretary. So what? There's another moment right behind it where you can do something different, try to repair things. Get my harmonica back . . . or not. Either way, I can't really get sore at you for what you did because one day you're going to be dead."

"Dad?"

"Where *is* that pot, anyway? The bag you got for my Hohner?"

Harry hugged his kid for a long time. It was a rock star's hug. Meaningless.

Matty never smoked weed again. He didn't even jaywalk.

Harry and Debbie were eating breakfast in silence when the pet store delivered their new cat. Debbie answered the door and initially refused to sign for it.

"This is not the way this is going to be from now on, is it?" she snapped over her green tea.

"What?"

"Just blindly signing away all our problems?"

Harry rose and confronted her with a bit more backbone than he'd ever shown before.

"Debbie, most people would give their right arm to be able to do that. The office will pay all our bills and take care of what we need."

"We don't need a cat, Harry. We *want* a cat. We go to the pet store or the pound and we make a fucking connection with the fucking cat and then we bring it home. We don't have it shipped."

"I don't have time to do that. I have to write songs. And record an album. So that we can have this luxury."

"Yes, but I don't want the luxury. I'd rather have you

available for . . . cat browsing." She was losing face. The phrase stuck in her mouth and crinkled her lips. She found herself giggling.

"Can we please sign for the cat?" Harry begged. "The guy's standing outside with the cat, Deb."

"You sign for it. I don't approve."

"Fine."

Harry opened the door, signed for the cat, and awkwardly ducked back in.

"Deb?"

"What?" she cried, exasperated. She'd walked over to reheat her tea but found herself smoking instead.

"Do you have a couple of dollars? For a tip?"

"Oh, I forgot. Rock stars never carry cash. They sign for everything."

"Debbie, come on. It's chilly out here. The poor cat is shaking."

She found her purse and pulled out a five. Harry handed it to the delivery man, took the cat in, and checked it out.

"He looks like Neil," Harry observed.

"He's not fucking Neil," Debbie shouted. "Neil was *our* cat!" She inhaled her chemicals and calmed a bit.

"He's a fine cat," Harry said. "We don't have to call him Neil 2 or anything like that. He can develop his own personality."

"Like you'll even be around for that. *I'm* going to have to name this cat."

"Just call him kitty," Harry suggested, "till I get home. I have to get to rehearsal."

"I just wanted to let you know that tonight you're taking me to the movies. And dinner."

"Okay. Great. I can't wait. Really."

She kissed him.

"I'm glad you're home."

"I'll call you at 6."

"Okay."

Debbie put her cigarette out and picked up the plastic carrying case.

"Now let me see this fuckin' cat."

I stopped by the high school on the way home from the car dealership. It was a little early for lunch, but I knew from her blogs that sometimes Motorrrju sneaked out of class and hit the parking lot for a smoke. I idled in the lot behind the wheel of my new purchase, cherry-red Mustang convertible. I put the top down and lit up a smoke, then, worried that it would mask that new-car smell, chucked it out.

Some jock kid with yellow hair and a football jersey walked out.

"Hey," I called. "Hey, sporto."

The kid walked over.

"Yeah?"

"Where's Natalie Levine?"

"I don't know, man. I'm a senior."

"So? That a big deal? I'm 38."

He looked me over.

"Aren't you in the Jane Ashers?"

"Yeah. You dig us?"

"I think you guys are overrated."

"Listen, what's your name?"

"Doug."

"Doug, here's a hundred dollars." I handed him a bill from my wallet. "There's another one in it for you if you bring Natalie out here in two minutes. Are you down?"

"Yeah."

"You're about it?"

"Yeah."

"Good. Go be about it. Hurry the fuck up. I got rehearsal."

The kid swiped the money and booked it back into school.

I reached into the paper bag at my feet and pulled out a bottle of beer, popped it open, and had my breakfast. I lit another cigarette, this time taking care to hold it out the window. I heard some kind of stampede behind me, turned around, and saw Natalie standing there in front of about 20 high school kids. She was wearing a ripped-up yellow-and-black-striped mohair sweater and red plaid trousers. Her hair had grown in a bit. She'd dyed it platinum blond and pushed it out of her eyes with a cheesy tortoiseshell headband. She looked beautiful to me. I pulled my racing shades down, killed the beer with another gulp, and cut the engine. I got out and walked over to Doug, showed him the second C-note, then pocketed it myself.

"Thanks for the discretion."

"What are you doing here?" Natalie wondered. I could tell that at least part of her was glad to see me. At least she liked the attention she was getting from her classmates on account of my showing up, anyway. I'd be lying if I said she seemed purely happy to see me. But I was determined to fix that.

"Nat, can we have some privacy here?"

She pulled a cigarette out of my pocket, turned around to look at her classmates, then swiveled back to me.

"Probably not."

"All right, get in the car."

"I can't. I have to go back to class." She looked at the car. "Is that new?"

"Yeah. It is. I picked it up this morning."

"It's hot."

"It's yours."

I handed her the keys. A shudder went through the kids.

"What? A 38-year-old man never bought any of you a car before?" I exhaled their way. "Get the fuck outta here, would you please?"

They didn't budge. Didn't matter, though. Motorrrju was behind the wheel already. I jumped into the passenger seat and rolled up the windows.

"It's a stick," she lamented.

"Yeah. It's a Mustang. You don't want an automatic transmission on a car like this."

"I can't drive a stick."

"It's all right. I'll teach you."

"Sandy, you shouldn't have bought me a car."

"I told you I'd buy you a car. I owe everything to you. Really." I touched her cheek. "Did you miss me?"

"I'm not telling you."

She pulled a beer from the bag. I pushed it down.

"Don't drive drunk in this. Okay? Promise me."

She stared at me.

"What?"

"Nothing."

"What? Come on."

"You're different. I was right."

"I'm exactly the same, Natalie."

"No. Only a rock star would say 'Don't drive drunk' after driving over here drunk. You're a rock star now. I hate rock stars."

"Aw, get over it. I mean, it's not like you're offering perfection. You've got problems too. For starters, you're a fucking minor."

"Yeah, but I don't have to do anything but age. You have a lot of work to do, Sandy. I don't want to date some immature . . . thing. I want a real person."

"I'll get mature."

"Okay, well, you grow, and I'll age, and we'll see what happens."

I smiled. She leaned over and kissed my cheek.

"Thanks for the Ford. I like red."

"I took a guess."

I leaned in and opened the glove compartment. Pulled out a little digital camera. Took a snap of her behind the wheel, smiling wide and surveying the big, impressive dash. She looked ready for the world, and I wanted to be there with her one day. Maybe when I'm older.

We didn't do much serious rehearsing. We just jammed and fucked around all day. We tried to write some riff-based stuff that Harry could maybe put lyrics to, but ended up playing a bunch of covers, badly. I think we were a little thrown by all the workmen. I'd hired a crew from the old yard to soundproof the place. I thought I'd want to gloat, especially with Dennis the foreman, the guy who'd insisted on calling me "Klein." But when they all got there, it just felt weird. I paid them in cash up front and then sent them to an early lunch, which I also paid for. Gloating is fun only in theory. In practice, it's hard work. You have to really commit to being an asshole, and once you're in a better place, you start worrying about things like karma. You have more to lose. Maybe that's not a pure take on karma. I'm just saying I didn't rub it in that I was a rock'n'roll star and they still drove hilos and ate chocolate breakfasts out of a vending machine.

Harry called Ben Jim Morrison to find out if his father had contacted the office again. Ben assured him that he would call him as soon as anything happened in that area. Harry thanked him for that, and for the cat, and asked if it was possible to track down a piano.

"I think maybe I need one. To write. What do you think?"

The last question was addressed to me and Rudy across the room. We shrugged.

"Sure. Whatever it takes," Rudy offered. "Get a piano. Get a marimba. We got an album to do."

"I'd like some timpani mallets," I quipped. "And a genuine Indian guru." I was quoting Dr. Hook and the Medicine Show, but I did have karma on the brain. I decided to get stoned.

"Your father? What's all that about?" I asked as I packed the bong.

"It's nothing." Harry looked around. "This place is really comforting." He pulled out a pen and wrote something down on a napkin.

"Idea?" Rudy asked hopefully.

"I don't even know," Harry replied fretfully. "Maybe the piano will help."

I put the bong down and coughed violently. The weed took over, and I decided I was happy . . . and hungry.

"Oh . . . oh, shit. I totally forgot. Oh, get your coats," I urged.

"You wanna get some food?" Rudy inquired.

"Yes. Yes. I have something to show you, man. You'll get a kick out of this. Follow me."

We piled into Harry's Volvo and drove the short distance to the diner. We all took a booth and ordered coffee, then I got up and walked to the jukebox. I put a dollar into that can, hit the push-button selector, and the slick, pink-lit flaps under the glass slid up and over each other like they were greased.

Harry and Rudy had followed me, and I said, "Look at E-12."

"Oh my God, there we are."

E-12 at Dil's Diner in Dean, Ohio, in case you're ever passing through, was and still is "Let's Go Steady Debbie" by the Jane Ashers. Our eggs tasted especially good that day.

Ben was waiting for us when we got back to the garage. He was munching a peanut butter, jelly, and bacon sandwich. The grease from the bacon was glistening on his beard.

"Your mother? She is a culinary genius nonpareil. May she live to be a hundred." Ben patted Harry's back warmly. "Genius must run in the family."

"Ben, that's *my* mom in there," I told him.

"Ah. Well, then, I guess it skips a generation. I'm just fucking with you, Sandy."

Ben pulled out a fax from some vintage piano shop in Pittsburgh and handed it to Harry.

"I got you a hell of an instrument today, my friend. It'll be here in the morning. All you have to do is sign for it. They'll bill us."

"Right. Of course."

"It's a Baldwin. Bone white. Used to belong to Neil Sedaka."

Harry laughed. "Sedaka?"

"He wrote 'Laughter in the Rain' on it."

"Wow, so it's, like, cursed," Rudy cracked.

" 'Laughter in the Rain' is a beautiful love song," Ben protested. "You write something as beautiful as 'Laughter in the Rain' and we'll keep talking. Otherwise I'm done here."

Ben playfully pushed Rudy on his way out and winked at Harry.

" 'Laughter in the Rain,' " he uttered once again, as if it was some coded assurance that everything was going to be okay.

We played for another hour and a half, and then Harry excused himself to go meet his 32-year-old wife for "date night." Rudy, Minna, and I ordered a pizza and watched a DVD of *The Rolling Stones: Rock and Roll Circus*, then *Don't Look Back* on the new 62-inch plasma TV I'd kitted out the living room with. Surround sound and everything.

"Is this a crib, yet? It's almost a crib, right?" I asked Rudy, wondering if the young Bob Dylan had ever asked anyone if he'd achieved cribitude.

"Harry, hello! I saw you on television," the maître d' at Finley's greeted them warmly as he guided Harry and Debbie to their table.

"Really? We were on television?"

"Yes, I think you were. MTV."

"Oh, I don't watch it."

"All this must be very exciting for you. And Mrs. Vance, you look beautiful this evening. We have two lobsters in the tank for you."

They were the last pair of fresh lobsters in Dean, and they were way off the menu for anyone else. The pair of times Harry and Debbie had splurged on a meal at Finley's in the past, this guy had never said anything besides "Your table is ready. *Bon appétit*" to either of them. Now he was guiding them to the best table in the place.

"Maybe we can put your photo up behind the bar, next to Ruby Dee's."

Harry glanced at the wall of celebrity Ohioans above the narrow strip of mirror behind the shelved bottles. The great Ruby Dee was there, next to autographed photos of Jack Nicklaus and Nancy Cartwright (who does the voice of Bart Simpson). Not bad company.

"So, how are you?" Harry asked her once they sat down and had a bit of privacy. "For real. Are you okay?"

"You sound like a shrink. I'm fine, Harry. Really. I'm holding it together."

"That's such a relief."

"Well, don't get used to it. We can't do this forever."

"It won't be forever. There's an end to this."

"Is there?"

"There was before."

"Is this anything like it was then? At all?"

"No."

"Is it anything like you thought it would be?"

Harry had no answer. He didn't know. He wished his wife would stop interviewing him and just speak to him. Reach him somehow. He didn't want to think about anything. He just wanted . . . dessert. Can a dream technically come true if it happens after one's already stopped dreaming about it?

The waiter approached. "We have some delicious specials this evening. We have a very large grilled artichoke with a smoked tomato vinaigrette. That's an appetizer. For two . . ."

They ordered the most expensive bottle of red on the wine list. He had the steak with broccoli rabe. His body was telling him he needed some greens and vitamins or it'd start rebelling against him, and he complied. She had the lobster with a side of pasta.

When they'd finished eating, he grabbed her hand and squeezed it.

"I needed that."

"It was delicious," she allowed. The waiter brought over a couple of sambucas, little espresso beans drowning in the concave base of the glass.

They toasted and clinked and drank.

"I'm getting a little drunk," Debbie confessed.

"Me too. Don't worry—we'll call a cab. Believe me, I can't drink and drive. I'm a . . . role model."

"Jesus."

"I know. It's ridiculous. But I am. Or they tell me I am."

"No. It's not that." She laughed. "It's just there's a family at the table by the bar. They're staring."

"Shit. I knew this would happen. What do I do?"

"Just smile back. Be nice to your fans. They keep us in artichokes and expensive *vino*."

Harry turned and smiled at the balding man. He was big and fat, not just beer-bellied but built like someone who was once muscular. He wore a cheap brown corduroy suit jacket, chino pants, a blue-and-white-striped oxford, and a navy polyester tie. His wife was also fat, but she'd probably always been. Purple-auburn hair. Heavy makeup. Ice blues and fruity oranges. They looked about fifty upon first glance. They dressed like middle-aged substitute teachers, anyway. They were probably much younger. Their son was slight. Wispy. He wore a black and yellow Nirvana T-shirt with a frowning smiley on it. He was playing with his food until he saw Harry. Then he just locked in and looked ecstatic.

Harry nodded. The man rose and grabbed his kid, who ran like an excited pooch right over to their table.

"Hello," Harry said slowly, a little put out, straining to be polite.

"Hi there. My kid is a big fan. We saw you there when we came in. Didn't want to bother you while you were eating, but would it be possible to get an autograph? We all think you're really great. My wife had her card game the other day, and all the ladies were humming the Debbie song. I really love it too. I'm a musician. Well . . . I teach music. At the high school. I used to be in a band."

Harry looked over at the man's wife. She was blushing. "She's shy," the man explained.

Harry didn't notice the color draining from Debbie's face as she examined the man. He was busy scribbling his name on the kid's place mat when she screamed. The waiter ran over.

"Is everything all right, Mrs. Vance?"

"You're Stagger!" she howled, and pointed at the balding man. "Stagger Wilkie. You're Unkillable!" The man looked befuddled.

"I . . . well, I'm not . . . I haven't . . . I'm Robert. Go by Robert now. Bob."

The kid looked up at his dad. Stagger turned to the kid. "I'm Bob," he assured him. "It's me. Bob." He turned back to Harry and Debbie. "I haven't gone by that name in years. Who . . . Did you know me? My band?"

Debbie jumped up and began scratching at his cheeks.

Stagger covered his face with his hands and whimpered. Even gone to flab, he was still massive enough to swat her like King Kong, but she had adrenaline and alcohol on her side. Vengeance too.

"You cursed our baby! You cursed our baby!"

His wife jumped up and waddled over to the table to reflexively protect the poor kid, who'd started to cry. Like Matty, he evidently hadn't known his dad had once rocked. Sort of. Badly. Darkly. And, apparently, no longer for a living. Stagger put his rock past behind him. And unlike Harry, it hadn't been dredged back up.

"You fucker! You killed my baby!"

The waiter tried to pull Debbie off him, but she was preternaturally stubborn, and very drunk. Harry finally joined in and together, with the man's wife and the waiter, the three subdued her. She spat at Stagger, "Get the fuck out of my sight, you fat cocksucker. And take your ugly family with you."

The man licked his hand, wiped the blood from his

cheek, and meekly retreated. They got their coats and headed out to the car, looking stunned. It'd be a long drive home for the Wilkie clan, full of explainin'.

"These are the kind of people who love you?" she asked. "These are your fans?"

"No. I mean, they're mostly kids. The kid was a fan. I don't like the word *fan*."

"I don't give a shit what you like."

"Deb—"

"Your *fan* cursed our baby."

"I can't help it if he likes our songs. Thousands of people like our songs. They can't all be cool. Or even good people."

"Why not?"

She was irrational. Inconsolable. For the night, anyway. By breakfast she'd be happily recounting to Matty how she dismantled the former death rocker, but Harry knew that she'd been shaken badly.

The night before, while failing to sink into sleep, he'd made some kind of peace with the fact that all this was going to be messy in ways he could only half imagine. But after that altercation, he wanted everything to be pure and safe again, only for Debbie. Only so that he'd know she'd be okay. He worried about leaving her. Wondered if he'd made a mistake by letting this thing of his back into their lives. He wondered if he'd ever write again. And whether Jim Morrison and Elvis and Tupac and Richie Manic faked their own deaths, and if so, how. If this balance between family and rock'n'roll wasn't meant to hold, that could be an option, couldn't it? Lord knows they still sold records.

Harry paid the check for both tables, apologized, and

got a cab to take them home. In the morning, Ben Jim Morrison gave him a lift to pick up the car.

"Do the . . . Great-Aunt. Do the Great Auk. Do the Grebe." Harry was flailing.

"What's a grebe?" Rudy asked.

"It's a bird. Like the auk. The dictionary says it's one of several great diving birds. It's like a loon. You can hold your nose and pretend to dive while you're doing the dance," Harry offered.

"Why are you writing a dance song?"

" 'Cause I can't fucking think of anything. Okay?"

He rose from Neil Sedaka's bone white piano and kicked the bench over, then picked Minna's dictionary off the top and continued to thumb through it. We'd dug it out because we thought it might help, but we needn't have bothered. Once we'd hit the "Do the . . ." phase, trolling around for dance crazes, we'd sunk too low for a dictionary to rescue us. Harry's muse was at home, making dinner, and he couldn't write about her anymore. What Harry lusted for—cocaine, girls, maybe ego satiation—he couldn't think about, much less write and sing about. And the prospect of his father materializing made him bite his lip till it bled. The normal stuff was too boring, and the weird stuff was still too confusing.

"Well, you know, this is why producers make a lot of money," Tracey laughed into the phone. "For what you spent loading that garage with soundproofing you could have moved into Electric Ladyland here. We could have posted Phil Spector's bail and met his producer's fee. I'm trying to say that you could have been done by now. We could be selling records at this point, not struggling to make them."

"Okay," I agreed. "What do we do?"

"Sandy, are you ready to do this the right way? We don't like to interfere, but we do have momentum now and it would be practical to captialize on it, wouldn't you agree?"

"Yes. Absolutely."

"Sandy . . ."

"Yeah?"

"It's going to be okay. Tell Harry it's going to be okay. I know he's too ashamed to call me himself, but he's got nothing to be ashamed about. We have total faith in all of you. New York was wonderful. The reviews were uniformly raving. It's all good. Do they still say 'It's all good'?"

"We never said it."

"Yes. Well, it's all good. We anticipated this. And we have a plan. When I hang up I'll ring Ben at the office and work out the details, but in order to calm you down, I'll frame everything for you right now, okay?"

"Thank you."

"I'm going to tell Crispin to book a flight for the three of you."

"What about Ben? Ben can book the flight."

"Crispin's booking it. One-way. I want you to come to New York tomorrow morning. Leave Ben in Dean. This is *business*."

"He's gonna be pissed."

"Tell him to buy more fish. Tell him it's very important. The fish."

"Fine."

"We will put you into a rehearsal studio for a few days
and see if we can't find you a real producer. Don't focus
on new material. Just play. We'll clean up and rush-
release a proper EP of the old material, then put the Jane
Ashers on tour. With the Spurts. I'll have our booking
agent focus on West Coast dates. Only a few, but media-
centric cities. L.A., of course. San Francisco. Nice and
warm. Beaches. Have you ever been to the beach?"

"No."

"Go to the beach. Look at the ocean. Sound good?"

"All right. Yes. I'd like to see the ocean."

"The ocean is a powerful thing. It will stimulate some
creativity. Loosen you up. We'll kit out the bus with a
mini-studio in the back. You can write on the road. Like
Led Zeppelin in 1969."

"Zeppelin."

"They weren't too bad, were they, Sandy?"

"No."

"Then we'll have sustained buzz, we'll have the new
songs, we'll have the old songs in killer shape, and we'll
go back in and make the full-length album the right way."

"Okay."

"Sound advice?"

"Yes. Sound advice. Thank you."

"I'm going to conference in James now. Are you
ready?"

"Yes."

"Harry, how are you? How's Ohio these days?" asked
James.

"This is Sandy."

"Where's Harry?"

"He's . . . he can't talk right now."

"Okay. Listen, Sandy, you can relay all this to the guys. *Headphones* magazine wants to do a cover story on the Jane Ashers. They only want Harry on the cover. They're saying they want the whole band, but that means they want to shoot the whole band and crop them out, run the cover with just Harry. Do you have a problem with that?"

"I'm not wild about the idea. Will they interview me at least?"

"Absolutely," James said.

"Okay, well, we'll have a band meeting about it."

"You do that. But keep in mind I already said yes."

"You did?"

"It's *Headphones* magazine, Sandy. They're the second-largest music magazine in the country, and the only American mag with any cred, really. It's a good match. Joe Green is the writer. He's going to conduct the interview at the Vegas tour stop."

"You already booked the tour too?"

"House of Blues. At the Mandalay Bay. Right downstairs from where you'll be staying. The venue is actually in your hotel. Isn't that great? And if you don't gamble, you'll keep all your money. All right, I have to get going, but I'm going to fax over the full list of what you can and can't discuss with *Headphones*, okay? I'm giving you back to Tracey now."

"Where's he going?" I asked Tracey when James had gotten off.

"First school play. *Nutcracker*. Very basic rendition. Two-year olds, y'know."

"Oh, right, his kid. How does he do it?"

"How hard is it, really?"

"Do you have kids?" I asked Tracey.

"Oh, no, Sandy. I'm in the closet."

"All right, Tracey. I have to go put the backbeat to a new dance craze now."

Once the new plans had been relayed to Harry, he hung up the phone, walked into the kitchen, and sat down. The chicken Debbie had prepared was savory. She'd become a good cook after all those years.

"What was all that?" Debbie asked.

Harry was happy that she'd finally calmed down after the Finley's fiasco, and he was reluctant to bring up anything potentially jarring. He gulped his wine hard. Part of him was sad and worried. Another part was excited. He didn't want to feel either one too intensely. He'd been hoping for a quiet dinner, maybe some catch-up with the TiVo.

"I have to go back to New York. In the morning."

She rose, walked to the kitchen, and scooped some more mashed potatoes onto his plate. She seemed to stay in there for a long time. Harry stared around the lilac house at the arches and high ceilings, the thick walls and solid floors. Once inside, it didn't feel so safe.

Debbie returned from the kitchen and smiled.

"Well, you better eat, then. Get your strength up."

She put the plate in front of him, wrapped her arms around his neck, and kissed his scruffy cheek.

"I never did thank you for writing that song for me," she whispered.

too much, too late

10

"Crispin, if anyone claiming to be my father calls the office at any time, I wanna be notified immediately. Okay? *Immediately.* Please," Harry instructed before boarding the bus.

"Huh? What? Yeah. Harry, sure. You got it," the kid assured him. "I'll make sure that's the top priority for whoever's answering the phone."

"Top priority. Please."

"All right. Okay. Easy. Relax, man. You got it. Word is bond. Word is bond."

"What is that?"

"What?"

" 'Word is bond.' "

"Wu Tang, nigga."

For all the abject hairiness leading up to it, the excitement over pulling out of Manhattan in our silver and black Prevost tour bus, almost fifteen years too late but still on a nation-conquering and sold-out rock'n'roll tour, was intense. A tour bus is like a bachelor apartment on wheels. Twenty minutes into New Jersey, I realized that it's possible to be best friends with someone all your life and not really know their living habits— what kind of underwear they prefer, whether they snore or not. Man, we found out a lot about each other really fast, even about Charlie, who did not hang upside down when he slept, as we suspected. Twelve bunks. Two toilets you're never supposed to shit in (there was a big sign taped to the door "Don't Shit in Me") for some reason. I saw it as a real egalitarian thing. Whether you were Mick Jagger or Britney Spears or the drummer in some Warped Tour band, nobody is allowed to shit in the tour bus toilet. I don't know why. Maybe nobody wanted to empty the tank.

A shower. A kitchenette with a microwave, little fridge, coffeemaker, and wet bar. A U-shaped entertainment center/social area at the back, with a TV with PlayStation or whatever, satellite cable, and a stack of DVDs Crispin had bought us (including the requisite *This Is Spinal Tap*, which every rock band on every tour bus in every country owns—it's as indispensible, I'm told, as brake fluid and shocks). As promised (word is bond), Tracey and Hillary provided a little four-track recorder, laptop, and mike for our Led Zeppelin–inspired writing/recording. The Prevost, which was commanded by Soapy, our driver, a former professional rugby player with a shaved head and an impressive collection of mesh jerseys and T-shirts, was nicer than Minna's house, and definitely more plush than Rudy's nonmobile bachelor apartment. It could have been a home. Some bands have to tour for years in an Econoline van or a VW bus, right?

This was cool for most of us, but not for Harry. Harry had a real home. Harry had a real everything. He'd sit in the back and stare out the window and chop lines of coke, ignoring the acoustic guitar by his side. Nothing got recorded. Nothing was even written. Not even "Do the Grebe." When not drinking with Charlie and the Spurts guys, who sometimes rode with us and crashed on our bus since it was nicer than theirs, I'd watch him and wonder if he was counting the miles off the green road signs.

Now I'm 75 miles away from Debbie. Now I'm 110 miles away from the kid. I wonder what they named the new cat.

Charlie was a sweet kid. So were the Spurts. The band had been on the road for about a year and a half already and seemed to know the crew at each venue stop. They'd been raised well and always took time to introduce us. In return, we always invited them to play Halo or whatever stupid game transfixed them for hours on our bus. Rudy and I weren't about to waste this on video gaming. But the Spurts were happy to gather around that glowing tube for hours during our downtime. Like they were born to be rock stars and didn't mark time the way normal people did.

The Spurts revered Harry the most, so it didn't seem to matter much that he offered them the least socially. They'd give him cigarettes and dibs on the good noodle soup or burritos. They'd bring him wacky souvenirs from the truck stop gift shops, trucker hats and bumper stickers with slogans like "Keep Honking, I'm Reloading."

Sometimes Rudy and I would just stare at each other and smile. "Can you believe this? We're in Portland. We're in Seattle. We're in San Francisco. We're in Phoenix . . . that's in Arizona!" When we'd pull into the venue and walk up the ramp to the load-in area, I'd always marvel about how much it reminded me of the yard where I'd worked after our breakup. Same cement dock. Same steel gate. Same trucks. Only this time I was being delivered. In every way.

Harry came around just before the shows too. It's hard not to smile and indulge in some optimism when you're in front of all that love. Nothing, nothing at all will ever compare to the sound of that crowd. Zeppelin compared it to the ocean, right? It *is* like the ocean. And like Tracey promised, the ocean is inspiring. You don't even have to be a hippie or a surfer to get off on it. You sit backstage and you're thinking, *Every one of those people knows who we are. They want us. They love us!* Every feeling of insecurity you ever had—every girl who ever blew you off, every teacher who ever told you that you were a fool, every disappointment, every doubt—that wave just washes them all away. So you dive in. And when the audience of 3,000 teenagers and another 2,000 men and women our age (who were probably only there because they thought if we bring it, old and

ugly as we are, they can have some of it too) totally sur-
renders to you, you have the illusion of total power. Do
you know that feeling, when you're in a crowd yourself,
and the band onstage plays a song and everyone knows
it? You've been walking around thinking you're the only
person in the world who feels that strongly about that
music, and when you're exposed to this communal
recognition and you realize that that song means something to the guy next to you too, and you're all here together, that's a celebration: *I'm not the only one who
listened to this album alone in my room when I was sad.*
Now, think about how it must feel to provide that beau-
tifully comforting realization. It's *addictive*. It's why rock
stars think they're a bunch of hairy Jesuses.

But then there's the comedown. . . .

"We are the Jane Ashers from Dean, Ohio. Thank you
and good night."

Every morning, the oceanic Zeppelin buzz was gone,
and we couldn't wait till the next city and the next load-
in and the next sound check and the next showtime to
get it back. You can relate to stars who have their own
lines of clothing and fragrances after lingering too long
in the ocean.

Watching your lead singer coming down off the wave,
glum as gunk, staring out the window 3,000 miles away
from his one true love is antithetical to partying hard. If
anything, Harry's conflict made me that much more determined to forget about Motorrrju for the time being
and just swim. After nearly fifteen years of delays and
repairs, the beach was open.

All the Ashers did cocaine. Even Harry. I guess he
figured if he had to have one vice, maybe it should be

one that validated his tension, that Bowie astronaut feeling. Besides, it was just there. I don't know *why* it was there. I hadn't thought it would be there anymore. I'd thought it was strictly a '70s, early-'80s kind of thing. Fleetwood Mac and *Tusk*, you know? But it never went away. That's one of the dirty secrets of rock'n'roll. Coke has always been there and will always be there. If you're a rock star, you do coke. You just do. And maybe you should. Someone's got to, or else all that coke will go to waste. What you *shouldn't* do is do so much coke that you're convinced that there's a layer of skin slowly sealing your mouth together and in a matter of minutes you won't be able to speak or breathe or sing backup, and you have to find a scissors or a knife really fast and jam it in there or else the devil is going to silence you forever. I mean . . . don't ever do *that*. Okay? Seriously, though, I think we all did the drugs and drank as much as we did out of sheer nervousness. We wanted the experience, but sometimes it was too much and we had to dull it and blur it to make it comfortably unreal. That's all.

When Harry was on coke, he didn't call Debbie. He just remained in our little rolling cocoon, where the lights were low and the white lines on the highway and the coffee table disappeared into each other. On your way to a new city, you told yourself that there were different rules up ahead. You'd sort your head out then. Someone or something would require it. But I never felt a shift or any real pressure to clean up. Every city was the same. And after Soapy wandered into the crowd or among the crew and scored for us, every city was fun. After a few hours, every city was gone.

It's one way to travel.

When Harry was drunk, on the other hand, he'd call home. He'd get all sweaty and whiny and "I miss you, baby! I all kinds of miss you."

When he was high, it was "We need fire. Don't you think we should have some fire for that song? Hey, remember that song 'Fire' by the Crazy World of Arthur Brown? Can someone download that song? I need to hear that song right now! Someone download that song." It was "Where are we in the charts, Crisp?" It was "I need some clothes. When we get to L.A., I think we all need to buy some clothes, man. Maybe we should all play in suits again. Hey, can you throw a party for us in L.A.? Can we meet Arthur Lee? I wanna meet Arthur Lee. Who wants to meet Arthur Lee? Rudy?"

"I'd like to meet Sofia Coppola. And Francis Coppola. I'd like to meet some Coppolas."

"Forget that. When the fuck are we going to meet Winona *freakin'* Ryder?" I'd demand. "Would someone please bring her to the show? Aren't we rock stars now? Where is she?"

By Phoenix, third to last stop on the tour (which we'd dubbed "No Sleep Till 40," as Rudy, the oldest Jane Asher, was about to turn the big 4–0), the ocean had taken all of us under, and I didn't even remember what the surface looked like anymore. Looking back, I think all we needed was a break between shows. Maybe some time at SeaWorld in San Diego. Or a day in Joshua Tree National Park or something. Rudy became the first Jane Asher to get arrested after a punch-up in a karaoke bar in Scottsdale, Arizona, with Charlie, Crispin, and a bunch of groupies. I was on the bus with my latest Motorrrju substitute. Rudy had been mixing green chartreuse (Rudy is the only human being I know who can pound that stuff) with the blow we'd picked up earlier at a nearby pool hall, and for reasons I don't even wanna *start* pondering, he got up and did a version of "Sisters Are Doin' It for Themselves," by the Eurythmics (with Aretha Franklin). He was heckled mercilessly, as he should have been. One thing led to another, and both things led to blood and teeth and hair flying. Then the hospital. And, once patched up, the pokey. Crispin called Soapy from the police station pay phone. He was in a bad panic, and we had to drive over there and bring him his checkbook so bail could be posted.

"I didn't even know you were a feminist," I kidded Rudy as he climbed onto the bus at 6 that next morning, rejoining us for our dawn-lit crawl toward Phoenix.

"Mmrthalrightpf," he mouthed through a wired-up jaw.

"No more cocaine," Soapy warned us as he got behind the wheel. "It makes you sing crap techno. From now on we stick to liquor like gentlemen!"

The show at the Celebrity Theater in Phoenix was our only shitty gig ever. Not a bad average. Even the Beatles admitted to playing a few, although they were drowned out by the mania. Watching the Spurts play from the side of the stage was not a good idea, for starters. I think maybe we got a little intimidated. They were furious that night. The songs they'd been playing for two years over and over again across the world seemed brand-new and exciting to them and, by direct extension, to the crowd.

No disrespect to the Copper State, but it was, after all, Arizona. Not L.A., where "they've lost it" rumors can start. We hadn't played many shows, but by then we'd done enough to know that sometimes, no matter where you are, you can suck or you can transcend. A make-or-break big-city show just won't happen for whatever reason. The band doesn't come together. And a show in San Jose for 500 stoned surfers could be the best rock'n'roll show you'll ever play in your professional life. You can't put your finger on exactly why. That said, I had a hunch we were not going to blow Phoenix away. Crispin had lost his cell phone somewhere on his late-night spin through the underbelly of Scottsdale, Arizona. He'd purchased a new one after setting up the mobile office at the venue and bumming a ride from one of the venue's crew. While they were loading us in and we were enjoying some dinner from the catering table, he was trying and failing to make sense of his lost messages and saved numbers. As we munched our chocolate chip cookies and smoked our cigarettes and drank our tea, Harry was monitoring him, visibly perturbed. He didn't have the Buddha-like glow that I'd seen surrounding him before a really great gig. He looked dour and full of dread. When the Spurts began their set a few hours later, it got worse. And after our first and only shitty show (even "Debbie" didn't gel up there), all his dread was confirmed.

We had no coke residue for the building of artificial

276

confidence. The run-in with the cops the night before had made us paranoid, and we ditched it all . . . up our noses, another reason why our show might not have been life-changing for the kids in the crowd. We were fiending and trying to come down with Scotch. Charlie skulked off into the crowd. Every once in a while, he liked to hang with people his own age. Crispin canceled the meet-and-greet postshow hugfest, but a few diehards remained outside the dressing room, determined to make a connection with us. Most of them were teens, breaking curfew and just thrilled to see some alternative rock (John Waite had been there last night, tomorrow Joe Satriani was set to roll into town). One of them was 60 years old.

Harry Vance Sr. tugged on the stocky Mexican security guard's navy windbreaker. His hands shook with nerves, not age. He looked good for 60. A little leathery, probably no more or less than anyone else who'd left the Bay Area for the arid desert climate and harsh rays of Phoenix. He still had his hair, and it was the same color as Harry's but thinned with age and brushed to the side rather than piled high. He didn't wear glasses, but the resemblance was instantly apparent. This was not an imposter.

"Excuse me, officer," he addressed the guard.

"I'm not a police officer."

"Oh, I'm sorry."

"What do you need?"

"Well, my boy is in there. And I was wondering if you could please ask someone if it would be all right for me to come in. I bought a ticket." Harry senior reached into his loose fitting jeans and showed the man his floor seat ticket.

"Lots of people bought tickets. Do you have a VIP pass?"

"Well . . . no."

The guard looked him over. Maybe he believed his pitch. He *was* the old guy out among the kids and thirty-something well-wishers.

"What's your name?"

"Harry Vance. The first."

"You're Harry Vance's dad?"

"That's right."

"Hang on . . ."

Harry was searching the backstage area for Crispin when the security guard found him.

"Yo, Harry, man. There's someone out there claiming to be your father. What do you want me to do?"

Harry froze. He smiled. Shook his head. Then froze again. The guard immediately felt bad and took a step back toward his abandoned post in front of the closed dressing room door.

"What does he look like?"

"He looks like you, man."

Rudy and I looked up from our whiskey shots. I walked over to Harry and handed him the bottle. He took it and swigged. Pulled out his sunglasses and put them on. Took another swig.

"Bring him back," he said. "Bring him in."

"All right. Wow. Hey. This is something," Harry senior gushed nervously. If you've never been in a dressing room at a medium-sized venue, it's really not much. Very plain and functional. It was clear to all of us the guy was nervous. It was clear to most of us what was happening, and I guess he sensed that.

"Hi." The old man stood before the son he hadn't seen in nearly 36 years. "How are ya?" he asked.

Harry stared at him. Didn't move or speak.

"It looks like you're doing real well. I saw the show. Boy . . . what a performance."

"Does Mom know you're here?"

The old man looked worried but resigned to whatever was coming.

"Harry . . ."

"Answer me. Does my mother know that you're here? In Phoenix, Arizona? Does she know where you are?"

"No. She doesn't."

"How come I know you're here? Because Mom's not a rock star? What do you want? Money? You want money? Crispin, give my father some money."

Crispin shrank further into the couch next to us.

"Uh, Harry . . . I don't have any cash. I have my checkbook."

"I don't want money," the older man assured us. "That's not why I'm here."

I didn't want to get up. It wasn't my business.

Harry moved closer to his dad. Looked him over thoroughly.

"Do you know how old I am?" Harry asked.

"I sure do. You're 38. I remember the day you were born."

"Do you remember the day you left?"

"I do remember the day I left too. I certainly do."

Harry looked around.

"Could you guys give us a minute?" he asked.

"Yeah, sure, Harry," Crispin said. "We'll see you on the bus."

He gathered up his stuff. Rudy and I followed. We both patted him on the back as we hid in the corner of the big room and pretended to talk about guitars and food.

"Sit down," Harry said. "You want a drink?"

"Sure. Thank you. That would be fine. Just one, though. I'm driving."

"Oh, yeah? You live far from here?"

"Over in Scottsdale."

"You listed?"

"Yes."

"Under your own name?"

"Yes."

"Not hiding or anything?"

"No."

"Nice place?"

"It's not fancy. But we like it."

"You have a family there?"

"I have a wife."

"Kids?"

"I have a kid. You're a grandfather. Did you know that?"

"No."

"But you knew that I would be playing the Celebrity Theater tonight."

"I saw it in the paper."

"Oh, yeah? Just saw it in the paper? I heard you were trying to reach me at the office."

"I was."

Harry's father grabbed the bottle. This wasn't going well. "Do you mind if I pour it into a glass?"

"Do you want to know his name?" Harry asked, ignoring the question.

"Who?"

"Your grandson. His name's Matt."

"Is that right."

The old man lifted his glass. "Well, cheers to that. I'm a grandfather."

Harry raised the bottle. Clinked with his father's glass. Drank.

"Can you take your sunglasses off?"

"Why?"

"I want to see your eyes, that's why."

"No, I'm leaving them on."

"Why?"

"Shut up! Shut up! Why did you leave me?" he shouted inside himself. He gulped, wiped his mouth, and took another shot. Outside he had to play it cool. He was, after all, a rock star now.

"Why'd you split?" Harry asked. He was laboring to sound cool. He sounded like a boy.

"I don't know how to say it. It was such a long time ago."

"I remember it. You left for San Francisco with a girl. So you ended up in Scottsdale with a wife. Is it the same person?"

"No."

"You left her too?"

"She left me."

Harry rose and took off his glasses For a minute, he and his old man locked eyes. The same eyes, green and intense. Harry squinted hard, trying to see without his prescription. Maybe he'd have found some peace here if his normal glasses weren't on the bus. Maybe something in the old man's face would have explained it all.

Harry senior downed his drink and rose as well. He grabbed his son's hand and pumped it.

"Listen, son—"

Harry shook loose. "I'm not your son."

"Harry, you must know there are no guarantees in life. Your mother and I . . . Well, people change. Life is . . . Well, it's a little . . . messy."

Harry saw himself in his father. And when he did, he saw himself sitting on the bed in his son's room. He saw himself shaking off his own accountabilities by blaming the messiness of life. He didn't like this picture. He put down the bottle. He'd been clenching it too tightly, like a weapon. It was worrying him. He just let it go.

Harry senior loosened up and seemed relieved. He laughed. "Besides, you know Dean is . . . well, it's not reality, is it? You *have* to get out. If you don't, you'll go nuts. Right? Nuts? Come on . . ." The old man moved in like he was about to get a cleansing hug.

He got a left hook in the jaw instead. He hit the floor, stunned. Some blood dripped from the corner of his mouth. Some of it was the younger man's blood, from the cut on his knuckle he'd gotten when he hit one of the old man's teeth. And some of it was from where that tooth had been in the old man's mouth. Harry picked the tooth up from where it lay on the floor and put it in his pocket. He walked over to the mobile office, picked up a pen, and scribbled out a number on a notepad. He ripped off the sheet and tossed it at the fallen man.

"I want you to call my mother in the morning. I want you to tell her where you are and that you're never coming back to Ohio. Will you do that for me?"

Harry senior nodded. Harry left him there in the dressing room. He grabbed his bag and got on the tour bus. It was his turn to walk out. We all followed.

"Well, you showed him," Rudy cheered.

"Look, it's all over now," I promised him, hoping the closure would somehow fix him but knowing it would take more than that. Once the satisfaction faded, the hole in him would still need filling up.

I got off the bus, walked back to the dressing room, and found the old man.

"How's your face?" I asked him. He shook his head in silence. I offered him a cigarette, which he declined. I picked up a beer and extended it.

"For your eye. Don't open it."

He held the sweating Bud to his swollen face.

"I want you to give me your number."

"Does Harry want it?" he asked.

"No. *I* want it."

"Are you gonna call me?"

"What do you think?

He put down the beer and wrote the number out. I thanked him and pocketed it.

"By the way . . ." I turned around and slugged him hard in the gut. He doubled over, teared up, and groaned. "Nobody talks shit about Dean except Deaners."

Once on the bus, I handed Harry the slip of paper. He didn't have to ask what it was.

11

In the end, it was the pot roast that killed us. But I'm jumping ahead slightly.

After the incident with his father, Harry resolved to call home and apologize to his own kid for telling him that life was "messy." He'd decided that living in a messy world was no excuse for neglect. Not when you're a father. He probably swore he'd tell Debbie he'd love her forever. Maybe he even made a mental note to find out what they named the cat. I'm sure he committed to all of these things before he passed out anyway. But he was very drunk, having padded his courage with swigs of Jack in that room with his father.

too much, too late

Surging with adrenaline, he didn't realize how lit he'd made himself. As he fell asleep, he told me later, he replayed his father's excuse in his head: *Well, it's not reality, is it?*

When Harry came to, we were already in Vegas, and there was business to deal with. Promotional duties and the mechanics of a big rock'n'roll machine seemed urgent and meaningless at the same time, and put Harry off his phone call home. He decided he wasn't going to do anything until he figured himself out. He was going to shut down. That would be reality. An utter blank. He'd become something that couldn't be rejected or deconstructed or considered in any way. He'd forget himself and everything around him and embrace nothingness. Until sound check.

We checked into the Mandalay. Some nights were hotel nights, some were bus nights. This would be the former, thanks to the planned *Headphones* interview. Harry stood in the lobby and stared at the parrots in their golden cages, the Japanese tourists checking in, the bustle and smoke. He shook his head and decided he needed air.

"Where are you going?" Crispin asked worriedly.

Harry didn't reply. He just kept moving.

"Wait. You have to see the pool, Harry," he insisted. "It has actual waves in it. Or we could go look at the sharks. There's an actual coral reef here full of sharks."

Harry didn't respond.

"Or you can watch them from the room. There's a shark channel on the television. In the room. Simulcast from the tank. You can see sharks," he explained. "Sometimes manta rays too."

Harry pushed him out of the way and headed toward the sliding doors and the Strip.

"Where are you going? Harry!"

"A walk," was all he said.

"Ah. Okay. Stretch your legs. Good idea. You sure you don't want me to go with you? Or get you a car or something?

"No."

"All right. Hey, Harry. Listen, man. I'm really sorry about your father. I let that happen. My slip-up, I guess, huh? I know you wanted to be prepared for that kinda shit."

"It's all right, Crisp."

"Okay. I just wanted to say so. It won't happen again. With any other . . . anything. Nobody gets in. Okay? Nobody, uh . . . penetrates the . . . thing."

Harry wanted no more of the "thing." He wanted to put possessive specifics to every description. *My family.* He felt too weak and corrupted and far away from Debbie to reclaim himself. He couldn't adjust the expensive lenses that had replaced his old, nerdy spectacles. Everything remained blurry, distorted, and ugly anyway. This was starting to seem normal to him.

Harry took the escalator up to the tram station and walked the elevated path into the Excalibur casino. The *bling blink blink bling* of the slots, unending and no longer exciting, was just noise and color and loss—loss of money, of time, of hope, all for the chance of hitting one jackpot. *But for what?* he wondered. *You're still gonna bloat, and hide your desires, and damage your children. And*

too much, too late

if rock'n'roll really is the answer, the beauty and truth and grace in a world that's bereft of all that, then why did Elvis end up here? Why is Elton John here now? And when will it be my turn to offically and finally lose my family and every last little bit of soul? Harry decided to just give in to waste. To drown. To do something prematurely and not belatedly for once.

As he drank five Irish coffees there in fake Manhattan, then staggered into a men's room to puke, he was still telling Debbie he loved her and he was sorry. In his head. While he was doubled over in the stall, the world spinning, he heard someone bang on the door.

"I'm all right," he gurgled.

"Are you Harry Vance?" some guy called from the other side.

"Yeah. What?"

"I got tickets to the show is all. I just wanted to say what's up. You fucking rock."

"Thanks."

"You gonna rock tonight?"

"Sure."

"All right! Rock."

The man disappeared. Harry never saw his face.

"I only have one speed—balls out," Joe Green sniffed. Harry stared at him from across the table.

"Gene Wilder. *Stir Crazy*."

Harry didn't reply. Joe lit up a cigarette. He already had one burning in the ashtray.

"We don't walk around thinking of Gene Wilder

anymore, do we? As a people, I mean. He's just . . . receded. But in the '80s, right? In the '80s."

Green had uncombed brown hair, a yellowy pallor, and stubble. He wore a musty black velvet jacket that buttoned snugly thanks to the paunch that stretched his V-neck T-shirt. His skinny legs were encased in a pair of Levi's 517 Flex jeans. Worn black cowboy boots on his feet, and a cheap-looking iridescent black scarf knotted tightly around his neck, which didn't seem to be supporting his head too well. His nose ran. His eyes were shielded by a huge pair of black sunglasses. He wore a silver ring on his fuck-you finger and drank vodka tonics with lime, one after the other after the other. Didn't carry a pen. Just a cheap Radio Shack tape recorder that he'd forgotten to turn on.

"You like Vegas?" he asked. "I love Vegas. The hotels are so cheap, I finally get to stay someplace decent. Usually they shoot me off like a space monkey. Stick me in a Hampton Inn by the airport. I gotta spend forty bucks for a cab ride into the city. I don't drive. I know how to drive. But I don't drink and drive, so I never drive. Do you drive?"

He wiped his nose, pulled down his shades, and eyed Harry's veal piccata. They were dining together in some Italian place in the casino.

"You going to eat that veal? Maybe we should get it wrapped up? No? You want another drink? Yeah? Diphthong is paying for this, right? You can, like, sign for it? Yeah. Cool."

Joe signaled for another round. He jabbed his fork into Harry's veal, airlifted it over to his plate, and dug in. "This is almost like a junket. How come there are no junkets anymore? You know how in the '70s you read about journalists getting flown out to L.A. and treated like kings? What the hell happened? I've been doing this seven years, I've never been on one fucking junket. I've been on *junk*." Joe picked up his recorder. Held it close to Harry. "So . . . should we do this now?"

Harry shrugged, then picked up his drink and gulped it.

"Did you like working in a hardware store?"

Harry shrugged.

"Do you like being a rock star?"

Harry looked around for the waiter.

"What's the best thing about being a rock star, Harry? Besides getting to hang out with guys like me."

Joe flagged down the waiter.

"We're doing great. We just need another round here. And keep them coming every ten minutes. Thanks. We're in room . . . We're in his room. Rock star."

Joe winked at the waiter. Harry stared down at his congealing dinner.

"Do you gamble?"

"No."

"My dad's a gambler. If he were here, he'd be over in the sports book room betting on horses. What does your dad do?"

"I don't know."

"Okay. Whoa. This isn't exactly Bangs/Reed here." Joe looked at Harry desperately. "I gotta file something at some point. Why don't I stop asking you questions and you tell me something? Whatever you wanna say, Harry."

"Why?"

"Why? 'Cause this is our job, man. This is what we do. I mean, I've been thinking about getting out. Transitioning over to one of those men's magazines. Stop writing about the rock. Start poeticizing about tits and cheese and razors. Alligator shoes. Did you know that Condé Nast has its own cafeteria? *Headphones* doesn't even have Splenda. Like, what if I was a diabetic?"

"It doesn't matter."

"What doesn't matter? Diabetes?"

"Nothing matters."

"Great. So you're a funky-ass nihilist?"

"No."

"You're a Pisces?"

"It doesn't matter."

"We covered that. So what matters? Or . . . I've got it. More importantly, what matters to these kids? Why do you think they latched on to you? Why are you, a 37-year-old, 38-year-old, whatever-year-old hardware store guy, their hero?"

"It doesn't matter."

"To them it does. Not me. I don't listen to new music. But to them, you're it, Jack. I mean, do they wanna fuck you? Do they? These young girls? I bet they do."

"It doesn't matter."

" 'Cause correct me if I'm wrong, but I always believed that rock'n'roll was all about fucking. Going to the show was all about some kind of fuck-a-rama going on between the audience and the performer. The kids go crazy for the guy they wanna do, right? They're going crazy for you. So I'm wondering, do they wanna do you, these kids? What do you think?"

Harry didn't reply.

"Okay, like, Van Morrison, for instance, has a lot of soul. And I'm sure a lot of kids in college still light cherry incense and sit in their rooms and listen to *Astral Weeks* and feel deep. But do they wreck themselves and think of doin' it with Van Morrison? Is it rock'n'roll? It's poetry maybe, but can it be rock if you don't wanna slam Van? Van's not sexy anymore. Too old and wise or something. Smells funny, I bet. Although in *Them*, Van, he was kind of badass, wasn't he? Kind of sexy. When he was singing 'Gloria' Van was rock'n'roll. He was fuckable. Wouldn't you agree? And I'm positing to you that eternally, this is what rock is all about, Harry. So where do you fit in? How can you justify this phenomena? Phenomenon. Whatever. I mean, are you a man or are you a boy? Right?"

"I don't anymore," Harry slurred, and choked a bit.

Joe nodded. "Me neither." He lit another cigarette and stared off a little sadly.

"So, are you fucked up? Anything good?"

"It doesn't matter."

" 'Cause I'm a little fucked up. Nothing good, though. I could use something . . . good."

The waiter brought another round.

"This place is great, huh? Posh."

Harry craned his neck toward the engraved crystal panels surrounding the bar. He started pulling at the pink linen tablecloth, wadding it into his fists, upending the fresh cocktails.

"You wanna get some air? Go out by the pool? They got elephant heads out there. Spouting water, I guess. Fountains, you know?"

"No."

"You want me to throw you to the sharks? Just kidding."

Harry got up and walked away. Joe followed.

"Hey . . . hey, Vance. Where are you going?"

Harry disappeared into the rows of slot machines. Vanished amid the tourists and the cocktail waitresses and the *bling blink blink bling*.

"You need to sign for the drinks, man!" Joe called. "Hey! Hey! What's your room number?"

The Spurts were once again amazing. I began fantasizing that their drummer would OD or something and they'd ask me to join. I'd be a Spurt. Harry didn't say a word to any of us backstage. He hid in the bathroom stall up until showtime, bouncing a pink Spalding ball against the locked metal door. All he said to the crowd was "Good evening" and "Thank you, good night." Never turned to look at us as we played. Never took off his sunglasses. And insisted on hitting the stage dressed in an oversized powder-blue T-shirt with "Vegas" written on it in rhinestones. He sang well. We played all right. I just wish we'd have come together, since it would be our last show ever.

Our tour came to an end midday in Los Angeles. It was supposed to go all night. We were set to play a sold-out concert at the Staples Center with the Spurts and some hot local band called Mathlete as our support acts. We were at capacity in L.A. like we were during every other stop on the tour, but the L.A. stop was a big sports arena. Hardly a low-key gig to stimulate the creative juices. Hillary and Tracey were set to fly in for the show. Lots of celebs on the guest list—sitcom stars, rockers older than we were.

We arrived in L.A. early. The idea was to give us a much-needed half day's downtime in the West Hollywood Hyatt before the show. The Hyatt—aka the "Riot House," as you probably know—is a great, historic place for rock'n'roll. In the '70s, Led Zeppelin rented out entire floors for uninterrupted debauchery, and Iggy did laps in the pool on the roof while Tom Waits loitered in the coffee shop. But today that coffee shop is a fancy-ass Thai restaurant, and more important, there's no fucking pot roast on the room service menu. I've spent hours, probably whole days in total, wondering what might have been if they'd been able to scare some up in the kitchen. I'm sure that for most touring bands pulling off the road into L.A., a decent hamburger and a cold beer are plenty. I, like 99.9 percent of my itinerant brethren, could give two fucks about whether my meat was pot roast. To Hebrews like me, it's brisket anyway. My grandma, she made brisket. Bob Dylan's ma probably made brisket. Harry's mother, and more crucially his wife, Debbie, made pot roast. Pot roast is a weird food. You're almost obliged to eat it with a family.

So we were all in the Hyatt. The tour bus was idling on Sunset Boulevard, waiting to take us to the venue, which isn't really anywhere near L.A. proper. Harry had the biggest room of us all. He hadn't demanded it. That wasn't really his style, even with the whole world jerking him off. Crispin, probably taking cues from the Diphthong twins, figured he was collecting a lot of drama, and hopefully some writing material, as we moved along, and needed the extra space to store it. Otherwise, from the outside, things didn't seem too crazy. If you were watching us on a surveillance camera, L.A. was no different from the previous night's show in Vegas—from the lobby to the elevator to the room door, anyway. Harry registerd under the name Dabney Coleman. (I always checked in as Chuck Mangione.) After that, I assumed that his make-himself-at-home ritual was probably the same as it had been earlier in Portland and San Francisco, when he and I were still sharing a suite. Up to the room. Put on the classic rock station and the TV on mute, CNN or the Cartoon Network. Crank up the air conditioner to its highest setting and open the blinds and the glass doors and let all that fake air flow right out. If there was a balcony, as there was in San Francisco and L.A., Harry'd step out, light a smoke, and stare at the world, which I guess also seemed containable and controllable from that perspective and height, recycled air blowing the real air away as it fought to invade the room. The aforementioned decent burger and cold beer would come next. Then maybe a couple of shots if the band was gonna hang and psych ourselves up for the show. Finally a phone call to Debbie and the kid. I'd call Ma maybe, but mostly I'd call down to the truck and see if Soapy or the crew had any line on where to get us high and/or laid after the gig. Then it'd be the gig, the hotel, the party, the bed, and the bus, and everything all over again. It was a good routine. It worked. Time slipped into the future. I could have done it forever. It was an almost perfect existence. World events could not affect us. We were on the road.

adjustable shelf and thrown it against a wall, shattering the picture tube. Chopped the desk in half with who knows what? Iron, maybe? Maybe the ironing board too. Shredded the pillows and bedspread. Thrown one chair onto the balcony, probably in an attempt to kill some poor Mexican valet 40 feet below. Smeared the walls with coffee grounds, complimentary lotion, shampoo, conditioner, beer, matches, orange soda, and crushed ice.

"What's wrong?"

"He was hungry," she said.

The only thing he seemed to have left intact was the telephone. I saw the cord running under the closed bathroom door.

"Harry?" I called out. "Harry, man, open the door."

"He won't come out," she said.

"Who the fuck are you?" I asked, giving her my hard look, the one I picked up after a night in the police station when I was 16 and got caught spray-painting "Reagan Smells Bad" on the side of Harrison High. It's a good back-off look—it worked on a couple of big homeboys, so I've been favoring it ever since.

"Get outta here. Go on," I ordered.

"Can I get my clothes?" she asked.

"Fuck, yes, you can get your clothes. Get your ugly fucking clothes!"

She grabbed her white jean skirt and a faded black jean jacket and scuttled down the hall naked. For the record, I would have let her fix herself up in the room, but it didn't occur to her. I never saw her again, but I see her now as I write this. Actually, I see Sissy Spacek.

I don't know why. Bad memories are weird things, and I guess sometimes you recast movie stars in your bit parts just to jazz up the pain.

"Harry! Open the fucking door, please!"

"Sand?" The voice was crushed.

"Yeah! Don't make me break it down, all right? It's the only thing in the room that isn't already broken. What did you do? What's going on?"

The door opened a crack. I pushed it farther and peered in. He was naked too. He still held the phone receiver, now lowered, indicating some kind of surrender. His eyes were ringed black and bloodshot. His hair was limp and clumped with sweat and grease. Coke boogers and blood dripped from his nostrils. Greenish spittle clung to the corners of his lips. He licked his dry lips and wiped away some tears with his free hand.

"Pot roast," he whimpered. "They won't bring any."

"Who? Room service?"

"And I can't call her. I can't call home, Sand. I forgot the number."

"You want pot roast?"

"Yeah. They won't bring any, Sand."

"Why?"

"I can't call her anymore. I can't."

"Who? Debbie?"

Sobbing, he dropped the phone and pushed the door open, walking past me, like I wasn't even there. He stepped over all the rubble as though the maid had just cleaned up, and stood out on the balcony, dick blowing in the wind. For a second I thought he was gonna jump, but instead he fell to the cold, yellow concrete and curled up in a fetal position.

The city might have belonged to Jim at one point, but tonight it belonged to us. Didn't it? Still? About 20,000 kids did, anyway, and you know that's the part of the population that really counts when you do what we do for a living. We did still do this for a living, didn't we? We were still living, weren't we? It didn't feel like it. A wave of depression fell over me, and then, more fatally, a wave of anger. I decided I needed some backup. In hindsight, I wish I'd never called in Crispin, never shouted at him with stupid indignation that he needed to pull his weight with this, that I was the talent and he was the tour management, his salary coming out of our advance, and therefore he had to deal with such messes and earn his stupid salary. Who knows what would have happened if I'd stayed in the room, tidied up a bit myself, taken some responsibility for the situation, for my friend. I could have easily found the poor guy some brisket. I was a rock star. Instead I *behaved* like a rock star. If I'd behaved like a human being, I'd probably still be a rock star. Instead, I called in the suits, and then went up to the rooftop pool after all, to brood and smoke and pace and drink instead of helping my friend find his way back to some place that warmed and comforted him. I tell myself that I did the wrong thing, but to be honest, I only knew it was wrong after it killed us. And my regret over doing the wrong thing will always be colored by the consequences, not any real sense of fraternity or morality. I can't even regret well. The future was certain and the end was near. Who knew it at the time? I mean, I knew things were bad, but they'd been bad for several major cities. I figured Crispin was a better cleanup guy than me. He'd get us to the Staples

Center on time 'cause that was his job. He'd duke the front desk for the room damages and throw my man in the shower like Martin Sheen in the opening scene of *Apocalypse Now.* A few hours later, Harry'd be in the dressing room laughing it off, high on the adrenaline and anticipation over an hour and a half of serious arena rocking.

But we'd never play music together again. Never even see each other again. The last time I saw Harry Vance, he was whimpering about meat, with lipstick on his ass.

We all had different reactions upon hearing the news an hour later, just around the time we'd have been loading ourselves in for the ride to the arena. Charlie, he started crying. He was just a kid, after all. A real kid, not some arrested middle-aged kid. Rudy, he was Mr. Keith just before a show, right? He couldn't blow his cool, even with us, so he just shrugged and said, "Yeah, okay." I tried to punch Crispin in the mouth when he told me the show was not going to go on. Then I tried to stab him with the mother-of-pearl-handled hunting knife/coke knife I'd bought that morning at some truck stop in Barstow. I was pretty drunk on gin. Maybe over-tired. I'm glad he didn't tell me the full story then. I might have killed the guy.

epilogue

Whenever I can't sleep, I sit here in the garage and wonder what the guy from Supertramp with the high voice is doing now. What is Greg Dulli doing right now? What do we do between the end of the road and the big reunion tour? What do you call this purgatory I'm in? I don't call it rock'n'roll suicide, and even though the road sign says Dean, it no longer feels much like Dean either.

Out here, it's quiet like a grave except for an occasional car rolling by and the hum of the old mini fridge. I pace in here and chain-smoke and listen to our EP over and over, the one Diphthong packaged up and rush-released. The one that was called simply *The Jane Ashers*, since we couldn't convene to agree on a title. You have to all be in one room to agree on something, and that isn't going to happen for a long, long time.

After L.A., Harry packed up Debbie and Matty and left Dean for some undisclosed location westward. I knew where he was going, and I didn't try to stop him. He was going to use that phone number I'd given him. He'd made his decision. He'd come up with his answer to the question Joe Green posed to him in Las Vegas. He *was* a boy, and he'd never be a man in a rock'n'roll band. Just like he'd never be a man hiding from a rock'n'roll band. In order to raise his own son right, and truly grow up himself, he had to fix himself for real. He had no idea whether or not his father was a patient man, but he knew it was going to take some time and he'd better start immediately. It felt funny. He was already married. Already a father. Already a millionaire. Already a legend. And this was his very first commitment. As long as Harry Vance Jr. and Harry Vance Sr. were both alive and breathing, my lead singer and his family had a shot. Unlike in rock'n'roll, in real life Harry Vance was not too old.

Charlie went back to New York City and ironically enough joined the Spurts after Marco Salinger was gored by a walrus in the Arctic. It is, to date, my favorite rock'n'roll death; the ante has been upped. Rudy went back to film school. He eventually got his Ph.D. I don't know what comes after a Ph.D., but whatever it is, he's going to get that too. I hardly see him anymore, but when I do, I call him "Doctor."

The Jane Ashers debuted at number one on the charts,

which is, I believe, unprecedented for an EP. It sold seven million copies worldwide, becoming the greatest indie rock album that's not really an indie rock album ever. It won a bunch of awards. In November, Diphthong released a live record, some rarities, and an album of Jane Asher songs covered by artists named Jane. Jayne County. Jane Child. Joan Osborne (Hillary said it was "close enough"). All of this is thrilling and some of it is amusing. But none of it can provide answers for me. Here, on my own, I try to process what happened. Try to touch and taste it. Make some sense of it all. Sometimes it feels like I dreamed up our success. Or read it all. Like maybe everything happened to someone else.

One afternoon, must have been somewhere in 1992, we were in here, taking a break from rehearsal, and Archie, as he frequently did, rolled and fired up a horse-dick-sized joint. He started sucking, and soon his eyes began to cross. He stared out at the garage wall for 10 minutes or so, and I watched his expression shift from zoned out to concerned and finally mortally terrified. Then he turned to me and in this childlike, quivering, broken little voice he whispered, "Sandy?"

"Yeah, Arch?" I said.

"How do we know we're alive?"

"What's that, Arch?"

About five more minutes went by. He was still staring, his eyes darting, unfocused.

"I was just thinking," he said, "how can we tell for sure that we're alive? Right now. Like maybe we're dead and we don't know it."

Without saying anything, I got up and punched him in the left arm. Really hard on the elbow bone, so the pain must have vibrated all up and down. It's the kind of punch that takes a good long time to shake off. He grabbed his arm and started rubbing.

"You feel that?" I asked.

"Yes! Fuck!"

"I guess you must be alive."

On nights like tonight, I wish someone would come in here and punch me like that. I haven't left rock'n'roll behind, even if it seems to have left me behind. And therefore I am probably a little too old. The clock on my wall is probably a little too loud.

It's three-thirty in the morning. Ma is asleep and I can't wake her up, 'cause she's old even if she doesn't act it. None of my friends and fans is online or in our chat room. Not even Motorrrju, who totaled her Mustang after plowing into the batting cage while doing stoned donuts around the bases on the high school diamond. She was fine, but her mom and dad made it official—she wasn't allowed to talk to me. Maybe by the time she's 18 I'll have figured things out a bit more. I never really thought I could win her over with a car. But I will win her over . . . with something. Sometimes wondering how I'll accomplish this is the only thing that keeps me sane. I check off the days, one after another, counting down till she reaches the age of consent and I reach an age of enlightenment. Forty-two? Forty-three? Until then, it's just me and Winona on the wall. I've replaced my kit with a big metal desk, so I face her while I write. Sometimes Winona looks confused. Sometimes I think I hear her say, *Sandy, what happened to the kit?* Or *Sandy, you guys were almost as good as the Replacements.*

marc spitz

I'm hungry, craving cold roast beef with Russian dressing. I'm out of cigarettes, searching the garbage for cigarette butts. I don't feel like a rock star. And I know what a rock star is supposed to feel like.

So, like I asked a bit earlier, what happens if you come close to burning out, and you also come close to fading away, but ultimately do neither. What *do* you do?

That is what I am going to figure out in the next year and a half or so. I already know the answer isn't "Sleep, peacefully." But I choose to believe that there is a place for all of us was-es, with our sad memoirs and our unhealthy bodies and our thriving ghosts. We will all become men . . . some day.

about the author

MARC SPITZ is a senior writer at *Spin* magazine. His work has also appeared in *Maxim, Nylon,* the *Washington Post,* and the *New York Post,* as well as on MTV, M2, and VH1. Spitz is the author of *How Soon Is Never?* (Three Rivers Press, 2004) and co-author (with Brendan Mullen) of *We Got the Neutron Bomb: The Untold Story of L.A. Punk* (Three Rivers Press, 2001). Seven of his plays, including "Shyness Is Nice," "Worry Baby," and "Gravity Always Wins," have been produced in theaters of varying size and cleanliness.

Spitz lives in Manhattan with his girlfriend and a basset hound named Joni Mitchell.

A poignant, hilarious novel of what happens when you're 30-something, strung-out, disillusioned... and utterly sure that getting the Smiths back together will change your life.

a novel

how soon is never?

marc spitz

Also by Marc Spitz

There is a light and it never goes out ... or is there?

0-609-81040-5 $13.00 paper

"A genius idea for a first novel: hapless N.Y.C. music journalist tries to get the Smiths back together. We're feeling nostalgic already."
—*Seattle Weekly*

"Spitz's debut novel has all the key elements of the [Nick] Hornby playbook."
—*Washington Post*

"Irresistible . . . For anyone who has ever had a jones for a rock band."
—*Baltimore Sun*

"Funny, sad, and appropriately ridiculous in retrospect."
—*The Stranger*

THREE RIVERS PRESS • NEW YORK

Available from Three Rivers Press wherever books are sold
www.crownpublishing.com